WOMEN WRITING THE WEIRD

Edited by Deb Hoag

doghornpublishing.com

Editor: Deb Hoag
Editor-in-Chief: Adam Lowe
Cover art by Ashlyn Fenton
Design and typesetting by Adam Lowe

Published by Dog Horn Publishing, 2012

Selection © Dog Horn Publishing, 2012
Contents © the contributors, 2012
Cover illustration ©Ashlyn Fenton, 2012

The moral right of the authors has been asserted.

First published in the United Kingdom in 2012 by
Dog Horn Publishing
45 Monk Ings
Birstall
Batley
WF17 9HU

doghornpublishing.com

British Library Cataloguing-in-Publication Data
A cataloguing record for this book is available on request from the British Library

ISBN ISBN: 978-1-907133-26-8

Printed and bound in the UK.

WEIRD

• Eldritch: suggesting the operation of supernatural influences; "an eldritch screech"; "the three weird sisters"; "stumps . . . had uncanny shapes as of monstrous creatures" —John Galsworthy; "an unearthly light"; "he could hear the unearthly scream of some curlew piercing the din" —Henry Kingsley

• Wyrd: fate personified; any one of the three Weird Sisters

• Strikingly odd or unusual; "some trick of the moonlight; some weird effect of shadow" —Bram Stoker
wordnetweb.princeton.edu/perl/webwn

WEIRD FICTION

• Stories that delight, surprise, that hang about the dusky edges of "mainstream" fiction with characters, settings, plots that abandon the normal and mundane and explore new ideas, themes and ways of being. —Deb Hoag
doghornpublishing.com/women_writing_the_weird.html

THE WILD WOMEN ARE LOOSE!

Women are usually considered the more gifted with the word, written and spoken; the more cunning and craft-wise subtle of our species. When you look for the best of women's fiction, and qualify that with fiction that breaks boundaries and takes risks, what you get is the tasty array of fiction that we present you with here: stories that will thrill, delight and shock you; stories with heart and mind and heat and depth.

When I put out a call for weird fiction, I deliberately left the definition of "weird" wide open. More than one person tagged me. "What do you mean by 'weird', exactly? How do you define it? What *is* it?"

The reply was simple. "I'll know it when I see it. Something odd. Something unusual. What have you got that no one else would take, because it wouldn't fit into a neat little package? That's what I'm looking for. Think you have something that qualifies? Send me what you've got."

The responses took my breath away, rich and varied and puzzling and maddening.

Come with us as we pull back the curtain and show you our wares. Step into the mind-blowing box with no doors, but with windows into the multiverse. And look for us out there, in magazines and books, online anthologies and lethal collections of wit and wisdom. We're everywhere; you've just never realized how weird we can be.

Deb Hoag
September, 2011

STORY LIST

SECTION ONE

Ys by Aliette de Bodard	8
Blood Willows by Caroline M. Yoachim	31
Six Reasons Why My Sister Hates Me by Aimee C. Amodio	36
Catfish Gal Blues by Nancy A. Collins	39
Bird in the Hand by Flavia Testa	52
Beneath the Skin by C.M. Vernon	54
Guadalupe of the Bowery by Ann Hagman Cardinal	67
A Stray Child by Rachel Turner	78
Hate Therapy by Wendy Jane Muzlanova	82

SECTION TWO

In the Meantime by Janice Lee	88
The Scene Changes by Mysty Unger	92
The Difference Between My Girlfriend and a Sea Captain by Katie Coyle	97
Safe as Houses by Helen Burke	111

In Any Mistake by Janis Butler Holm — 114

Lion Man by J.S Breukelaar — 116

Phat is a Four-Letter Word by Deb Hoag — 128

Minnows by Carol Novack — 142

SECTION THREE

Capps and Cavities by Moira McPartlin — 148

Fall Any Way You Can by Tantra Bensko — 155

The Gorilla in the Phone Booth by Nancy DiMauro — 158

Gretel by Firelight by Roberta Lawson — 172

The Strawman by Candy Caradoc — 177

The Seasonal Witch by Rachel Kendall — 183

Prayers for an Egg by Sara Genge — 187

Brain Box by Gina Ranalli — 198

The Bunny of Vengeance and the Bear of Death by Eugie Foster — 200

SECTION 1

Eldritch: *suggesting the operation of supernatural influences*

Ys
by Aliette de Bodard

Aliette de Bodard lives and works in Paris, where she has a day job as a Computer Engineer. In her spare time, she writes speculative fiction informed by her love of history and mythology: her Aztec noir fantasies Servant of the Underworld *and* Harbinger of the Storm *have been published by Angry Robot, while her short fiction has appeared in venues such as* Asimov's, Interzone *and the* Year's Best Science Fiction. *She has been a finalist for the Hugo, Nebula and Campbell Award for Best New Writer. Visit her website at* aliettedebodard.com.

"I wrote 'Ys' in homage to the seacoast of Brittany in France—where my father's side of the family hails from, and where I spent years as a child," said Aliette. "It is part of a series of fantasy stories set in France (the other being 'Mélanie', set in a Paris university, and which is available online at the World SF blog). The original legend of Ys has the sunken city vanish forever after Ahez betrays her father's trust, but I thought it was appropriate to have it resurface in more ways than one. Françoise is a composite of several people I knew who had to abandon art for practical purposes (whether it be science or other dayjobs); and I packed a lot of familiar locations into the short story."

September, and the wind blows Françoise back to Quimper, to roam the cramped streets of the Old City amidst squalls of rain.

She shops for clothes, planning the colours of the baby's room; ambles along the deserted bridges over the canals, breathing in the smell of brine and wet ivy. But all the while she's aware that she's only playing a game with herself—she knows she's only pretending that she hasn't seen the goddess.

It's hard to forget the goddess—that cold radiance that blew salt into Françoise's hair, the dress that shimmered with all the colours of sunlight on water—the sharp glimmer of steel in her hand.

You carry my child, the goddess had said, and it was so. It had always been so.

Except, of course, that Stéphane hadn't understood. He'd seen it as a betrayal—blaming her for not taking the pill as she should have—oh, not overtly, he was too stiff-necked and too well-educated for that, but all the same, she'd heard the words he wasn't saying, in every gesture, in every pained smile.

So she left. She came back here, hoping to see Gaëtan—if there's anyone who knows about goddesses and myths, it's Gaëtan, who used to go from house to house writing down legends from Brittany. But Gaëtan isn't here, isn't answering her calls. Maybe he's off on another humanitarian mission—incommunicado again, as he's so often been.

Françoise's cell phone rings—but it's only the alarm clock, reminding her that she has to work out at the gym before her appointment with the gynaecologist.

With a sigh, she turns towards the nearest bus stop, fighting a rising wave of nausea.

"It's a boy," the gynaecologist says, staring at the sonographs laid on his desk.

Françoise, who has been readjusting the straps of her bra, hears the reserve in his voice. "There's something else I should know."

He doesn't answer for a while. At last he looks up, his grey eyes carefully devoid of all feelings. His bad-news face, she guesses. "Have you—held back on something, Ms. Martin? In your family's medical history?"

A hollow forms in her stomach, draining the warmth from her limbs. "What do you mean?"

"Nothing to worry about," he says, slowly, and she can hear the "not yet" he's not telling her. "You'll have to take an appointment with a cardiologist. For a fetal echocardiograph."

She's not stupid. She's read books about pregnancies, when it became obvious that she couldn't bring herself to abort—to kill an innocent child. She knows about echocardiographs, and that the prognosis is not good. "Birth defect?" she asks, from some remote place in her mind.

He sits, all prim and stiff—what she wouldn't give to shake him out of his complacency. "Congenital heart defect. Most probably a difformed organ—it won't pump enough blood into the veins."

"But you're not sure." He's sending her for further tests. It means there's a way out, doesn't it? It means . . .

He doesn't answer, but she reads his reply in his gaze all the same. He's ninety-percent sure, but he still will do the tests—to confirm.

She leaves the surgery, feeling—cold. Empty. In her hands is a thick cream envelope: her sonographs, and the radiologist's diagnosis neatly typed and folded alongside.

Possibility of heart deformation, the paper notes, dry, uncaring.

Back in her apartment, she takes the sonographs out, spreads them on the bed. They look . . . well, it's hard to tell. There's the trapeze shape of the womb, and the white outline of the baby—the huge head, the body curled up. Everything looks normal.

If only she could fool herself. If only she was dumb enough to believe her own stories.

Evening falls over Quimper—she hears the bells of the nearby church tolling for Vespers. She settles at her working table, and starts working on her sketches again.

It started as something to occupy her, and now it's turned into an obsession. With pencil and charcoal she rubs in new details, with the precision she used to apply to her blueprints—and then withdraws, to stare at the paper.

The goddess stares back at her, white and terrible and smelling of things below the waves. The goddess as she appeared, hovering over the sand of Douarmenez Bay, limned by the morning sun: great and terrible and alien.

Françoise's hands are shaking. She clenches her fingers,

unclenches them, and waits until the tremors have passed.

This is real. This is now, and the baby is a boy, and it's not normal. It's never been normal.

That night, as on every night, Francoise dreams that she walks once more on the beach at Douarnenez—hearing the drowned bells tolling the midnight hour. The sand is cold, crunching under her bare feet.

She stands before the sea, and the waves part, revealing stone buildings eaten by kelp and algae, breached seawalls where lobsters and crabs scuttle. Everything is still dripping with brine, and the wind in her ears is the voice of the storm.

The goddess is waiting for her, within the largest building—in a place that must once have been a throne room. She sits in a chair of rotten wood, lounging on it like a sated cat. Beside her is a greater chair, made of stone, but it's empty.

"You have been chosen," she says, her words the roar of the waves. "Few mortals can claim such a distinction."

I don't want to be chosen, Francoise thinks, as she thinks on every night. But it's useless. She can't speak—she hasn't been brought here for that. Just so that the goddess can look at her, trace the minute evolutions in her body, the progress of the pregnancy.

In the silence, she hears the baby's heartbeat—a pulse that's so quick it's bound to falter. She hears the gynaecologist's voice: *the heart is deformed.*

"My child," the goddess says, and she's smiling. "The city of Ys will have its heir at last."

An heir to nothing. An heir to rotten wood, to algae-encrusted panels, to a city of fish and octopi and bleached skeletons. An heir with no heart.

He won't be born, Francoise thinks. He won't live. She tries to scream at the goddess, but it's not working. She can't open her mouth; her lips are stuck—frozen.

"Your reward will be great, never fear," the goddess says.

Her face is as pale as those of drowned sailors, and her lips purple, as if she were perpetually cold.

I fear. But the words still won't come.

The goddess waves a hand, dismissive. She's seen all that she needs to see; and Françoise can go back, back into the waking world.

She wakes up to a bleary light filtering through the slits of her shutters. Someone is insistently knocking on the door—and a glance at the alarm clock tells her it's eleven a.m., and that once more she's overslept. She ought to be too nauseous with the pregnancy to get much sleep, but the dreams with the goddess are screwing up her body's rhythm.

She gets up—too fast, the world is spinning around her. She steadies herself on the bedside table, waiting for the feeling to subside. Her stomach aches fiercely.

"A minute!" she calls, as she puts on her dressing gown, and sheathes her feet into slippers.

Through the Judas hole of the door, she can only see a dark silhouette, but she'd know that posture anywhere—a little embarrassed, as if he were intruding in a party he's not been invited to.

Gaëtan.

She throws the door open. "You're back," she says.

"I just got your message—" he stops, abruptly. His grey eyes stare at her, taking in, no doubt, the bulge of her belly and her puffy face. "I'd hoped you were joking." His voice is bleak.

"You know me better than that, don't you?" Françoise asks.

Gaëtan shrugs, steps inside—his beige trench coat dripping water on the floor. It looks as if it's raining again. Not an unusual occurrence in Brittany. "Been a long time," he says.

He sits on the sofa, twirling a glass of brandy between his fingers, while she tries to explain what has happened—when she gets to Douarnenez and the goddess walking out of the sea, her voice stumbles, trails off. Gaëtan looks at her, his face gentle: the same face he must show to the malnourished Africans who come to him as their last hope. He doesn't judge—doesn't scream or accuse her like Stéphane—and somewhere in her she finds the strength to go on.

After she's done, Gaëtan slowly puts the glass on the table, and steeples his fingers together, raising them to his mouth. "Ys," he says. "What have you got yourself into?"

"Like I had a choice." Françoise can't quite keep the acidity out of her voice.

"Sorry." Gaëtan hasn't moved—he's still thinking, it seems. It's never been like him to act or speak rashly. "It's an old tale around here, you know."

Françoise knows. That's the reason why she came back here. "You haven't seen this," she says. She goes to her working desk, and picks up the sketches of the goddess—with the drowned city in the background.

Gaëtan lays them on the low table before him, carefully sliding his glass out of the way. "I see." He runs his fingers on the goddess's face, very carefully. "You always had a talent for drawing. You shouldn't have chosen the machines over the landscapes and animals, you know."

It's an old, old tale; an old, old decision made ten years ago, and that she's never regretted. Except—except that the mere remembrance of the goddess's face is enough to scatter the formulas she made her living by; to render any blueprint, no matter how detailed, utterly meaningless. "Not the point," she says, finally—knowing that whatever happens next, she cannot go back to being an engineer.

"No, I guess not. Still . . . " He looks up at her, sharply. "You haven't talked about Stéphane."

"Stéphane—took it badly," she says, finally.

Gaëtan's face goes as still as sculptured stone. He doesn't say anything; he doesn't need to.

"You never liked him," Françoise says, to fill the silence—a silence that seems to have the edge of a drawn blade.

"No," Gaëtan says. "Let's leave it at that, shall we?" He turns his gaze back to the sketches, with visible difficulty. "You know who your goddess is."

Françoise shrugs. She's looked around on the Internet, but there wasn't much about the city of Ys. Or rather, it was always the same legend. "The Princess of Ys," she said. "She who took a new lover every night—and who had them killed every morning. She whose arrogance drowned the city beneath the waves."

Gaëtan nods. "Ahez," he says.

"To me she's the goddess." And it's true. Such things as her don't seem as though they should have a name, a handle back to the familiar. She cannot be tamed; she cannot be vanquished. She will not be cheated.

Gaëtan is tapping his fingers against the sketches, repeatedly jabbing his index into the eyes of the goddess. "They say Princess Ahez became a spirit of the sea after she drowned." He's speaking carefully, inserting every word with the meticulous care of a builder constructing an edifice on unstable ground. "They say you can still hear her voice in the Bay of Douarnenez, singing a lament for Ys—damn it, this kind of thing just shouldn't be happening, Françoise!"

Françoise shrugs. She rubs her hands on her belly, wondering if she's imagining the heartbeat coursing through her extended skin—a beat that's already slowing down, already faltering.

"Tell that to him, will you?" she says. "Tell him he shouldn't be alive." Not that it will ever get to be much of a problem, anyway—it's not as if he has much chance of surviving his birth.

Gaëtan says nothing for a while. "You want my advice?" he says.

Françoise sits on a chair, facing him. "Why not?" At least it will be constructive—not like Stéphane's anger.

"Go away," Gaëtan says. "Get as far as you can from Quimper—as far as you can from the sea. Ahez's power lies in the sea. You should be safe."

Should. She stares at him, and sees what he's not telling her. "You're not sure."

"No," Gaëtan says. He shrugs, a little helplessly. "I'm not an expert in magic and ghosts, and beings risen from the sea. I'm just a doctor."

"You're all I have," Francoise says, finally—the words she never told him after she started going out with Stéphane.

"Yeah," Gaëtan says. "Some leftovers."

Francoise rubs a hand on her belly again—feeling, distinctly, the chill that emanates from it: the coldness of beings drowned beneath the waves. "Even if it worked—I can't run away from the sea all my life, Gaëtan."

"You mean you don't want to run away, full stop."

A hard certainty rises within her—the same harshness that she felt when the gynaecologist told her about the congenital heart defect. "No," she says. "I don't want to run away."

"Then what do you intend to do?" Gaëtan's voice is brimming with anger. "She's immortal, Françoise. She was a sorceress who could summon the devil himself in the heyday of Ys. You're—"

She knows what she is; all of it. Or does she? Once she was a student, then an engineer and a bride. Now she's none of this—just a woman pregnant with a baby that's not hers. "I'm what I am," she says, finally. "But I know one other thing she is, Gaëtan, one power she doesn't have: she's barren."

Gaëtan cocks his head. "Not quite barren," he says. "She can create life."

"Life needs to be sustained," Françoise says, a growing certainty within her. She remembers the rotting planks of the palace in Ys—remembers the cold, cold radiance of the goddess. "She can't do that. She can't nurture anything." Hell, she cannot even create—not a proper baby with a functioning heart.

"She can still blast you out of existence if she feels like it."

Françoise says nothing.

At length Gaëtan says, "You're crazy, you know." But he's capitulated already—she hears it in his voice. He doesn't speak for a while. "Your dreams—you can't speak in them?"

"No. I can't do anything."

"She's summoned you," Gaëtan says. He's not the doctor anymore, but the folklorist, the boy who'd seek out old wives and listen to their talk for hours on end. "That's why. You come to Ys only at her bidding—you have no power of your own."

Françoise stares at him. She says, slowly, the idea taking shape as she's speaking, "Then I'll come to her. I'll summon her myself."

His face twists. "She'll still be—she's power incarnate, Françoise. Maybe you'll be able to speak, but that's not going to change the outcome."

Françoise thinks of the sonographs and of Stéphane's angry words—of her blueprints folded away in her Paris flat, the meaningless remnants of her old life. "There's no choice. I can't go on like this, Gaëtan. I can't—" She's crying now—tears running down her face, leaving tingling marks on her cheeks. "I can't—go—on."

Gaëtan's arms close around her; he holds her against his chest, briefly, awkwardly—a bulwark against the great sobs that shake her chest.

"I'm sorry," she says, finally, when she's spent all her tears. "I don't know what came over me."

Gaëtan pulls away from her. His gaze is fathomless. "You've hoarded them for too long," he says.

"I'm sorry," Françoise says, again. She spreads out her hands—feeling empty, drained of tears and of every other emotion. "But if there's a way out—and that's the only one there seems to be—I'll take it. I have to."

"You're assuming I can tell you how to summon Ahez," Gaëtan says, carefully.

She can read the signs; she knows what he's dangling before her: a possibility that he can give her, but that he doesn't approve of. It's clear in the set of his jaw, in the slightly aloof way he holds himself. "But you can, can't you?"

He won't meet her gaze. "I can tell you what I learnt of Ys," he says at last. "There's a song and a pattern to be drawn in the sand, for those who would open the gates of the drowned city . . . " He checks himself with a start. "It's old wives' tales, Françoise. I've never seen it work."

"Ys is old wives' tales. And so is Ahez. And I've seen them both. Please, Gaëtan. At worst, it won't work and I'll look like a fool."

Gaëtan's voice is sombre. "The worst is if it works. You'll be dead." But his gaze is still angry, and his hands clenched in his lap; and she knows she's won, that he'll give her what she wants.

Angry or not, Gaëtan still insists on coming with her—he drives her in his battered old Citroën on the small country roads to Douarnenez, and parks the car below a flickering lamplight.

Françoise walks down the dunes, keeping her gaze on the vast expanse of the ocean. In her hands she holds her only weapons: in her left hand, the paper with the pattern Gaëtan made her trace two hours ago; in her right hand, the sonographs the radiologist gave her this morning—the last scrap of science and reason that's left to her, the only seawall she can build against Ys and the goddess.

It's like being in her dream once more: the cold, white sand crunching under her sandals; the stars and the moon shining on the canvas of the sky; and the roar of the waves filling her ears to bursting. As she reaches the bottom of the beach—the strip of wet sand left by the retreating tide, where it's easier to draw patterns— the baby moves within her, kicking against the skin of her belly.

Soon, she thinks. Soon. Either way, it will soon be over, and the knot of fear within her chest will vanish.

Gaëtan is standing by her side, one hand on her shoulder. "You know there's still time—" he starts.

She shakes her head. "It's too late for that. Five months ago was the last time I had a choice in the matter, Gaëtan."

He shrugs, angrily. "Go on, then."

Françoise kneels in the sand, carefully, oh so carefully. She lays the cream envelope with the sonographs by her side; and positions the paper with the pattern so that the moonlight falls full onto it, leaving no shadow on its lines. To draw her pattern, she's brought a Celtic dagger with a *triskell* on the hilt—bought in a souvenir shop on the way to the beach.

Gaëtan is kneeling as well, staring intently at the pattern. His right hand closes over Françoise's hand, just over the dagger's hilt.

"This is how you draw," he says.

His fingers move, drawing Françoise's hand with them. The dagger goes down, sinks into the sand—there's some resistance, but it seems to melt away before Gaëtan's controlled gestures.

He draws line upon line, the beginning of the pattern—curves that meet to form walls and streets. And as he draws, he speaks: "We come here to summon Ys out of the sea. May Saint Corentin, who saved King Gradlon from the waves, watch over us; may the church bells toll not for our deaths. We come here to summon Ys out of the sea."

And, as he finishes his speech, he draws one last line, and completes his half of the pattern. Slowly, carefully, he opens his hand, leaving Françoise alone in holding the dagger.

Her turn.

She whispers, "We come here to summon Ys out of the sea. May Saint Corentin, who saved King Gradlon . . . " She closes her eyes for a moment, feeling the weight of the dagger in her hand—a last chance to abandon, to leave the ritual incomplete.

But it's too late for that.

With the same meticulousness she once applied to her blueprints—the same controlled gestures that allowed her to draw the goddess from memory—she starts drawing on the sand.

Now there's no other noise but the breath of the sea—and, in counterpoint to it, the soft sounds she makes as she adds line upon line, curves that arc under her to form a triple spiral, curves that branch and split, the pattern blossoming like a flower under her fingers.

She remembers Gaëtan's explanations: here are the seawalls of Ys, and the breach that the waves made when Ahez, drunk with her own power, opened the gates to the ocean's anger; here are the twisting streets and avenues where revellers would dance until night's end, and the palace where Ahez brought her lovers—and, at the end of the spiral, here is the ravine where her trusted servants would throw the lovers' bodies in the morning. Here is . . .

There's no time anymore where she is; no sense of her own body or of the baby growing within. Her world has shrunk to the pen and the darkened lines she draws, each one falling into place with the inevitability of a bell-toll.

When she starts on the last few lines, Gaëtan's voice starts speaking the words of power: the Breton words that summon Ahez and Ys from their resting-place beneath the waves.

> "Ur pales kaer tost d'ar sklujoù
> Eno, en aour hag en perlez,
> Evel an heol a bar Ahez."

A beautiful palace by the seawalls
There, in gold and in pearls
Like the sun gleams Ahez

His voice echoes in the silence, as if he were speaking above a bottomless chasm. He starts speaking them again—and again and again, the Breton words echoing each other until they become a string of meaningless syllables.

Françoise has been counting carefully, as he told her to; on the ninth repetition, she joins him. Her voice rises to mingle with Gaëtan's: thin, reedy, as fragile as a stream of smoke carried by the wind—and yet every word vibrates in the air, quivers as if drawing on some immesurable power.

> "Ur pales kaer tost d'ar sklujoù
> Eno, en aour hag en perlez,
> Evel an heol a bar Ahez."

Their words echo in the silence. At last, at long last, she rises, the pattern under her complete—and she's back in her body now, the sand's coldness seeping into her legs, her heart beating faster and faster within her chest—and there's a second, weaker heartbeat entwined with hers.

Slowly, she rises, tucks the dagger into her trousers pocket. There's utter silence on the beach now, but it's the silence before a storm. Moonlight falls upon the lines she's drawn—and remains trapped within them, until the whole pattern glows white.

"Françoise," Gaëtan says behind her. There's fear in his

voice.

She doesn't speak. She picks up the sonographs and goes down to the sea, until the waves lap at her feet—a deeper cold than that of the sand. She waits—knowing what is coming.

Far, far away, bells start tolling: the bells of Ys, answering her call. And in their wake the whole surface of the ocean is trembling, shaking like some great beast trying to dislodge a burden. Dark shadows coalesce under the sea, growing larger with each passing moment.

And then they're no longer shadows, but the bulks of buildings rising above the surface: massive stone walls encrusted with kelp, surrounding broken-down and rotted gates. The faded remnants of tabards adorn both sides of the gates—the drawings so eaten away Françoise can't make out their details.

The wind blows into her face the familiar smell of brine and decay, of algae and rotting wood: the smell of Ys.

Gaëtan, standing beside her, doesn't speak. Shock is etched on every line of his face.

"Let's go," Françoise whispers—for there is something about the drowned city that commands silence, even when you are its summoner.

Gaëtan is looking at her and at the gates; at her and at the shimmering pattern drawn on the sand. "It shouldn't have worked," he says, but his voice is very soft, already defeated. At length he shakes his head, and walks beside her as they enter the city of Ys.

Inside, skeletons lie in the streets, their arms still extended as if they could keep the sea at bay. A few crabs and lobsters scuttle away from them, the click-click of their legs on stone the only noise that breaks the silence.

Françoise holds the sonographs under her arms—the cardboard envelope is wet and decomposing, as if the atmosphere of Ys spreads rot to everything it touches. Gaëtan walks slowly, carefully. She can imagine how he feels—he, never one to take unconsidered risks, who now finds himself thrust into the legends of his childhood.

She doesn't think, or dwell overmuch on what could go wrong—that way lies despair, and perdition. But she can't help hearing the baby's faint heartbeat—and imagining his blood draining from his limbs.

There's no one in the streets, no revellers to greet them, no merchants plying their trades on the deserted marketplace—not even ghosts to flitter between the ruined buildings. Ys is a dead city. No, worse than that: the husk of a city, since long deserted by both the dead and the living. But it hums with power: with an insistent beat that seeps through the soles of Françoise's shoes, with a rhythm that is the roar of the waves and the voice of the storm—and also a lament for all the lives lost to the ocean. As she walks, the rhythm penetrates deeper into her body, insinuating itself into her womb until it mingles with her baby's heartbeat.

Françoise knows where she's going: all she has to do is retrace her steps of the dream, to follow the streets until they widen into a large plaza; to walk between the six kelp-eaten statues that guard the entrance to the palace, between the gates torn off their hinges by the onslaught of the waves.

And then she and Gaëtan are inside, walking down corridors. The smell of mould is overbearing now, and Françoise can feel the beginnings of nausea in her throat. There's another smell, too: underlying everything, sweet and cloying, like a perfume worn too long.

She knows who it belongs to. She wonders if the goddess has seen them come—but of course she has. Nothing in Ys escapes her overbearing power. She'll be at the centre, waiting for them—toying with their growing fear, revelling in their anguish.

No. Françoise mustn't think about this. She'll focus on the song in her mind and in her womb, the insidious song of Ys—and she won't think at all. She won't . . .

In silence they worm their way deeper into the cankered palace, stepping on moss and algae and the threadbare remnants of tapestries. Till at last they reach one last set of great gates—but those are of rusted metal, and the soldiers and sailors engraved on their panels are still visible, although badly marred by the sea.

The gates are closed—have been closed for a long time, the hinges buried under kelp and rust, the panels hanging askew. Françoise stops, the fatigue she's been ignoring so far creeping into the marrow of her bones.

Gaëtan has stopped too; he's running his fingers on the metal—pushing, desultorily, but the doors won't budge.

"What now?" he mouths.

The song is stronger now, draining Françoise of all thoughts—but at the same time lifting her into a different place, the same haven outside time as when she was drawing the pattern on the beach.

There are no closed doors in that place.

Françoise tucks the envelope with the sonographs under her arm, and lays both hands on the panels and pushes. Something rumbles, deep within the belly of the city—a pain that is somehow in her own womb—and then the gates yield, and open with a loud creak.

Inside, the goddess is waiting for them.

The dream once more: the rotten chairs beside the rotten trestle tables, the warm stones under her feet. And, at the far end of the room, the goddess sitting in the chair on the dais, smiling as Françoise draws nearer.

"You are brave," she says, and her voice is that of the sea before the storm. "And foolish. Few dare to summon Ys from beneath the waves." She smiles again, revealing teeth the colour of nacre. "And fewer still return alive." She moves, with fluid, inhuman speed; comes to stand by Gaëtan, who has frozen, three steps below the empty chair. "But you brought a gift, I see."

Françoise drags her voice from an impossibly faraway place. "He's not yours."

"I choose as I please, and every man that comes into Ys is mine," the goddess says. She walks around Gaëtan, tilting his head upwards, watching him as she might watch a slave on the selling-block. Abruptly there's a mask in her hand—a mask of black silk that seems to waver between her fingers.

That legend, too, Gaëtan told her. At dawn, after the goddess has had her pleasure, the mask will tighten until the man beneath dies of suffocation—one more sacrifice to slake her unending thirst.

Françoise is moving, without conscious thought—extending a hand and catching the mask before the goddess can put it on Gaëtan's face. The mask clings to her fingers: cold and slimy, like the scales of a fish, but writhing against her skin like a maddened snake.

She meets the goddess's cold gaze—the same blinding radiance that silenced her within the dream. But now there's power in Françoise—the remnants of the magic she used to summon Ys—and the light is strong, but she can still see.

"You dare," the goddess hisses. "You whom I picked among mortals to be honoured—"

"I don't want to be honoured," Françoise says, slowly. The mask is crawling upwards, extending coils around the palm of her hand. She's about to say "I don't want your child", but that would be a lie—she kept the baby, after all, clung to him rather than to Stéphane. "What I want you can't give."

The goddess smiles. She hasn't moved—she's still standing there, at the heart of her city, secure in her power. "Who are you to judge what I can and can't give?"

The mask is at her wrist now—it leaves a tingling sensation where it passes, as if it had briefly cut off the flow of blood in her body. Françoise tries not to think of what will happen when it reaches her neck—tries not to fear. Instead, as calmly as she can, she extends the envelope to the goddess. When she moves, the mask doesn't fall off, doesn't move in the slightest—except to continue its inexorable climb upwards.

Mustn't think about it. She knew the consequences when she drew her pattern in the sand; knew them and accepted them.

So she says to the goddess, in a voice that she keeps devoid of all emotions, "This is what you made."

The goddess stares at the envelope as if trying to decide what kind of trap it holds. Then, apparently deciding Françoise cannot harm her, she takes the envelope from Françoise's hands, and opens it.

Slowly, the goddess lifts the sonographs to the light, looks at them, lays them aside on the steps of the dais. From the envelope she takes the last paper—the diagnosis typed by the radiologist, and looks at it.

Silence fills the room, as if the whole city were holding its breath. Even the mask on Françoise's arm has stopped crawling.

"This is a lie," the goddess says, and her voice is the lash of a whip. Shadows move across her face, like storm-clouds blown by the wind.

Françoise shrugs, with a calm she doesn't feel. "Why would I?" She reaches out with one hand towards the mask, attempts to pull it from her arm. Her fingers stick to it, but it will not budge. Not surprising.

"You would cast my child from your womb."

Françoise shakes her head. "I could have. Much, much earlier. But I didn't." And the part of her that can't choke back its anger and frustration says, "I don't see why the child should pay for the arrogance of his creator."

"You dare judge me?" The goddess' radiance becomes blinding; the mask tightens around Françoise's arm, sending a wave of pain up her arm, pain so strong that Françoise bites her lips not to cry out. She fights an overwhelming urge to crawl into the dirt—it doesn't work, because abruptly she's kneeling on the floor, with only shaking arms to hold up her torso. She has to abase herself before the goddess—before her glory and her magic. She, Françoise, is nothing; a failure, a flawed womb. An artist turning to science out of greed; an engineer drawing meaningless blueprints; a woman who used her friend's feelings for her to bring him into Ys.

"If this child will not survive its birth," the goddess is saying, "you will have another. I will not be cheated." Not by you, she's saying without words. Not by a mere mortal.

A wave of power buffets Françoise, bringing with it the smell of wind and brine; of wet sand and rotten wood. Within her, the power of the goddess is rising—Françoise's belly aches as if fingers of ice were tearing it apart. Her baby is twisting and turning, kicking desperately against the confines of the womb, voicelessly screaming not to be unmade, but it's too late.

She wants to curl up on herself and make the pain go away; she wants to lie down, even if it's on slimy stone, and wait until the contractions of her belly have faded, and nothing remains but numbness. But she can't move. The only way to move is towards the algae-encrusted floor, to grovel before the goddess.

Gaëtan was right. It was folly to come here; folly to hope to stand against Ahez.

Françoise's arms hurt. She's going to have to yield. There's no other choice. She—

Yield.

She's a womb, an empty place for the goddess to fill. She has been chosen, picked out from the crowd of tourists on the beach—chosen for the greatest of honours, and now chosen again, to bear a child that will be perfect. She should be glad beyond reason.

Yield.

The mask is crawling upwards again—it's at her shoulder now, flowing towards her neck, towards her face. She knows, without being able to articulate the thought, that when it covers her face she will be lost—drowned forever under the silk.

Everything is scattering, everything is stripped away by the power of the goddess—the power of the ocean that drowns sailors, of the storm-tossed seas and their irresistible siren song. She can't hold on to anything. She—has to—

There's nothing left at her core now; only a hollow begging to be filled.

And yet . . . and yet in the silence, in the emptiness of her mind is the song of Ys, and the pattern she drew in the sand; in the silence of her mind, she is kneeling on the beach with the dagger still in her hand, and watching the drowned city rise from the depths to answer her call.

Slowly, she raises her head, biting her lips not to scream at the pain within her—the pain that sings yield yield yield. Blood floods her mouth with the taste of salt, but she's staring at the face of the goddess—and the light isn't blinding, she can see the green eyes dissecting her like an insect. She can—

She can speak.

"I—am—not—your toy," she whispers. Every word is a leaden weight, a stone dragged from some faraway place. "The child—is—not—your—toy."

She reaches for the mask—which is almost at her lips. She feels the power coiled within the silk, the insistent beat that is also the rhythm of the waves, and the song that has kept Ys from crumbling under the sea—and it's within her, pulsing in her belly, singing in her veins and arteries.

The mask flows towards her outstretched fingers, clings to them. It's cold and wet, like rain on parched earth. She shakes her hand, and the mask falls onto the ground, and lies there, inert and harmless: an empty husk.

Like Ys. Like Ahez.

"You dare—" the goddess hisses. Her radiance is wavering, no longer as strong as it was on Douarnenez. She extends a hand: it's empty for a split second, and then the wavering image of a white spear fills it. The goddess lunges towards Françoise. Out of sheer instinct, Françoise throws herself aside. Metal grates on the stones to her left—not ten centimetres from where she is.

Françoise pushes herself upwards, ignoring the nausea that wells up as she abruptly changes positions. The goddess is coming at her again with her spear.

Françoise is out of breath, and the world won't stop spinning around her—she can't avoid the spear forever. The song is deep within her bones, but that doesn't help—it just adds to her out-of-synch feeling.

The spear brushes past her, draws a fiery line of pain on her hand. She has to—

Behind the goddess, Gaëtan still stands frozen. No, not quite, she realises as she sidesteps once more, stumbling—the nausea rising, rising, screaming at her to lie down and yield. Gaëtan is blinking—staring at her, the eyes straining to make sense of what they see.

He raises a hand, slowly—too slowly, damn it, she thinks as she throws herself on the floor and rolls over to avoid the spear.

It buries itself into her shoulder—transfixes her. She's always thought she would scream if something like that happened, but she doesn't. She bites her lips so fiercely that blood fills her mouth. Within her, the pattern she drew on the sand is whirling, endlessly.

The pattern. The dagger. She fumbles for it, tries to extract it from her trousers' pocket, but she can't, she's pinned to the ground. She should have thought of it earlier—

"Your death will not be clean," the goddess says, as she withdraws the spear for another thrust.

Françoise screams, then. Not her pain; but a name. "Gaëtan!"

His panicked heartbeat is part of the song within her—the nausea, the power shimmering beyond her reach. He's moving as if through tar, trying to reach her—but he won't, not in time. There's not enough time.

But her scream makes the goddess pause, and look up for a split second, as if she'd forgotten something and only just remembered. For a moment only she's looking away from Françoise, the spear's point hovering within Françoise's reach.

Françoise, giving up on releasing the dagger, grasps the haft of the spear instead. She pulls down, as hard as she can.

She's expected some resistance, but the goddess has no weight—barely enough substance to wield the spear, it seems. Françoise's savage pull topples her onto the floor, felling her like harvested wheat.

But she's already struggling to rise—white arms going for Françoise's throat. At such close quarters, the spear is useless. Françoise makes a sweeping throw with one hand, and hears it clatter on the stones. She fumbles, again, for the dagger—half-out of her pocket this time. But there's no time. No time . . .

Abruptly, the white arms grow slack. Something enters her field of view—the point of the spear, hovering above her, and then burying itself in the goddess's shoulder.

"I don't think so," Gaëtan says. His face is pale, his hair dishevelled, but his grip on the spear's haft doesn't waver.

Françoise rolls away from the goddess, heaving—there's bile in her throat, but she can't even vomit. She finally has her dagger out, but it doesn't seem like she will need it.

Doesn't seem...

The goddess hisses like a stricken cat. She twists away, and the spear slides out of her wound as easily as from water. Then, before Gaëtan can react, she jumps upwards—both arms extended towards his face.

The spear clatters on the ground. Françoise stifles the scream that rises in her, and runs, her ribs burning. She's going to be too late—she can't possibly—

She's almost there, but the goddess's arms are already closing around Gaëtan's throat. There's no choice. There never was any choice.

Françoise throws the dagger.

She sees everything that happens next take place in slow motion: the dagger, covering the last few hand-spans that separate Françoise from the goddess's back—the hilt, slowly starting to flip upwards—the blade, burying itself at an angle into the bare white skin—blood, blossoming from the wound like an obscene fountain.

The goddess falls, drawing Gaëtan down with her. Françoise, unable to contain herself anymore, screams, and her voice echoes under the vast ceiling of the throne room.

Nothing moves. Then the goddess's body rolls aside, and Gaëtan stands up, shaking. Red welts cover his throat, and he is breathing heavily—but he looks fine. He's alive.

"Françoise?"

She's unable to voice her relief. Beside him, the goddess's body is wrinkled and already crumbling into dust—leaving only the dagger, glinting with drowned light.

Within her, the symphony is rising to a pitch—the baby's heart, her own, mingling in their frantic beat. She hears a voice whispering, *the Princess is dead. Ys is dead. Who shall rule on Ahez's throne?*

Once more she's lifted into that timeless place of the beach, with her pattern shining in moonlight: every street of Ys drawn in painstaking detail.

At the centre of the city, in the palace, is its heart, but it's not beating as it should. Its valves and veins are too narrow, and not pumping enough blood—it cannot stave off the rot nor keep the sea from eating at the skeletons, but neither will it let the city die.

And it's her baby's heart, too—the two inextricably tied, the drowned city, and the baby who should have been its heir.

She has a choice, she sees: she can try to repair the heart, to widen the arteries to let the blood in—perhaps Gaëtan could help, he's a doctor, after all. She can draw new pathways for the blood, with the same precision as a blueprint—and hope they will be enough.

She wants the baby to live—she wants her five months of pregnancy, her loss of Stéphane, not to have been for nothing, not to have been a cruel jest by someone who's forgotten what it was to be human.

But there are skeletons in the streets of Ys; crabs and shells scuttling on the paved stones; kelp covering the frescoed walls; and in the centre of the city, in the throne room, the dais is rotten—to the core.

She hears the heartbeat within her, the blood ebbing and flowing in her womb, and she knows, with absolute certainty, that it will not be enough. That she has to let go.

She doesn't want to. It would be like yielding—did she go all that way for nothing?

But this isn't about her—there's nothing she can offer Ys, or the baby.

She closes her eyes, and sees the pattern splayed on the ground—and the heart at the centre.

And in her mind she takes up the dagger, and drives up to the hilt into the pattern.

There's a scream, deep within her—tendrils of pain twisting within her womb. The pattern contorts and wavers—and it's disappearing, burning away like a piece of paper given to the flames.

She's back in her body—she's fallen to her knees on the floor, both hands going to her belly as if she could contain the pain. But of course she can't.

Around her, the walls of the palace are shaking.

"Françoise, we have to get out of there!" Gaëtan says.

She struggles to speak through a haze of pain. "I—"

Gaëtan's hands drag her upwards, force her to stand. "Come on," he says. "Come on."

She stumbles on, leaning on his shoulder—through the kelp-encrusted corridors, through the deserted streets and the ruined buildings that are now collapsing. One step after another—one foot in front of the other, and she will not think of the pain in her belly, of the heartbeat within her that grows fainter and fainter with every step.

She will not think.

They're out of Ys, standing on the beach at Douarnenez with the stars shining above. The drowned city shivers and shakes and crumbles, and the sea is rising—rising once more to reclaim it.

Then there's nothing left of Ys, only the silvery surface of the ocean, and the waves lapping at their feet. Between Françoise's legs, something wet and sticky is dripping—and she knows what it has to be.

Gaëtan is looking at the sea; Françoise, shaking, has not the strength to do more than lean on his shoulder. She stares ahead, at the blurry stars, willing herself not to cry, not to mourn.

"You OK?" Gaëtan asks.

She shrugs. "Not sure yet," she says. "Come on. Let's go home and grab some sleep."

Later, there'll be time for words: time to explain, time to heal and rebuild. But for now, there is nothing left but silence within her—only one heartbeat she can hear, and it's her own.

I'll be OK, she thinks, blinking furiously, as they walk back to Gaëtan's car. Overhead, the stars are fading—a prelude to sunrise. I'll be OK.

But her womb is empty; and in her mind is the song of her unborn son, an endless lament for all that was lost.

BLOOD WILLOWS
by Caroline M. Yoachim

Caroline M. Yoachim is a writer and photographer living in Seattle, Washington. Her fiction has appeared in Asimov's, Fantasy Magazine, Beneath Ceaseless Skies, *and* Greatest Uncommon Denominator, *among other places. She is a member of Codex, a graduate of the Clarion West writers workshop, and was recently nominated for a Nebula Award for her novelette "Stone Wall Truth." For more about Caroline, check out her website at* carolineyoachim.com.

"Blood Willows" first appeared in Flash Fiction Online *in the March, 2010 issue. I liked it so much that when I had the opportunity to put together this anthology, I immediately thought of Caroline and her haunting tale of a woman who takes going green way too far . . .*

Stephen cradled Mara in his arms. She was light, but awkward to carry because of her trees. A blood willow grew from her shoulder and hid her face behind a curtain of crimson leaves. Its trunk was pale and gnarled.

They'd taken this path to visit her father's grove, back when Mara could walk. Now a cottonbone tree grew from her thigh and locked her knee perpetually straight. The roots extended down her leg and dangled from the tips of her toes.

Natasha and Evan toddled along behind him with Grandma Angie between them.

"See the cottonbone trees?" Angie pointed at a grove. "Grew a long time to get that big."

The bleached-white cottonbones stretched up into the clouds. Scattered among them were the smaller blood willows, with branches sagging down to the ground instead of reaching to the sky. Bright red blossoms dotted the branches like a troupe of ladybugs.

"Will Mommy bloom too?" Natasha asked, noticing the flowers.

"We'll see," he answered.

"Stephen," Mara called, "come look at this."

She stood in front of the bathroom mirror with her shirt knotted up above her rounded belly. He smiled. "Are the twins playing soccer in there?"

"No, this." She pointed to a red bump on her hip.

"Bug bite?"

"It's been like this for three days. I've been nauseous, but I thought it was the twins." She picked at the bump with her fingernail and winced.

"Well that's why it hasn't gone away. You're picking at it," he scolded, laughing and grabbing her hand.

There was a dot of blood on her fingernail. He wiped it away and opened the medicine cabinet to look for a bandage. When he turned around, Mara was crying.

A blood willow sapling was growing from her hip.

Mara's clearing was covered with moss. Stephen set Mara down on the blanket of green. Her breath came in gasps.

"The other way," she said.

He turned her to face her father's grove. Stephen had never met him. Mara insisted he was there in the grove — that the curve of his pelvic bone formed the base of a cottonbone tree and his heart hid inside the trunk of a blood willow.

Grandma Angie took the twins to his grove, and Evan hoisted himself up into the cottonbone branches. Stephen turned to call him down, but Mara whispered, "Let him. Papa so rarely gets to play with his grandchildren."

"He's not there," Stephen said. He pulled the blood willow branches aside so he could see Mara's face. Her eyes were clear blue, but unfocused.

"He'll be so happy that I'm here."

Already her roots dug into the ground around her.

Natasha ran up, nearly slipping on the slick moss. "Mommy, Grandpa is blooming! I picked you flowers."

One corner of Mara's mouth curled into a smile. "Hang them where I can see them, okay?"

Natasha draped the bright red blossoms over the cottonwood on Mara's leg.

"Give Mommy a kiss."

Natasha obliged, then wandered back to her grandpa's grove.

"I don't want to be alone," Mara said.

"We'll stay."

Stephen stroked the side of her neck. He could feel the bulge of the roots beneath her skin.

"And after?" Mara asked.

"We'll stay." He didn't know what else to say.

"Hold still," Stephen said.

Mara lay face down on the bed. A cottonbone sapling poked out from her shoulder blade. It was as thin as hair, and silver-gray. He gripped it with the tweezers.

"Ow, ow, ow."

"I haven't started yet."

"Leave it."

"We can't. The doctor said to pull them early."

He yanked. Mara buried her face in the pillows. The sapling dangled from the tweezers, three inches of roots stained red with her blood. He chucked it in the trash. Mara rolled over, revealing a blood willow on her stomach.

"It's getting worse." He ran his fingers over the stretch marks the twins left behind.

"The seeds are in my blood," she said. "We'll never keep up. Pull this one, then let them be."

He grabbed the willow with the tweezers and tore it out. She cried from the pain, and he hurled the offending tree against the window. The sapling left a trail of Mara's blood as it slid down.

The sun set, and the air turned crisp and cool.

"Should I take the twins home?" Angie asked.

"I don't want to be alone," Mara whispered through the roots in her throat.

"I'll stay," Stephen said.

Mara didn't answer. Natasha and Evan pushed in under her branches.

"Time to go home, Mommy," Natasha told her.

Mara strained against her roots to bring one arm up and stroke Natasha's cheek. "Go with Grandma, and be good, okay?"

She reached for Evan, but he was too far away. Stephen nudged him forward.

"That goes double for you young man. You be good for Angie and Daddy."

"Bye, Mommy," he said. He put his head against her cheek. "I'll come climb you tomorrow."

Angie hugged Mara, then led the twins away.

Stephen leaned against the trunk of Mara's willow and cradled her head in his lap. They talked about the twins, about Angie, about anything that wasn't trees. When she got tired, he talked for both of them, a constant chatter so she'd know she wasn't alone.

"Stephen," Mara whispered. He stopped talking for the first time in hours. She coughed and gasped. Stephen brushed his fingers over her hip, her stomach, her neck. He remembered the trees they'd pulled, small victories before this final, crushing defeat.

Silence filled the clearing. There was no wind to shake the leaves, and no breath to rasp and rattle in Mara's chest.

Stephen stayed and talked to her trees. The sun rose, and in the warmth of morning, Mara's willow smelled faintly of flowers. He pulled her branches closer and squinted in the morning light. Scattered among her leaves were tightly curled red buds, flowers beginning to bloom.

SIX REASONS WHY MY SISTER HATES ME
by Aimee C. Amodio

Aimee C. Amodio was eleven when she told her parents she wanted to grow up to be a writer. She may not consider herself "grown up" but she does do that writing thing on a regular basis. Aimee lives in the Pacific Northwest with two neurotic dogs (they take after their mother). Visit her website at newroticgirl.com.

"I spent three years as caretaker for a family member with Alzheimer's disease. It's an incredibly cruel disease. I know what it's like to be responsible for someone you love, to be obligated to put their needs first, to feel like you can never get away. Mix that up with the long-standing obligation between sisters, and there you go.

"Until I was asked for a little history/inspiration behind 'Six Reasons,' I hadn't realized how much of it was tied into caring for my grandmother. But I don't hate her—I hate the disease that's stolen her away from us."

(One)

My sister Chiru has beautiful, rich, warm brown skin. Mine is like onionskin paper, yellowed and dry and fragile. The few wisps of hair that grow on my scarred scalp mock the thick, black waves that fall past her shoulders and would grow to her waist if she let it. She is poised and correct in her posture, where I am bowed and curled like a crescent.

She is perfect and I am flawed, and she hates me.

(Two)

My sister Chiru is brilliant, and speaks to computers. I mean this literally; she is a technopath. If it has wires and electricity for blood, it will bend to her will. She is rich, richer than I could ever be, simply by doing what comes naturally and disguising it under a title: network consultant.

She speaks the language of the machine so well and relates to the living so poorly. I am alive, and she must take care of me.

(Three)

My sister Chiru is a hero who walked bravely into the jaws of death and pulled me from them. That is to say: she threaded the maze of white corridors to return to the facility where we were created and free our siblings from locked room and computer-run incubators.

When Chiru is angry or afraid, machines explode. (Perhaps now you see why she could escape where none of the rest of us could begin to wake up from a druggy haze.)

Chiru was very angry that day.

In the end, she couldn't retrieve anyone but me; hundreds or thousands of fertilized eggs, clones in various stages of development, a few newly dissected in the name of Science all died while I lived.

I didn't know what I was doing. My first memory is orange and yellow and thick, dark smoke, the smell of meat, the roar and crackle, the white-hot bubbling of my skin. Instinct bent the lines of energy away from me, shielding me from the blaze while everyone else burned.

She called me Coda because I am the last one.

She hates me because I survived where all the rest died. I whisper this to myself every day as penance.

(Four)

My beautiful, brilliant sister Chiru has no gift for people.

That gift is mine.

I can perceive the thin strands that make connections between people: family, friends, lovers, coworkers are all connected by threads of energy. Across distance, across time, we are connected in a great and tangled web.

I can see the threads, and I can follow them. Manipulate them.

But we are all connected. Tug one thread, and another part of the tapestry unravels. There is a price to pay for every twitch of the lines. Saving myself — even though I didn't know what I was doing when I did it — wrecked a hundred other lives. I made a wall from bits of lives and wrapped it around myself as I burned. As we all burned.

Those lives I used left blank lines in the web, weak spots that will surely fail, and the more I try to fix things, the worse things get. It spirals out exponentially, great patches of darkness in the glittering universe I can see between people.

Chiru has to order pizza online because she hates talking to the delivery boy.

(Five)
I am the one they wanted, and she hates me.

(Six)
I am the successful experiment, and they hunt us.

She runs, she carries me, she tends my empty body while my mind travels, she spoons broth into my cracked lips. Nowhere is safe for long, so she hauls me from one hiding hole to another, whispering to the cash machines and airport ticket computers to change our names and hide our tracks.

They would perhaps leave her alone if she left me behind.

But she won't. I am all she has, the only person in the world she could possibly relate to, and she runs and carries and hates me.

CATFISH GAL BLUES
by Nancy A. Collins

"Catfish Gal Blues" was originally published in 999 *(Avon Books, 1999). Nancy has written more than a dozen novels, most of which involve races of creatures the author calls Pretenders, monsters from myth and legend passing as human to better hunt their prey. She is best known for her vampire character, Sonja Blue.*

I'm delighted to say I selected this story before I knew what a popular writer Nancy is. Now that I know, I'm doubly impressed with my own good taste.

Flyjar is the kind of Southern town where time doesn't mean much. Maybe that's because there's little in the way of change between the seasons—the difference between winter and summer a mere fifteen degrees on average. And when you're as poor as most folks in Flyjar, there's not a whole lot of difference between one decade and another—or century, for that matter.

The two constants in Flyjar are poverty and the river. The town clings to the Mississippi like a child to its mama's skirt, and its fortunes—for good or ill—have been tied to the Big Muddy like apron strings. At one time it had served as a regular fueling stop for the riverboats that once traveled up and down The Father of All Waters. But those days were long gone, and all that remained of "the good old days" were some deteriorating wooden piers along the riverbanks.

Since most of the wharves extended several hundred feet into the river, there were plenty of crappies, channel cat and garfish free for the taking, provided you had the know-how and patience to catch them, as Sammy Herkimer, one of Flyjar's better fishermen, was quick to tell anyone who'd listen.

There were several docks to choose from, but Sammy's favorite was the one at Steamboat Bend. It was a mile or so from town and, because of that, was not in the best of shape. Since it meant keeping an eye on where you walked, not many of the locals used it, which suited Sammy just fine. Then one day, while he was sitting on the dock, sipping ice tea from a thermos, he was surprised to find himself joined by, of all people, Hop Armstrong.

Hop was the closest thing Flyjar had to a fancy man, since the good Lord had seen fit to bless him with good looks, but skimped in the ambition department. When it came to playing guitar and getting women to pay his way, Hop was second to none. But when it came to physical labor . . . well, that was another story.

"Lord A' mighty, Hop!" Sammy proclaimed, unable to hide his surprise. "What you doin' here? Someone set fire to your house?"

"You could say that," Hop grunted. "My woman said I had to bring home supper."

"That a fact?" Sammy said, raising an eyebrow.

Hop's most recent sugar mama was Lucinda Solomon, the proprietoress of the local beauty parlor. Lucinda was good-looking and well-to-do, at least by Flyjar's standards. She was also notoriously strong-willed, and rumor had it that in living off Lucinda, Hop had finally met up with something approximating hard work.

Sammy glanced at the younger man's gear, noting with some amusement that while Hop had remembered to bring along his guitar, he hadn't bothered to pack a net. He returned his gaze to the river, shaking his head. After a long stretch of silence between the two, the older man spoke up abruptly.

"You know why they call this stretch of the river Steamboat Bend, Hop?"

"I figgered on account of it bein' a bend in the river and there was steamboats that used to come down it," he replied with a shrug.

"That's part of it, but it ain't the whole reason. A long time ago there was this big ole paddleboat that used to cruise up and down the river called *Delta Blossom*. She was a real fancy pleasure boat, with marble mantelpieces and crystal chandeliers and gold door-handles. When folks heard *Delta Blossom* was coming, they ran from the houses and fields to watch her pass. Anyways, one day, without any warning, *Delta Blossom* went down with all hands, right about there," Sammy said, gesturing towards the middle of the river.

"Why did she sink?" Hop asked, a tinge of interest seeping into his voice.

"No one's rightly sure. Some said the boilers blew out th' side of the boat. Some said there was a fire below decks. Maybe it got its hull punched open by a submerged tree. Who can really know, after all this time? But my old granny used to swear up and down that *Delta Blossom* was scuttled by catfish gals."

Hop scowled at the older man. "You funnin' with me, ain't you, Sammy."

"No, sir, I ain't!" he said solemnly, shaking his head for emphasis. "Before there was any white or black folk, or even Indians living in these parts, there was catfish gals here. They live in the river, down where it's muddy and deep. They got the upper-parts of women, and from the waist down are big ole channel cats. They keep their distance from us humans, and, for the most part, are peaceful enough. Some folks said the catfish gals sank the *Delta Blossom* on account of one of 'em gettin' caught in the paddlewheel and crushed."

Hop turned to fix the older man with a curious stare. "You ever *seen* one of them catfish gals, Sammy?"

"No, I ain't. But I ain't gone lookin' for them, neither. But my granny said they was why no one ever finds folks who are fool enough to go swimmin' in the river. They take the drowned bodies and stick 'em deep in the mud, until they get all blote up. That way their flesh is easier to eat . . . "

Hop grimaced . "Hush up about that! It's bad enough my woman's got me out here without you goin' on about catfish eatin' daid folks!"

"Sorry. I didn't realize you was sensitive on the subject."

After another stretch of silence, Sammy nodded towards the guitar.

"So—if you're here to fish, why the git-box?"

"Man can do more 'n one thing at a time, can't he?"

"I reckon so—but I don't recommend it. You'll scare off the fish."

"Mebbe I'll just charm me a catfish gal instead," Hop grinned.

"If anyone could, I reckon it'd be you," Sammy sighed as he reeled in his line. "Well, I caught me enough for one day. I better get on home so's I can clean this mess of crappies in time for supper. Good luck on charming them catfish gals, Hop. Y'all take care."

"Y'all too, Sammy," Hop replied absently, his gaze fixed on the river.

Hop had to admit that being out in the sunshine on a day like today wasn't all that bad. It wasn't too hot and there was a nice breeze coming off the water . . . plus, there was the added advantage of being out of his woman's line-of-sight.

Lucinda was far from an easy woman to please, and an even harder one to live with when riled. And she was most always riled. Hop knew the signs well enough by now to realize that his days of leisure at the feisty Miz Solomon's expense were drawing to their close, but he didn't like to jump ship unless he had a new girlfriend lined up. Unfortunately, for a man of his tastes and inclinations, Flyjar didn't have much in the way of available lady folk for him to choose from—so it looked like he was going to have to make do with Lucinda for a while longer.

At least Steamboat Bend was remote enough that the chances of Lucinda actually finding how hard he was—or wasn't—working at putting supper on the table was in his favor.

Hop pulled a forked stick from his tackle box and wedged it between the loose planks of the dock. After baiting the hook, he cast the line into the murky waters and propped the reel against the stick. Keeping one eye on the bobber, Hop leaned against the nearby wooden pylon and picked up his guitar.

There was not a time in his memory where music didn't come easy to him. Ever since he was knee-high, he'd been able to make a guitar do whatever it was he wanted of it. Playing guitar came as natural to him as breathing and eating— it was pretty much the same with women, too—and both were a lot more pleasant than chopping cotton or driving a tractor to make ends meet.

Hop scanned the deceptively calm surface of the river. It was so wide the current's strength was difficult to gauge with the naked eye. The only way to figure out just how powerful the river truly was was by the size of the driftwood, and the speed at which it went past. There were days when he'd seen full-grown oak trees race one another to the Gulf of Mexico. Today was relatively placid, with only a few deadfalls the size of railroad ties headed down river.

Hop found his mind turning to the story Sammy had told him. Not about the catfish gals—that was pure hokum if ever he heard it. What piqued his imagination was the *Delta Blossom*. Hop wondered what it must have been like back in those days, when the steamboats cruised the river, bringing glamour and wealth to pissant little towns like Flyjar.

To think that one of the grandest of the old paddle wheelers had come to its end a stone's throw from where he was sitting, taking its splendor to the Mississippi's silty floor . . .

All Hop had ever seen gracing the river were flat-bottomed barges and the occasional freighter or small leisure craft. These were hardly the kinds of vessels that sparked the imagination and quickened the heart. Folks didn't flock to the levees just to watch a barge pass by.

Hop wondered if there was still anything left of the old *Delta Blossom* at the bottom of Steamboat Bend. There was no way to know. What secrets the river held it did not give up readily. Still, it didn't keep him from idly hoping to spot the sunken pleasure ship's outline.

In his mind's eye, he could see the long-lost floating pleasure palace, white as new cotton with towering double-smokestack puffing away like a rich man's cigars as she made her way along the Mississippi. He could picture the southern belles in hoop skirts lining the ship's second story promenade, silk fans fluttering like caged birds, while riverboat gamblers in pristine linen suits and wide-brimmed hats tossed silver dollars and gold-pieces onto the felt of the gaming tables. Hop saw himself dressed like Clark Gable in *Gone With The Wind*, tipping his hat to the young ladies of fashion gathered in the *Delta Blossom's* grand salon for the evening's entertainment. What a swath he could have cut back then!

As his debonair phantom-self danced underneath the swaying crystal chandeliers with a young woman who looked a great deal like Vivienne Leigh, Hop's nimble fingers were quick to provide the music. Granted, *Goodnight Irene* wasn't around at the time, but it was his daydream, after all, wasn't it?

As he played, a sudden movement in the middle of the river caught Hop's eye. From where he was sitting, it looked as if a swimmer had surfaced in the middle of the bend, near where Sammy said the *Delta Blossom* had gone down, then just as quickly submerged. But that was impossible.

Swimming in the Mississippi was only slightly less hazardous to your health than brushing your teeth with lit dynamite. Every so often some fool would get drunk enough to try and brave the river—and disappear without a trace ten feet from shore. If the family were lucky, the body would turn up a few days later, fifty miles downstream, snagged in the branches of a tree on the floodplain, looking more like a drowned pig than a human being.

But what Hop saw hadn't looked anything like a floater popping to the surface. For one thing, it stayed in one place and didn't follow the current. Hop shaded his eyes against the sun, trying to get a better look, but there was nothing there. His attention was brought back closer to shore as the bobber on his line registered a strike. Hop dropped his guitar and snatched up the fishing rod, reeling in a ten-pound catfish.

It looked like Lucinda wasn't going to have anything to scold him about tonight, that much was for certain.

But as he headed back home, his fishing pole draped over one shoulder and his guitar slung over the other, Hop couldn't shake the feeling that he was being watched—and by something besides the catfish hanging from his belt.

That night as he was lying in bed, Lucinda snoring beside him, Hop got to thinking.

Maybe what Sammy Herkimer said about catfish gals wasn't all hogwash after all. He remembered reading in one of them yellow-backed magazines down at the barber shop about some kind of fish everyone thought was extinct being found in some foreign country a few years back. Besides, who was he to decide there weren't no such things as catfish gals, when he didn't know a soul who'd been to the bottom of the Mississippi and lived to tell the tale?

The very next day Hop went fishing without Lucinda telling him to.

He decided to try his luck again at Steamboat Bend. When he arrived at the dock, he was relieved to find he was alone. Hop set himself up on the dock just as he had the day before, but after a half- hour of sitting and waiting for something to happen, he put down the fishing rod and picked up his guitar to pass the time.

Halfway into *Moanin' At Midnight*, Hop heard what sounded like a fish slap the water near the pier. When he glanced up to see what had caused the noise, he nearly dropped his axe into the water below.

There was a human head bobbing in the water a hundred feet away from the dock. At the sound of his astonished gasp, the head ducked back down beneath the muddy surface without leaving so much as a ripple to mark its passing. Just as suddenly, there was a strike on Hop's line so powerful it nearly yanked his fishing pole into the river.

Although Lucinda was extremely pleased with the fifteen-pound catfish he brought home that evening, Hop didn't say anything about what he'd seen on the river. Something told him that whatever it was that was out at Steamboat Bend was best kept to himself.

The next day Hop didn't even bother casting his line into the river. He knew what was drawing the thing in the river to the dock, and it sure as hell wasn't the shiners he was using for bait.

He made his way to the very end of the landing, careful to avoid the loose and missing planks, and sat so his legs dangled over the edge. After a moment of deliberation, he decided *They Call Me Muddy Waters* would be an appropriate choice.

Just like before, the thing surfaced halfway through the song. Hop's heart was racing so fast it was hard to breathe, but he forced himself to keep playing. He didn't want to scare it off, so he kept playing, switching to *Pony Blues* once he'd finished with his first song.

While he played, Hop kept his head down, ignoring his audience as best he could. As he launched into *Circle Round the Moon,* he risked glancing in the thing's direction, only to discover it was almost directly underneath his dangling feet, staring at him with big, dark eyes that were almost all pupil.

Hop was surprised at how human the catfish gal looked. From what Sammy had said, he'd pictured a fish in a fright wig, but that wasn't the case. Her upper lip was extremely wide, with the familiar catfish whiskers growing out of them, and she had slits instead of a nose, but outside of that she wasn't *too* ugly. Hell, he'd seen worse looking women in church.

Her hair was a real mess, though, with everything from twigs to what looked like live minnows caught in the tangled locks. He couldn't see much of what she looked like below the waterline, although he did glimpse vertical slits opening and closing down the sides of her neck.

Hop couldn't help but smile to himself when he saw how the catfish gal looked at him. Half-fish or not, he knew what that look meant on a woman's face. He had her hooked but good and now was as good a time as any to reel her in.

Hop looked the catfish gal right in the eye and smiled. "Hello, lit'l fishie. You come to hear me play?"

The catfish gal's dreamy look was replaced by one of surprise. She glanced around, as if confused by her surroundings, then shot backwards like a dolphin walking on its tail.

"Please! Don't go!" he shouted, stretching out his hand to stay her retreat.

To his surprise, the catfish gal came to a sudden halt, regarding him curiously, bobbing up and down in the Mississippi as easily as a young girl treading water in a swimming pool.

"You ain't got nothin' to be scared of, lit'l fishie," Hop said, smiling reassuringly. "I ain't gonna hurt you none. Do you want me to play some more for you?" he asked, holding up his guitar.

The catfish gal nodded and lifted a dripping arm, pointing at the guitar with a webbed forefinger. Hop smiled and obliged her by picking up where he had left off.

By the time the sun was starting to go down, Hop's hands were cramping and his fingertips bloody. He'd played a little bit of almost everything—blues, bluegrass, honky tonk, camp songs, even a couple of nursery songs—trying to figure out what the catfish gal liked and didn't like: turned out she was partial to the blues—which made sense, seeing how that music was born on the banks of the Mississippi.

When he finally put aside his guitar, the catfish gal disappeared beneath the river's muddy surface. A few seconds later a large catfish came flying out of the water as if shot from a sling and landed on the dock beside him. Hop picked up the floundering fish and shook his head.

"I appreciate the thought," he said loudly. "But this ain't what I'm lookin' for." After he tossed the fish back into the water, Hop reached into his pocket and pulled out a silver dollar, which he held up between his thumb and forefinger, so that it caught the sun's fading rays. "If you want me to keep playin', you got to feed th' kitty. And this here is what the kitty eats."

The catfish gal popped back to the surface, stared at the gleaming coin for a long second, then submerged again. Hop shifted about uneasily as first one minute, then another, elapsed without any sign of the catfish gal. Maybe he pushed his luck a little too far too early . . .

Something heavy and wet struck his chest then dropped to the deck with a metallic sound. Hop picked up the flat, circular piece of slime-encrusted metal at his feet with trembling fingers. He scraped the surface with his thumbnail and was rewarded not by the gleam of silver—but the mellow shine of gold.

He gave out a whoop then looked around to see if anyone might have witnessed his good fortune, but he was alone on the landing, at least as far as human company was concerned. Talk about falling in a honey pot!

And all for the price of a song.

As summer wore on, Hop Armstrong became a regular visitor to Steamboat Bend, showing up early and staying till late, and always leaving with heavy, if somewhat damp, pockets. On those occasions Sammy Herkimer was fishing off the dock, Hop was forced to wait the old angler out, but for the most part he didn't have to worry about being discovered.

At first Lucinda had been suspicious of his new-found interest in fishing, but since he never came back smelling of perfume or wearing another woman's shade of lipstick on his collar, she eventually accepted his pastime as genuine. Of course, Lucinda had no way of knowing about the Folgers can full of old gold and silver coins he had stashed out in the garage, or of the bag of gold door-knobs hidden in the woodpile behind the house. Hop didn't see any need to tell her about his new found wealth, because that would lead to her asking him where he got it from, and then where would he be?

If he told Lucinda about the catfish gal, every man, woman and child in Flyjar would be lined up on the dock playing everything from a banjo to a Jew's harp trying to muscle in on his gig. The way Hop saw it, there was no call for him to ruin a good thing before he had to.

Once there weren't any more goodies coming his way from Lit'l Fishie, as he called her, he planned to take his Folgers can full of antique coins and gunnysack of doorknobs and head off to the big city—say Jackson or Greenville. Hell, he might even go as far as Biloxi—maybe even New Orleans! He didn't really care where he ended up, just as long as it was some place where the women were prettier and younger than those in Flyjar, and you could buy beer on Sundays.

Judging from how Lit'l Fishie was behaving during his more recent serenades, something told him it wouldn't be long before things dried up on her end, so to speak. She kept swinging back and forth between acting skittish—disappearing every time a bullfrog croaked—and making kiss-kiss noises with that saddlebag mouth of hers. Hop might not know much, but he sure as hell knew women, and Lit'l Fishie was showing all the signs of a sugar mama running short on cash.

As he set out for Steamboat Bend that day, Hop decided it was going to be his last serenade for the catfish gal—and his final day as a citizen of Flyjar. Now that he'd found his fortune, it was time for him to strike out into the world and collect his fame.

Hop scanned the sky, frowning at the approaching clouds. It had rained off and on since sunrise, and there were puddles all along the rutted cow path that lead to Steamboat Bend. As much as he disliked tramping through the mud, going out on foul-weather days meant he didn't have to worry about anyone snooping around.

Tightening his grip on his guitar strap, Hop hurried down the levee embankment and onto the deserted dock's wooden surface. He sat down on the end of the pier, as he always did, dangling his legs over the open water, and began to play *See My Grave Is Kept Clean*.

Normally Lit'l Fishie broke surface about fifty yards away the moment he started to play, then moved in until she was staring up at him like a snake-tranced bird. Hop knew that look all too well. He saw it all the time in the eyes of the women whenever he played at the juke joints. He knew that if he said the word, Lit'l Fishie would roll in cornmeal and gladly throw herself in a red-hot frying pan.

He had finished with Blind Lemon and started into Leadbelly, but the catfish gal had yet to put in an appearance. Hop frowned. Maybe she couldn't hear him. He didn't really know where she lived, exactly, but he was under the impression she didn't stray that far from the Bend. He changed from Leadbelly to Son House, on the off hand chance that she didn't care for *Cotton Fields*.

When Lit'l Fishie still didn't show herself, Hop's frown deepened even further. It was time to pull out the stops. He began to play one of her favorites: *Up Jumped the Devil*.

There was a bubbling sound directly below where he was sitting. Hop smiled knowingly at the shape lurking just below the murky water lapping against the pylon. Robert Johnson worked like a charm on women—whether they was two-legged or had gills.

"Why you so shy all of a sudden, darlin'?" he called out. "Why don't you show me that sweet, fishy face of yours?"

The bubbles at the end of the pier grew more intense, as if the water was boiling. Hop scowled and leaned forward, staring down between his dangling feet at the muddy water below.

"Lit'l Fishie—is that you?"

There was less than a heartbeat between the moment the thing with bumpy skin and gaping mouth filled with jagged teeth leapt from the water and when its powerful jaws snapped shut on Hop's legs. He was only able to scream just the once—a high, almost womanly shriek—before he was yanked, guitar and all, into the river.

The last thing Hop saw, before the silty waters of the Mississippi closed over him, was the catfish gal watching him drown, a sorrowful expression in her bruised eyes.

When Hop Armstrong went out fishing and never came back, most folks in Flyjar were of the opinion he'd found himself a new girlfriend and left Lucinda for greener pastures. A smaller group thought the handsome ne'er do well had gotten drunk and fallen through the dilapidated dock into the river below. In any case, no one really gave a good god damn, and after a couple of weeks there were other things to talk about down at the barber shop.

About three months after Hop disappeared, Sammy Herkimer snagged his line on something underneath the pier at Steamboat Bend. At first he thought he was just caught it on some waterlogged reeds. But when he reeled his line back in, he found Hop's git-box hanging off the other end.

The guitar that had charmed so many ladies out of their drawers and their life's savings was now dripping slime, it's neck splintered and body badly chewed up. Sammy shook his head as he freed the mangled instrument. He really wasn't surprised by what he'd found.

In a way, he blamed himself for what happened to poor Hop. After all, when he'd told him about the catfish gals, he'd forgot to mention they weren't the *only* critters that made Steamboat Bend their home.

One thing about them gator boys: they sure are jealous.

BIRD IN THE HAND
by Flavia Testa

Born in Tehran, Iran, Flavia Testa was a foundling of the Iranian Revolution. Her parents were diplomats for the UN so she lived all over the world. This has allowed her to observe, react and live a variety of realities. Images, emotions, and situations have been cultivated in her imagination coupled with artisitic abilities and the pleasure of writing has turned all these things into a creative hobby of illustrating and writing.

Here's a gal with a novel take on how to end a relationship . . .

You cannot clip a bird's wings and expect it to fly. Regina walked home quickly that afternoon. Her feet were well paced back and forth, rhythmic and precise. She walked home with a small, white cardboard box pressed tightly to her side. Making her walking slightly awkward, as one arm dangled asymmetrically back and forth. Her head looked stiff and pointed. No one would distract her now. Beneath her curved, rich chocolate eyebrows, her brown eyes of determination gleamed fiercely.

No one seemingly paid her any mind. The warm fall air didn't faze her, the colourful rows of maples dropping leaves gently on the sidewalk did not grab her attention, the warm sun that shone from the sky did not touch her skin.

She walked, fast.

She wrestled her free hand into her tight skirt pocket and pulled out a bunch of keys. She shuffled them until she found the right one and put it straight into the keyhole. Click, turn, unlock. She kicked the door open with the point of her Manolo and walked into a tiny, thin, light filled hallway with a dirty red carpet running along the floor. Her white heeled pointed shoes sinking softly into the yarn, leaving dented impressions of heels. The door had closed behind her. Her arm tight around the box.

At the second to the last door to the left she inserted another key, turn, click. She walked inside, and stopped. She inhaled deeply.

Her windows were open, the warm air from the street filled the room. She was high enough off the road that she could see outside but no one could see inside. She liked it that way.

She walked over to a small table between the two tall windows. An antique black iron, semi-rounded cage sat empty. She looked at it for a moment, then opened the small gate.

She opened the box. There, lifeless, small, wrinkled and detached, was a penis.

She picked up the formerly vibrant bird between her long agile fingers and placed it softly on the bed of the cage and closed the door. She peered through the tiny bars with her now sad brown eyes.

"Shh, shh," she whispered. "Now my cunt is free for another."

BENEATH THE SKIN
by C.M. Vernon

Though she likes writing YA science fiction and fantasy novels, C.M. Vernon has a penchant for good, twisted horror in the short story market. People who are familiar with her fantasy and sci-fi work are often surprised by this darker side. Vernon lives in Arizona with her family. They love to travel, listen to books on CD, and watch their favorite sci-fi sitcoms together; Fringe, Dr. Who, *and* Eureka *are the current favorites. Find her online at colettevernon.com, fictorians.com and twitter.com/cmvyawrite.*

"I wanted to write an interesting transformation story, but I didn't want another vampire, zombie, or werewolf angle," says Vernon. "I wanted something that really creeps me out, and hasn't been seen for a while. I have the typical aversion to spiders, scorpions and the like, but for some inexplicable reason beetles have always seemed bizarre and, well, creepy to me. When I did some research and found the Anthia Sexguttata, not only does it have a "sexy" name, the markings on its back reminded me of painted moons—a great catalyst. From there, the story grew."

Vernon definitely succeeded in her goal to provide creepy, crawly goodness. You'll never think the same way about bug bites again . . .

In the glaring afternoon sun, Kelley didn't notice the ordinary ground beetle, six white spots across its glossy-black carapace. Its scientific name was Anthia Sexguttata, or so any reasonable scientist would have explained. Kelley wouldn't have given it any thought, either way.

Escaping from the shadow of a rock, it scuttled quickly across the warm Indian dirt. Laughter drifted from the shade of a leafy, Sal tree. The other tourists, an overweight couple from Connecticut and two old ladies from somewhere in the Southwest, held lazy conversation while waiting for Kelley to finish her search.

The beetle reached her blue Nikes as she shifted her stance, bringing up her binoculars. It stilled in the brown grasses, waiting.

"I think I see one," Kelley said. "Yes, look . . . between the trees down there. It's a big one."

Rahul Pradesh, her handsome Indian guide, chuckled at her girlish enthusiasm. "Ah, I knew you would be finding one. Bandhavgarh Fort is the best place in all of India to see the tiger. We have more here than any other places."

The beetle reached her shoe and climbed, latching onto her laces as it ascended.

Kelley placed a hand on Rahul's arm. "Thank you for suggesting this. You don't know how much this trip means to me, being able to see and experience India. I feel like a new person."

"It is my honor, Miss Kelley."

"Please, just Kelley. We're friends right?" She didn't move, but smiled at Rahul hopefully.

"You haven't told me, Miss—" She frowned. "I am meaning Kelley. Why have you come here, all alone?"

She hesitated. "I just got divorced. My husband . . . ex-husband was a tightwad."

"Tightwad?"

"He never spent money on anything that wasn't absolutely essential to life." The beetle reached her long gray hiking sock. "At least, so I thought. Apparently, his girlfriend saw more cash than I did. I paid the bills, but money I thought was going to IRAs and such went into her pocket . . . or more likely, tucked safely between the surgically-enhanced hooters he gave her."

Rahul let her talk. Kelley was grateful for a quiet ear, someone to just listen, and not tell her what to do with her life.

Using its tarsal claws, the beetle carefully climbed the thick hiking sock, squeezing through the stiff folds of her jeans.

"I decided to take the settlement money and get away then take the vacation I've always wanted. When I get back, I'll be just another forty-something loser divorcee with no prospects and a dead-end job, but at least I'll have —" Kelley swiped at the back of her leg, clawing at the cuff of her jeans. "There's something . . . a bug or—" She screeched. "Get it off!"

The beetle dug its spiny claws into her skin, holding tight. In between each attempt to brush it off, it moved upward, in sight of its target.

"Calm. Miss Kelley, calm." Rahul placed his hands out in a placating gesture. "Just calm and we will be finding it."

She forced herself to stand still though her hands trembled. Rahul reached his hand up her pant leg. The fat man and his wife pulled away from the group, slowly waddling closer with wide-eyed curiosity.

Kelley screamed again. "Ow! What's it doing? It's biting me!"

The beetle had arrived. It pushed against the soft flesh in the crease behind Kelley's knee. With clicking mandibles and the sharp claws of its front fossorial legs, the beetle made a rough incision through the skin. Blood oozed, coating its hard shell. The slick fluid made it that much easier to insert its head into the small gap. Carving its way through the tissue, it squirmed forward.

Rahul's fingers clamped onto the beetle's slippery abdomen. "I've got it!"

Warm acid shot across his skin.

"Aayee!"

The blood-slick beetle slipped between his fingers, quickly pulling itself into the crevice between Kelley's muscle and tendon.

Rahul cursed in Hindi. "He got away. He is in the leg."

"In the . . . in the . . . " Kelley's eyes rolled up.

Rahul reached out with his free hand, unable to slow her fall. Her head hit the ground before her body pinned him to the dirt. Struggling to pull his hand free, he yelled behind him. "You! Mota—fat man from Conicut! Run down hill! Get help! She is fainted!"

The man's eyes went wide. "Me?"

"You see any person else? Run, mota!"

"It's Connecticut," the man grumbled as he toddled down the path, his wife huffing to catch up.

Rahul checked Kelley's skull. She didn't appear to be wounded, but he couldn't be sure. Did she have time to wait for help?

"I hope I'm right." Rahul hoisted Kelley onto his back into

a fireman's carry, grunting with the effort. He was not a large man. Kelley, though thin and shapely, was not a small woman. He groaned, struggling down the path.

Kelley sat on a mat of woven kora grass trying to come to terms with Rahul's words. Next to him, an old man squatted close to the dirt-packed ground, feet pulled in close to his buttocks and arms wrapped around his shins so that he seemed like a piece of folded paper. He had no shirt and wore an old-fashioned dhoti, like a dirty white robe, the long white fabric lending him an ancient air. His deep wrinkles, thick white beard laced with black, and unsmiling face disconcerted her, but not as much as his crude suggestion.

Kelley stood and moved against the wall, away from the old shaman. "He wants to do what?"

"He says you are having a moon beetle in your leg. It has moved to your hip." Rahul pointed to his hip bone. "He says we must be removing it now, or it will be making you a night monster."

"A night monster? What do you mean? Is that some kind of Indian disease?"

Rahul shook his head. "It is a legend."

The old man gestured to Kelley, speaking in rapid Hindi.

Rahul nodded to the old man then turned to her. "It is said that the famous warrior from many centuries ago, Arjuna, grew haughty. He was saying that the men under his command had all power, greater than the God Vhnu and greater than the heavens. Brahma, the troublemaker God, created a small insect, something that could be crushed under a man's foot, to torment Arjuna and show his warrior's weakness. The beetle entered an unsuspecting warrior through the foot. Later, the moon shone upon the warrior. He transformed into a terrible beast, killing all of Arjuna's valiant men. Arjuna finally killed the beast then crushed the beetle as it escaped. Every hundred years, the beetle is born anew. It is said that Brahma helps it find a host whenever men must be reminded again of their weakness before the gods."

Rahul shook his head, lowering his eyes. "It is a silly story; silly superstition. Even so, you are needing the beetle removed. He will kill the beetle."

The old man slipped a sharp hunting knife from behind his rags of loose clothing. He mimed stabbing the knife, speaking again to Rahul in their chant-like language.

Kelley swallowed, suddenly light-headed. "Is he saying he's going to stab me with that knife?"

"We were wanting to do it sooner, but you woke. No worries. Madin is good with the knife—very quick."

"But he wants to stab me!"

"We must be killing the beetle when it is not ready." His fingers crawled up his arm. "It will be moving if it knows we are after it."

Kelley jumped up. "No way am I letting an old man stick me with a knife. It's only an hour flight to New Delhi. I'll find a doctor there."

Madin stood, speaking loudly and gesturing wildly with his knife. Rahul argued back until the man finally relented. "Be going back to America, crazy woman," Madin said in heavily accented English. "Take the monster to them."

Rahul ushered Kelley from the hut, the tips of dried palm fronds scraping across her skin as if trying to hold her as she exited through the small door. The little thatched hut appeared incongruous among the mud-walled houses and richer cement structures of Katni. Usually the scenery, so mundane to the inhabitants, would have fascinated Kelley.

The beetle squirmed against her hipbone, sending a flash of pain that made her stumble. She grasped Rahul's arm. "Get me to the airport. Please hurry."

Rahul nodded, ushering her past a multi-storied apartment complex, the broken plaster creating designs across the sun-dulled blue paint, and into the resort's old jeep.

Getting a plane to New Delhi was the easy part. Getting registered at the hospital was like dodging her way through a carnival. She didn't have much time left. Her flight would leave in three more hours. After much pleading with the attendants, nurses, and anyone else she could bribe, they put her ahead of the other patients and escorted her to a room.

Dr. Chatterjee, an older man with clean-cut salt-and-pepper hair and bifocals scanned her hastily prepared chart. "You know, Miss—"

"Kelley. Just call me Kelley."

"Miss Brown, I'm a general practice physician. I don't have any expertise in . . . " He glanced down at the chart, his brow furrowed. "Insects?" His Indian accent leaned heavily to British, giving him a condescending air.

"A beetle." Kelley swallowed. "It climbed into my leg." She could feel her panic rising. "It's living somewhere inside of me and someone has to get it out. Please, you're a doctor, right? You could put me to sleep, do an x-ray and find it. Please, I've felt it moving. You've got to get it out!"

"You think it's inside of you?"

"I can show you. On my leg." She tried to pull the leg of her jeans up, but the denim wouldn't stretch. In desperation, she pulled them off her hips, completely unaware of the doctor's wide eyes and hesitant step back.

"Look!" She pointed to the scabby wound "It climbed into my leg. Last night, it was at my hip. Some crazy witch doctor was going to stab me with a Rambo knife to get it out. Maybe I should have taken him up on it. A few hours ago, I felt something in my gut. Please. You've got to help me."

The doctor nodded knowingly. "So the village shaman frightened you with their superstitions—the were-beetle myth."

"But I felt—"

"Put your clothing on, Miss Brown. You felt it, because a part of you believed him. There are some types of beetles that can be quite aggressive. I'm sure one of them climbed up your leg, got stuck, and caused some damage, but I can assure you, it didn't climb into the tissue. Beetles, even ones here in India, do not behave in such a manner."

"But I felt it squirming into my leg."

"Even if it managed to do so, it would quickly die and your body acids would absorb it. I assure you, there's no need to worry."

"But—"

"I have many patients. I'm sure you understand. If you will take your paperwork to the secretary at the front desk, she can handle your bill." He stepped out the door and she was left alone.

Kelley stared at the wall. Maybe the doctor was right. Maybe she had imagined the sensation because she'd been so paranoid, so frightened. She glanced at a digital clock on the counter. She had two-and-half hours to get to the airport, through security and onto her flight.

Gary McKeon, a forty-seven-year-old CIA operative finishing his London visit, stepped into the line of passengers making their way to the gate, heading for New York. A brunette woman, most likely in her early forties, stepped into line behind him, breathing heavily and sighing with relief.

"Worried you wouldn't make it?" Gary asked.

The woman nodded and smiled. "It's been a long couple of days. I just can't wait to be home, back on American soil."

Gary noticed her t-shirt with *I LOVE INDIA* painted in bold red across her admirable chest. "India didn't live up to your expectations, huh?"

The woman shivered as if reliving some horror. "Just at the end. I'll be fine though. I'm sure everything is fine."

He hitched his bag higher on his shoulder, hesitated, then put out a hand, "Gary McKeon. If there's anything I can do . . . ?"

They shook. "Kelley Brown. I'm okay. I'm just a little jumpy about an Indian superstition I heard on my trip. It's got me rattled and eager to get home."

Gary almost pursued the conversation, trying to think of

a way to get the woman's number. Even with shadows under her eyes and her long hair disheveled, she was a good-looking woman. Based on the slightly off-color tan line around her left finger, she appeared to be recently single as well. The airline attendant took his ticket and ushered him forward. He'd have to find her in the baggage claim area. He could make this work, he was sure.

Kelley found her seat by the window, wishing she had someone to pass the time with. Someone like the handsome man who'd stood in front of her. He was balding slightly but his dark hair and hazel eyes complemented a well-kept physique and easy smile. Instead, she had an empty seat and an old woman knitting at the aisle.

Kelley pulled the window shade down as soon as she had secured her seatbelt. She didn't have enough energy to talk anyway, she told herself. She was exhausted, it was night, and she didn't want even the pulsing light on the aircraft's wing to disturb her rest.

A few hours later, she rubbed absently at the lump in her neck, below the surface of her skin. It squirmed. She startled awake. Screamed. With an open palm, she slapped her neck, hitting herself again and again.

"What in the world?" The older woman, dark hair splattered with gray, pushed the assistance button. It wasn't necessary. The stewardess came running at the scream.

"Is there something wrong, miss?" The pale, blond-haired woman resembled a lemon in uniform. Her mouth twisted into a false smile. "Are you having a problem I can help you with?"

Kelley touched her neck. It had stopped moving. She shivered. She would have to find a twenty-four hour clinic as soon as they landed to get rid of the dead beetle.

"I'm fine." She couldn't tell the attendant she just squished a bug in her neck.

It took a couple of hours for exhaustion to overcome her

horror. She eventually fell asleep with her head crooked awkwardly into the seat.

She awoke feeling rested and refreshed. She felt for the bump in her neck. It was gone; had it dissolved somewhere in her body? She shifted uncomfortably in her seat, wondering if anyone in an American hospital would believe her any more than they had in India.

She opened the window shades. The bright light of a full moon hung large and overpowering on the horizon. Her skin prickled with gooseflesh. Eyes widening, her pupils dilated unnaturally. They expanded, pressing at her eyelids, burning. She threw her hands over them, trying to scream. Her breath caught in her throat. She convulsed. Pain shot through her skull.

"Are you all right, miss?" the older woman asked.

Kelley gargled, unable to respond. Beneath her shirt, skin rippled across her back, like molten lead, reshaping and hardening of its own volition. At the base of her ribcage, something pressed against her skin. She clutched her arms to her sides, doubling over in convulsing pain. The old woman pressed the overhead call button.

Kelley's jaw ached, stretching and enlarging. Two pricks of searing heat burned at the top of her head. Her buttocks bulged, pushing her forward. As the rest of her body pulsed and grew, bullet-sized spiracle holes opened from her hips to her underarms. Kelley could finally take a breath, but the air came not only from her mouth, but from the newly opened wounds along her torso.

The stewardess' shoes clicked against the plastic-coated runway. "Can I help you?" She glanced at Kelley. "There's an air-sickness bag in the seat-pocket in front of you." She sounded like an automated message, though she stood alive and in the flesh no more than three feet away.

Flesh, Kelley thought. Her mind withdrew as the beetle took control.

"Flesh." The beetle spoke through her. The desire to eat, tear, and crush these large beings, always hovering omnipotent above, made Kelley's jaw twitch.

"Please use the bag if you're going to be sick, ma'am." The

stewardess' voice was strained, thinly veiling her impatience.

Kelley uncovered her face, turning her multi-faceted eyes at the woman. "Human flesh." The voice sounded unnatural, raspy and deep, while still Kelley's.

The stewardess screamed.

Long antennae thrust up through Kelley's dark hair. Mandibles pushed through the skin along the jawbones like huge, reaching pliers. A pair of insect legs popped from the base of her ribs, through her t-shirt. Small spots of blood soaked into the white fabric around the new wounds. More dripped down her face, falling on her shirt and distorting the letters into strange blobs of red.

Kelley twitched her new tarsal claws, snapping her mandibles as she moved toward the stewardess. That high-pitched sound—it had to stop. Stepping over the older woman, either fainted or dead but blessedly silent, Kelley grabbed the obnoxious stewardess by the arm with one hand, her shirt with the opposite claw.

With one snap of her mandibles, the stewardess' head popped off her body. Her cries ceased, only to be filled with new ones; a disorienting cacophony of irritating noises. More than subduing the human beasts, she wanted to shut them up.

A tall man with a scruffy beard and a large gut grabbed a flowery, china vase from his wife's Debenhams' bag. "Out of my way!" He crashed it over Kelley's head.

She screeched, frantically clicking her mandibles. The back of her jeans ripped and the point of her large abdomen protruded. Acid spouted over the man, forcing him to the floor where he writhed as the acid ate at his flesh. His wife shrieked, bending down beside him. Their noises mixed with those splattered by the acid around them. Kelley covered her ears, anger rising. *Why couldn't they shut up?*

Using her mandibles, tarsal claws, and her bare hands, she tore at everyone within reach.

Gary struggled through the people around him, trying to get a visual on the disturbance near the front. He cannibalized a serving cart, managing to pull free a twisted rod of sharp metal. His other hand grabbed multiple, blunt-edged, butter knives. He forced himself over seats, and through the clogged aisle. He froze. *That beautiful, sweet woman. Why was he always attracted to the nut jobs?*

Kelley turned her large abdomen in his direction. Gary threw himself behind a row of seats. Acid splattered around him. A little girl's shrieking gained pitch. Gary peered over the seats. The girl's wounds were minor. Kelley's abdomen still twitched, but she'd used up her acid supply. He awkwardly jumped over two rows, jabbing at the beetle-thing with one of the rods, diverting her from the child.

Kelley's shirt tore, rising tightly beneath her breasts. Broad wings spread from her shoulder blades into the airplane's confined space. She couldn't raise her heavy body much more than a foot, banging her head against the top of the compartment. But her timing was right. The rod slammed into the flesh of her leg instead of her torso. She lifted her face and clamped her mandibles into the thick bulkhead. While her wings fluttered, she tore into the metal as if bearing through flesh.

Gary threw the sharper of his knives at her back. It clanked and fell; a useless scratch across her exoskeletal forewings. She dropped to the floor, ripping away a large chunk of fuselage. Air rushed from the compartment. Oxygen bags dropped.

The plane jolted, descending toward the runway.

Kelley lashed out around her, furiously sending pieces of the overhead bins in a wide arc. Gary swiped at the debris with his weapons, unable to attack and protect himself at the same time. Something sparked. The lights died.

A toddler screamed at the top of her lungs in the walkway, staring at a woman on the floor, covered in blood.

Kelley took a step toward the young girl, mandibles clicking.

Through the plane's gaping hole, moonlight illuminated Kelley's disfigured form.

Gary slammed the sharp rod through her back, between two ribs on her right side. Warm blood soaked into her red-splattered shirt. She reacted to the wound no more than a cockroach might to a stickpin. She turned, ripping the weapon from Gary's hands. With a human hand, she grabbed the back of his head. Eyes wide, he thrust a blunt knife into her chest where her human heart should have been. Writhing in discomfort, her grip tightened. She placed her cheek against his, reaching her large mandibles around the front of his neck. Gary scrambled in a panic, trying to find any weapon within reach.

A teenage boy in black goth, cowering between seats, handed him a chunk of thin, sharp metal, something Kelley had thrown aside. Gary latched onto it. He sliced it across the back of the monster's head. Kelley pulled back in surprise, releasing her hold. Gary sliced the shard of metal across the soft flesh of her throat. Blood spurted.

In the seat next to him he spotted an abandoned knitting bag, needles peeking through the top. He grabbed one, thrusting it between the mandibles attached to her jaw, right through the pharynx to her brain. She convulsed, her strange glass-like eyes distorting, growing smaller, finally returning to their natural mahogany brown. They rolled up into her head. Her blood-stained body fell from Gary's grasp onto the deck in front of the frightened, wide-eyed child.

The wheels hit the tarmac, the plane jolted and the spoilers flew up. The plane taxied to a special unloading area already swarming with official personnel. Gary stared at the dark-haired woman lying there in a pool of moonlight and blood on the floor of the plane. The only evidence of what she'd become were the bloody holes at her head and down both sides, now looking like gunshot wounds, and a scraped-up chin. This was not going to be easy to explain.

Gary tried not to roll his eyes as FBI Agent, Martin Klein, stared at the blood-smeared body. The man didn't fit the typical FBI profile, at least how the public tended to view them. He was short and stocky, mostly bald with a swath of short-cropped blonde hair running a low circuit around his head. His pompous gaze shifted to Gary. "You expect me to believe the woman turned into some kind of human beetle thing and attacked everyone on the plane?"

"I told you, Klein. Everyone will corroborate the story. I know it sounds crazy, but—"

"Crazy? It's beyond crazy. What did someone do, slip LSD into the drinks? Put PCP in the air system? They did something 'cause there's no way that I'm filling out a report about a massive bug killing ten people and injuring fifteen others on a commercial flight."

"Identical mass hallucinations are impossible. Whether you like the report or not, even her injuries support the story."

"How can you tell with all the bullets you plugged into her?"

"I didn't have my gun," *you idiot*. He bit off the words, but he couldn't suppress his patronizing tone. "Look at the blood in her hair—that's from the antennae. Along her face and jaw, the mandibles—huge pincer things." Gary shuddered as he pointed out the rest of the wounds caused by her transformation.

"You can see evidence of everything I've told you."

"Then why aren't they still there?"

"I don't know. When she died, she transformed back. I saw her when I boarded. She seemed tired, but otherwise—"

In the midst of their argument, neither man noticed the small bug wiggling its way from Kelley's ear canal. It limped, partly squished, as it skittered across her cheek, six shining dots, like molten moonlight across its back. It climbed from her down-turned nose onto the floor of the plane then paused, turning its antennae from one set of black, slick shoes to another. Neither man could hear the faint clicks and drag of the beetle scuttling toward its next target.

GUADALUPE OF THE BOWERY
by Ann Hagman Cardinal

I loved the sinister heat and urban sensibility to Ann's story. The slow slide from the mundane to the horrible, and the reaction of the characters as things begin to go wrong. There is, after all, no such thing as a free lunch.

Ann's first novel Sister Chicas—*co-written with two other Latina writers—was released in 2006 from New American Library, and she had recently completed two new young adult novels that currently reside with her agent. She is the Director of Alumni Affairs for Vermont College of Fine Arts (and a graduate with an MFA in Writing), as well as a columnist, blogger and social network marketing consultant. Just to mix it up, she also knits, skates and describes herself as "obsessed with zombie narratives."*

It was on the corner of Bleecker and Elizabeth Streets that he first experienced the vision. He had just left CBGBs, confining the night of blaring music, slam-dancing and blinding alcohol behind the front door like a stalking tiger. The evening was brisk, the fall air crackling around him as he crossed Bowery, his hands shoved deep into the pockets of his black jeans. Johnny staggered a little as he walked, his eyes following the darting, shiny tips of his boots, the sidewalk retreating as if it were being pulled out from under him. *What a freakin' night.* He had endured yet another reaming from his girlfriend, Karen, the issue of his inability to commit (or lack of desire to, but he couldn't say that to her . . . he'd never get laid) rising yet again, as if it were always there, ready to trap him like a loose shoe in deep mud.

He stopped abruptly on the corner of Elizabeth Street, holding his head in his hands as he swayed slightly, his eyes closed against the stinging wind. *Man, I shouldn't have had that last whiskey.* He tried to clear his head. A siren went by behind him, the sharp edges of its whine bruising his skull like the sound of his mother's voice, shrill and insistent in the otherwise quiet night, as she argued with his father about Johnny's latest sinful transgressions,. The throbbing in his temples dropped him to his knees, the concrete sidewalk scraping the skin through the thick cotton. As the siren retreated, he opened his eyes and looked upward, grateful for the reprieve. It was there, on the top of the corner building that he saw her, just as she had appeared in the plastic statue over his mother's kitchen sink.

She was lit from beneath, the green of her gown glowing like a wet palm leaf under the midday Puerto Rican sun. Her robe was surrounded with golden light that came to points around her whole body, mirroring the spikes on the dog collar around Johnny's neck. There was a child's face below her, gazing up, wings framing its plump cheeks, holding a slivered moon as if in offering. The Virgin's hands were reverently pressed together, and Johnny could feel her eyes on him like a jailyard spotlight, reminding him of his mother's shadowed form in the living room when he snuck in after meeting with a girl, their clandestine kisses betrayed by the redness around his lips, her maternal gaze exposing all his sins with her perfected piousness. His mouth opened as he gazed up. She was just a statue . . . wasn't she? Whatever or whoever she was, she was glorious. Johnny felt her beauty spill over the side of the four-storied building, coating him in its warmth. It was then that he caught the slight scent of roses, like the ones he passed in the farmers market when he cut class on Fridays during high school, their rainbow faces offering up their heady perfume. The fog of alcohol cleared, and he realized he felt both elated as never before and terrified beyond all imaginings. It was like . . . coming home, but to a home he had only dreamt of, insulated from the hatred that hissed around the dingy two-bedroom Bronx apartment where he had lived the first ten years of his life, before his mother left him.

Locked in her stern yet serene gaze, Johnny stood up, her eyes following him as he moved. He was certain it was a miracle, certain that she was alive. *Tell them, Juanito, bring others.* He heard her commanding yet silky voice in his head. Johnny turned on his heels and ran back to the club, anxious to share the news of this marvel with Karen, with his friends. And what a group of people in need of a miracle! He darted across the street, not even checking for oncoming cars on the early-morning avenue, and burst through the front door of the club, yelling, "Everybody! You have *got* to see this! It's a miracle!" But the tide of music that hit him drowned out his shouts. Catching sight of Karen halfway down the bar, perched flirtatiously on a torn, red leather bar stool, Johnny pushed his way through the crowd to her. He would start small, just tell one person. Karen would certainly listen. He sidled himself between Karen and the Mohawk-sporting guy who was hitting on her—a fact which was not lost on him, but in his elation he didn't even care—and grabbed her by the shoulders.

"Hey! Hands off, Johnny, I told you I wasn't gonna wait around for you!"

"Forget about that, Karen, this is important!"

"*Forget* about that?"

He could see the white heat building behind her sea-glass eyes like foam.

"What does that mean, forget about *us*?"

"No, no, that's not what I mean. Listen, I saw something down the street . . . *La Virgen* . . . a miracle!"

"Oh get off it, *Juanito*." Her voice slid over her lips like cheap scotch. "Virgin, ha! So you found a little trollop who convinced you she was pure. What makes you think I want to hear about it?"

"No, I mean *the* Virgin. The Virgin of Guadalupe! I want you to come see her."

Karen drew back and looked harder into his face. The edges of her voice softened slightly. "Are you on something, Johnny? You're starting to scare me."

He tugged gently at her wrist, urging her towards the exit. "Come with me, *mi amor*, please. I promise you won't be disappointed."

Karen hesitated, but allowed herself to be pulled. "Okay, Johnny, but I swear, if this is some twisted scheme to get me alone . . . "

Johnny led her down the street towards the corner, his skull tight and tingling with the anticipation. He stopped her on the corner of Elizabeth Street and pointed towards the glowing saint peering off the rooftop above. He didn't say a word. A moment this sacred should not be marred with mere language.

"That is what you brought me here for?" One hand went to her hip while she pointed with the other at the roof, her black rubber bracelets slipping down her forearm. "For Christ's sake, Johnny, it's a fucking statue on the top of a mission for local drunks!"

"Karen, what are you talking about? Are you blind? Look at her: she's alive! She's looking right at you! Can't you smell the roses?"

Karen stared at him for a moment; her eyes were soft but the line of her mouth remained tight. "Okay, Johnny, for real, what did you smoke tonight? Or are you making fun of me? Is your mother behind this 'let's ridicule the Irish *gringa* who will never understand our ways' little stunt? Yet another example of Doña Diego's sense of humor? 'Cause I'm not falling for it. I'm outta here." In a flurry of clicking heels she started back to the club, the scissoring of her long legs counterbalancing her swinging arms.

Johnny was about to call out to Karen when he heard the Virgin's voice.

Let her go, Juanito. She is not worthy.

"But if she didn't believe me, no one else will! How can I spread the word of your coming?" His voice sounded thin and about to break as it echoed off the buildings on the empty street.

Do not worry, mi amor. *Go home and sleep. Go back there tonight and they will all believe. Trust in me and I will provide.*

Johnny didn't even remember getting home, but he woke up in the late afternoon, sprawled on his twin bed, dressed in the same clothes and wondering if it had all been a dream.

That evening when he walked down Bleecker toward the

club, Johnny was surprised to see people congregating out front. He expected it to be busy—the Bad Brains were playing—but it was just 11:00, too early for this size crowd. When he got closer, he knew that something had happened; there was only the sound of muffled conversation coming from the club and the people inside seemed to have their heads together, showing their bare forearms to each other in groups. Johnny walked in and went up to Seth, the bouncer, who was also staring at the pale skin of his muscled forearm.

"Hey Seth, what's going on?"

"Oh, hey Johnny. Didn't you hear? Check this out, man." He shoved his forearm at Johnny, pointing to a bright, blood-red rose tattoo.

"Nice, Seth! You got some new ink. Where'd you have it done?"

"No man, you don't get it. I didn't. None of us did." Seth swept his arm around, indicating the humming crowd that had coagulated around the bar area.

Johnny's eyes swept the room and at first nothing seemed out of the ordinary. But then he noticed the same red rose on everyone's forearms. "Wha . . . "

"Fucking freaky, ain't it? We all woke up with them this morning. Everyone who was here last night, that is."

Johnny jolted and yanked up the sleeve of his shirt. Nothing. His eyes swept the crowd for Karen, but he didn't see her.

"That's weird, man. You were here last night, but you didn't get one."

Johnny took off towards the door, and shoved people aside as he tore out into the street, almost colliding with a fast-moving cab. He jogged in place as he waited for a break in the traffic; his legs couldn't stay still. When it was clear, he darted for the corner. He had to talk to *La Virgen*.

When he arrived at the street corner, he looked up at the building and gasped. She was gone! His breath sped up: he was gulping air like a fish on a dock. How could she have abandoned him, too? He dropped to his knees, feeling a cavity form in his heart. Then he heard his name being called. His eyes darted about, trying to find the source of the voice. A soft glow emanated from the nearby alley. He stood up and started for it, drawn to the light's warmth. Just as he got to the mouth of the alley, she stepped out in front of him.

His first thought was that she was much smaller than he had imagined. On her perch on top of the building she seemed twenty feet high. But standing before him now, she was a few inches shorter than Johnny. Except of course for her rays. Outlining her body were foot-long rubbery rays of gold that undulated with her slightest movement like Medusa's hair. Her green gown seemed to be its own light source; its fluorescence came off her like heat. Her skin was the color of *café con leche*, her lips stained red like blood. He was dazzled by the apparent softness of her skin, the life coursing below its surface, the cold marble replaced with warm flesh. But it was her eyes that shocked him most. She held him in her gaze as if she were searing his spirit with her long lash-curtained eyes, their lids quivering as if afraid to descend, even for a moment, over the electricity of her stare. He was terrified, but for a long moment he couldn't look away. There was movement at her feet and Johnny dragged his eyes from hers towards the hem of her gown. His breath caught in his throat as he met the lewd, smiling stare of a child-like face of a cherub whose chubby arms clutched a slivered shape like a golden watermelon rind it intended to devour. Johnny shuddered and took a step backward, almost tripping on a crack in the sidewalk.

"Juan, *mi querido* Juan."

It was the voice, her voice, but no longer confined in his head. He didn't want to look at her, but he couldn't help himself.

"Bring me to my followers. I gave them *rosas* so they would believe. Come." She stepped closer to him, her gown rustling belligerently. The aroma hit him then, the same rose scent as when he first saw her, but stronger, almost oppressive in its sweetness.

They walked together down the street, her hand resting lightly on his arm but burning his skin like fire. She seemed to glide above the ground, the cherub at her hem swaying along with her dress, his eyes occasionally darting up to his mistress with a look of fearful veneration.

Johnny began to feel different. As they approached the busy

thoroughfare, he felt a power surge through him, a potency which he now knew he had lacked his entire life. It was as if the last piece of a puzzle had suddenly snapped into place, the edges melding with the others until the image was whole. He stopped at the curb, the *whoosh* of the cars lifting his T-shirt. She pulled him forward, into the traffic, and he tried to jerk her back to the safety of the curb. At that moment, the cars just stopped, frozen along the two-way street while their drivers pumped the gas pedals, turned the keys, grinding the already running engines in their confusion.

They walked to the other side, slowly, as if in procession. When they arrived at the door of the club, Johnny heard the traffic roar back to live, the cars jerking forward as the gas pedals regained their powers. They walked through and the punks at the door parted, staring at her with mouths gaping. She smiled at each of them, her head bowing gently, the rays atop her head waving with each regal nod.

Johnny felt taller walking in with her. He could see the awe in each set of eyes as they bared their marked forearms the way a lesser wolf bares its neck in subjugation. It was then that he caught sight of Karen among the shocked faces, and he could see the respect in her eyes, the reverence. It was what he wanted from her all along. He started to imagine bringing Karen to her, giving the gift of the Virgin's blessing to his human love. It was Guadalupe's voice that drew him from his arrogant daydream. She was watching him gaze at Karen and for a moment, just a moment, Johnny could see her brown eyes flash and her mouth twist. But it passed so quickly he wondered if he had imagined it.

She stepped onto the low, black-painted stage, surveyed the sparsely lit club and declared, "Yes, this shall be my temple."

Johnny followed her eyes around the room, taking in the peeling paint and crumbling ceiling, the walls with their graffitied obscenities, the upside-down cross hanging from the opening band's microphone, the sour smell of stale beer and vomit filling his nostrils. He couldn't imagine how a saint could be comfortable in an environment that had so many sins soaked into its woodwork. Johnny looked over at the club's owner expecting protest, but his normally shrewd eyes were glazed over with adoration, his sleeves pushed up over strong working-class arms, exposing the same image as found on his clientele.

Johnny felt her fingers tighten around his arm, and pain shot up to his shoulder. "Now Juan, tell them I will need them to prove their devotion. They will give me proof of their love and I will care for them as my own children."

"Proof? What kind of proof do you need?" He fought to control a slight tone of aggravation that had edged into his voice.

She swept her eyes over the crowd, as a smile crept up the glazed clay-like surface of her cheek. "A sacrifice, as my Aztecs did so long ago."

Johnny's scalp began to sweat, his hair shifting as if alive. "S-s-sacrifice? You . . . you don't mean, *human*, do you?"

Her eyes snapped to him then, and he saw the flame return; this time there was no denying the rage that came off her like static. "Do you doubt my wisdom, Juan?"

He noticed she was no longer using the diminutive to address him. When he was a kid that was how he knew to stay out of his mother's way if he didn't want to bear the scars of one of her manic angry spells. "N-n-no, my Blessed Mother. But such an act is not accepted today. There are authorities and ethics . . . " His thoughts were jumbled, he wanted to scream at her, to push her off the stage, but he heard his mother's voice in his head, speaking of piety and loyalty to the saints, could hear her demand his silence, "*En boca cerrada, no entran moscas, Juanito.*" Flies don't enter a closed mouth. Was she testing his loyalty? His worthiness? He looked up at Guadalupe.

"Do not speak to me of such trivialities again, Juan. I have not the time for them." Returning a look of beneficence to her face, she gazed upon the silent crowd, her hand sweeping over their heads. "Who among you will give their flesh to honor me? To feed me."

Johnny felt the revulsion gurgle in his stomach as he gaped at the monster next to him on the stage. Did she actually intend to eat one of them? How could he have not seen it earlier? This twisted being was not the gentle Guadalupe of his mother's childhood stories. He was trying to think of something, anything he could do when a melodic voice rose above the crowd.

"I would be honored to give my life for you, my lady."

Johnny's head snapped up to see Karen making her way to the stage, a calm smile on her frosted lips, her eyes wide and empty. His stomach seized when he saw the tell-tale red mark peeking from beneath her sleeve.

"No! Karen, what are you thinki—" Johnny was abruptly shoved to his knees on the stage, the Virgin's hand on his shoulders like an anvil. The monster pinned him to the stage, the bent nail heads in the wood piercing his jeans and drawing blood. Karen continued walking, her delicate hand held out to the creature. He struggled to rise, but there was no fighting against the strength that held him down. Helplessly watching Karen's blank face, Johnny felt a heat growing in his chest, and his eyes searched around for some kind of weapon. He noticed the crucifix hanging from the microphone behind him. Just as Karen stepped up onto the stage, he tore the cross down, knocking the microphone stand to the ground in a clatter, and when the creature swung around at the noise, before he could think, he thrust the long end of the silver cross into its stomach. Its square corners tore through the glowing green fabric and a black stain immediately began to spread. The floral smell was now one of decay, rancid and sickly sweet.

Its screams pierced the night like a siren.

Karen stumbled back off the stage, holding her hands to her head. Johnny scuttled backwards until his back hit the massive black speakers behind him. He watched the creature howl and writhe, the rays around her flailing, the cherub at her skirts watching her with wide eyes and a slight smile, a drop of blood trailing down his tiny bow-shaped mouth.

Johnny looked around at the crowd, their eyes focusing as if they'd just awoken, their faces white while they watched the spectacle on stage. The creature dropped to the floor then, its gown pooled around it, the color slowly bleeding from its skin and clothes. The shrieks died down to a low but tortuous howl as it flattened out on the stage, rigidity setting in, its surface gray and pockmarked. The cherub's face seemed peaceful once again, content in its stony form.

At first Johnny felt a growing sense of panic, his bowels tightening with it. Then it was replaced by a warmth that spread outward to his limbs, as if he had stepped onto the hot sand of a sun-soaked beach. He knew what he had to do. Johnny gathered three of the stronger-looking men from the crowd, and together they hoisted the stone figure. The people silently parted when they walked through, their eyes carefully avoiding the statue. Traffic was light as they crossed Bowery and made their way down Bleecker. The mission doors were open and the group made its way into the lowly lit, cool interior. Johnny watched the old ragged men who sat on mismatched chairs scattered around the room for signs of surprise at the spectacle passing through their sanctuary, but saw nothing but wizened expressions on their lined faces. When they were about to enter the stairwell, Johnny saw an old man make the sign of the cross as his eyes fell on the statue.

The young men reached the fourth floor, the stairs ending in a landing with a bare, flickering bulb. It was then they saw the entrance to the roof, its red painted door yawning and hanging off its hinges, the wooden shards of nailed barricades scattered around the worn linoleum floor. They stepped out onto the tar roof, the cool night air startling them. Silently they walked to the edge and lowered the figure feet first onto the lit platform overlooking Elizabeth Street, the bottom fitting perfectly into the sharp-rimmed stone ring.

They stood for a moment and looked at her, the folds of the gown trailing down her back like water. Then one by one they broke free and walked back to the roof's door. Johnny was the last to go, his eyes staying on her not because they were forced to, but because he felt the way he had the week of his tenth birthday, when his mother dropped him off to live at his grandmother's apartment in the projects after his father left them. From her hushed Spanish he had gleaned phrases like "can't handle him" and "it is up to God to save him now." He had watched her stride away forever, vinyl handbag clutched over her arm, her heels clicking down the filthy institutional-gray hallway, the casual tilt of her head mocking his rising terror. Johnny surveyed the darkened city streets below, comforted by the sight of familiar storefronts and street corners.

He heard music on the night air, and looked down Bleecker and saw people spilling into the front door of CBGB's as if it were any other night. As if nothing had happened. With a smile, Johnny took a deep breath, the cool air filling his lungs and puffing out his muscular chest.

Johnny heard footfalls on the stairs behind him, and he turned and walked through the door to the stairwell without looking back. There, on the landing below him, were three old priests, their arms filled with tools and fresh two-by-fours. They waited for Johnny to pass through, and then wordlessly shuffled up the stairs to re-hang the roof's door and rebuild the barricade. As Johnny walked down the stairs, the metallic clang of hammers trailed behind him like a fading heartbeat.

A STRAY CHILD
by Rachel Turner

Rachel Turner is a 30-something-year-old half breed that seeks solace in the occasional twisted jolt that horror fantasy provides. By day she's a part-time college student and a full-time mom. By night she's a lover of the macabre, desiring to connect with fellow fans that only dark fantasy can attract. Learn more about her at realmcovet.blogspot.com.

"I came to write 'A Stray Child' while listening to Akira Yamaoka's Silent Hill *soundtrack,*" says Rachel. "*Feeling very inspired by the dark harmonies invoked from the melodies Yamaoka produces, coupled with the imagery that only* Silent Hill *games can induce, I was led to describe the sexual desire that resided within me.*"

I found this to be a troubling, arresting piece. The writer's energy screams off the page, and I spent more time than I like to admit turning it over in my head, trying to puzzle out some of the mysteries of it . . .

I feel the darkness rekindle me, it beckons forth the Protector. Her axe is ready in hand, dripping the blood of her most recent enemy's maw.

It has only been a fortnight since she last slumbered, her waking dreams now becoming a fully realized nightmare. She revels in this fury, for it is secretly a dream come true.

Increasingly tight, she grips her trusty friend, her only friend.

She traverses the depths of this self-made cavern. Her entrails guide her to her destiny. He skulks before her, like a deceitful jester, smelling her from the inside out.

"Dre-e-e-e-e-e-a-m-m-m my sweet princes-s-s-s-s. Dre-e-e-e-e-e-a-m".

His words are blaspheme and she toils subconsciously, the

warmth between her legs betraying her.

He always knew her before she even knew herself and she hated him for knowing of her Need.

The words clamored from her lips before she could give them the authority she desired to possess, dropping her only friend to the ground as its clatter echoed the empty halls of her hallow...

"Desecrate me"

"You kno-o-o-o-w-w-w that you are only fucking a facet of you-r-r-s-s-el-f-f-f?" He tore away her first layer of clothing.

She closed her eyes against the truth, wanting only to ingest the value of this meal that contained no nutrition. Visions of fingering a 10-year-old girl flashed through her imagination.

"The Protector comes to overcome. I'll eat you first and then I'll kill you."

"A-a-a-a-s you wish prince-s-s-s." He continued to strip her of her underwear.

Her bloody maid costume lay on the floor, she wore nothing but her boots now. Her friend lay only an arm's length away, but she no longer had any need for it. She moaned desperately as he opened her up from the throat down. The deeper he went inside her, the further she fell back inside herself. He would be in her for hours. Days even. Yes. This might take days.

She felt herself become one with his filth as he devoured her innocence. His flesh was the color of everything. He was covered in tendon and sinew. The slime from his accumulated rawness blended itself into her insides, becoming one with her flesh. Here she did not have to pretend.

Her howls were of satisfaction, an undying need to be satiated in the way that only she could render unto herself. After she killed him, there would be more. The fantasies would continue to grow more intense with every pulse. The notion of this brought her to climax.

He did not fill her desire though. He did not fuck faster or harder, but only remained banging her in that droning, disassociating manner. She grabbed him bodily to pull him further into her but her hands only slipped at the touch of blood and muscle. He wailed in sadomasochistic delight and the stench of his mouth caused her to vomit.

The fucking continued.

Her climax ended hours ago and he was still on top of her. She would lay there, maybe sleep, maybe sing a childhood tune until her fantasy told her she could be done.

There was still the business of the others she had to attend to. She thought of that little girl. She thought of what she had made her do. To herself, and to others. There were so many parts of herself involved.

So who was he?

He was the oldest one. Maybe not the original, but at least a close second or third. He had been her dumping grounds her whole life, as the Core dissipated into nothingness. He was once beautiful, far more beautiful than he was now. His hair long and healthy, skin smooth and soft. He had come to her in the night, saving her from all the memories her pretty little face could no longer recall. Each memory darkened him, made him less and less of who he originally was.

Everything around her was becoming rotten and desecrated.

"I'll have to kill you again, for this to be over. I don't want to, but it has to end sometime."

"W-e-e-e know. W-e-e-e always-s-s-s know-w-w-w. Why do you remind u-s-s-s-s? Always-s-s-s- remind u-s-s-s-s."

He would not ejaculate. He never had before. But she wanted him to. This time. She wanted to kill him while he did so. Maybe this time he would hate her enough to never come back. She hated making him turn this way. Her reality had taken control of her fantasies. And this is the misery they had brought upon her. Never any absolutes.

She changed her position—from lying in her vomit to on her knees. It gave her easier access to her friend. Her only friend. He resumed his monotonous pattern upon her, but as she reached for her weapon, his movements quickened. Noises that resembled ecstasy garbled from his throat and she wept for his loss. Though she knew he would be back, he would be less and less of who she wanted him to be every time.

She turned from her anal advantage of a position as his cock slid from her and rolled on her back. His cum released upon her abdomen and she wrapped her legs lovingly around him. His kisses repulsed her to an aching degree and she felt her love for him cultivate. She had conditioned her reaction to change from repulsion to hunger and thirst as each affliction grew more grotesque. The grip on her friend, her only friend, slackened but for a moment.

He raised himself up from her, still on his knees. Her blow was quick and steady as his life's blood flowed from the artery that led to his heart. His head made a quiet thump as it rolled on the floor next to her. She always imagined it to be louder. The silence pained her.

The warmth of his blood calmed her, soothed her. His headless body rested between her legs, in cold contrast to his blood. Visions danced in her head of making love to what was left of him, but she would save it for another day.

HATE THERAPY
by Wendy Jane Muzlanova

Wendy Jane Muzlanova has led a checkered life. She has had many different jobs, ranging from tomato picker to teacher, and many different husbands, ranging from Egyptian to Russian. She is, she says, a foul-mouthed polyglot. In addition to writing nasty stories and poetry, she also creates rather good visual art. In her free time, she destroys reputations, especially her own. When she grows up, she wants to be a spy. For more on Wendy's amazing adventures, visit her at soutarwriters.co.uk/wendymuzlanova

Take a look at what happens when a mild mannered gentleman is finally pushed too far. After all, he's just a boy who loved his mum . . .

There are some things, Victor knows, which he could never do. He could never be cruel to an old person, he could never hurt a child and most definitely, he could never take the easy way out and leave a wake of misery in his place. Victor has very strong beliefs about suicide.

But how can he deal with the hatred? Victor has come to realise that he will need to purge the feeling in some final and dreadful act of vengeance.

At first, he tried to talk himself out of it. But he couldn't. And he couldn't find the help he needed, anywhere. You can go to learn about Anger Management, certainly—but there are no approved therapies to banish hate. It's an emotion which is largely disapproved of, he knows. No one wants to hear him talk about it. People are frightened by hate. No one ever recommends that you embrace your hatred, run hand in hand with it towards a bloody sunset conclusion. He knows that he wants to be rid of his exhausting passion, but he doesn't want to trade it dishonestly and cheaply for compassion, forgiveness or even rational understanding.

He doesn't want to sell his hatred short.

He thinks he is a lot better off *not* understanding what makes The Scum tick and he doesn't wish to fraternise with That Scum in order to find out. Her lousy being might be contagious. When he sees her pinched, mean face, he wants to vomit. Even when he thinks of her, he wants to spit the foul idea of her out of his mouth. He wipes his clean hands on his trousers.

Victor is a normal man and much loved by his friends, who worry about him constantly, nowadays. If only he could let go, they say, if only he could rise above the situation. But he has always been a pathetically transparent man, an honest man. He is unable to feign peace and reconciliation. He is too true for his own good.

When his Beloved Mum became ill, The Scum had played the role of The Martyred Carer. In truth, she had never believed in anything except her own comfort and had nothing to lose anyway. She had lived a selfish life and had neither gathered nor given any love along the way. She proved to be a loudly complaining martyr. No silence kept. No dignity allowed.

Although he was a quiet and unassuming man, Victor had always had a keen sense of irony and he had a vague, if somewhat fixated concept of how he wanted The Death of the Scum to be played out. Too tricky, he thought, to nail her to a cross. He wasn't a practical man, not good with his hands. He felt sure that a cross of his own making would be destined to fall apart at just the wrong moment. He couldn't go wrong, however—he reasoned—if in some way, he could place the cross upon her. The Scum was the very opposite of charity and compassion. Victor had to teach her those lessons. How many times had she complained about My Cross To Bear?

When he was just a little boy, growing up in The Dread Shadow of the Scum, he used to help his father out with odd jobs. At least, he used to watch his Beloved Dad while he worked. All of his Dad's wonderful and mysterious tools were kept in a well-organised cupboard in the garage. The cupboard had been appropriated from his dead uncle's pharmacy. The drawers still bore the names of poisons and remedies and poisonous remedies.

Never touch the Stanley knife, his father warned him. *It could take your finger off.*

The little boy had stared warily at the shining silver triangle. It did look very sharp.

An adult now, he had still never held a Stanley knife, but he believed it would make a fine implement for carving. He bought one in a DIY store, no questions asked, of course. It wasn't as if he appeared to be buying The Young Boy's Torture Starter Kit. He had purchased the duct tape at another retail outlet. The Rohypnol he had stolen from an old friend who had never had any luck with conventional chat-up lines and these days preferred a more direct and complete seduction technique.

How could an old friend go so badly wrong?

He had waited, like the honest man he was, for the police to arrive. He had telephoned them himself, of course. He didn't want to be a bother and so he admitted his culpability the moment they came. He sat by the scene of the crime, his hate therapy complete, his want replete. He admired his meticulous mise-en-scène with a feeling of great satisfaction.. He felt like Poe and Tarantino all rolled into one, with a sideways nod at Lovecraft. He felt released. The policewoman threw up copiously through her fingers.

On the ward, no one knew what anyone had done—on paper, anyway—but everyone talked. At first, people were repulsed and fearful. After a short while, he acquired the status of hero. He was a Defender of Right. After all, That Scum had got what she deserved. What kind of pond-life could torment an elderly lady the way she had done? And—they reasoned—every good boy loves his Dear Old Mum.

Victor has settled quite happily into his new imprisonment. There are all the books he could wish to read, he has made new friends for life and nobody ever shits on his bed or spits in his dinner. They save all of that for Micky the Peed.

Victor's old friends from Outside visit him regularly and they don't worry about him anymore. He sleeps like a baby every night and no longer suffers from unwanted passion.

SECTION 2

Wyrd: *fate personified; any one of the three Weird Sisters*

IN THE MEANTIME
by Janice Lee

Janice Lee is a writer, artist, editor, and curator. She is interested in the relationships between metaphors of consciousness and theoretical neuroscience, and experimental narrative. Her work can be found in Big Toe Review, Zafusy, antennae, sidebrow, Action, Yes, Joyland, Luvina, Everyday Genius, elimae, *and* Black Warrior Review. *She is the author of* KĒROTAKIS *(Dog Horn Publishing, 2010), a multidisciplinary exploration of cyborgs, brains, and the stakes of consciousness; and* Daughter *(Jaded Ibis, 2011). Janice is co-editor of the online journal* [out of nothing] *and co-founder of the interdisciplinary arts organization Strophe. She can be found online at* janicel.com.

About "In the Meantime," Janice says, "I'm really interested in the ideas of cyborgs, not just from a physical point of view, but in terms of what their consciousness might be like. In this particular story I was exploring the relationship of language to our bodies, and because language shapes our perception, how our body which influences language, influences our perception of the world around us."

I found this quietly terrible and utterly sad . . .

When my arm was still attached to my leg, things seemed more ordinary, organic. It was easier to travel, paint pictures with my toes, though I realized that no matter how fast the brush strokes poured out of me, the language still eventually disappeared.

When my arm was attached to my right hip, the writing faded away less slowly, and I have to admit, my wrists were easier to slit, exposing the lack of flesh underneath. I wanted to see the pulsing, pulsing, that would have been more satisfying, but all I managed to do was short some wires, have myself thrown into solitary confinement where there were no words at all. Alterations are possible to a text, so with my finger sharpened to a point I etched the missing words onto the walls. It becomes a rule that language thwarts my perception, so in the meantime I watch the language fading. It could be a trick of the eye, I wasn't there to witness its installation, and it could be the landscape substituting itself for another, but I do remember the feeling of being able to display digits dangling from my waist.

When my arm was attached to my neck, I felt ultra-sensitive to everything: the sun, always strangely a little too warm, phrases always seeming to be in the wrong order. Such an emphasis on syntax stirred strange memories in me. I could see photographs that I didn't remember taking, though the light gradually subsided. It was hard to sleep in those days, the air always too dry, words traveling from one eye orbit to the other, like the wires were crossed somewhere. My hand always woke me up too soon, before the sun even, and then I had to endure the gradual warming of my face as the daylight approached. It was unbearable.

When my arm was attached to my head, that's when things started to feel strange. It was as if I was viewing the world through a filter, another lens, constantly zooming in on words and absorbing the letters so thoroughly that they always looked off. I kept wondering, *who is messing with the words?* Though I suspected little out *there* had changed. When I sat in the waiting room, the walls always startled me with their whiteness. Once I grabbed some crayons from the children's table and scribbled portraits of my family onto the walls. It was an urge. They didn't understand, and I was reprimanded for my actions. *It's not my fault*, I declared.

In more recent days, though, I felt I would gladly go back in time to any of the previous arrangements, even to feel the sun burning the skin under my fingernails. The lack of an arm at all was such an obtrusion to everyday life. Simple things like buying condoms and acne cream at the store proved such a task, or even putting my socks on in the morning. I couldn't even access the language I used to be able to, so had to spit them out in the shower, the words, but in the dampness they dissipated almost immediately. I demanded some accommodation to this situation, but they just laughed at me, as if this situation was laughable, as if they knew what this felt like.

Then, they told me of my next and final arrangement, and I jumped at the opportunity. *Anything but this*, I thought. *It begins tomorrow, so get a good night's rest*, they advised me.

I had a dream last night that it was the next morning already. I was crouching under the kitchen table, cradling myself. Cradling myself? I realized I had two arms, one attached to each shoulder. *Why was I hiding?* I thought. This is the ultimate fix. Then I looked up, out beyond the table legs, and saw what it was that I was hiding from. The excess of language was alarming, each word with its gradations, each gradation followed by a shadow, my arms shivering from fright. Some of the words were enormous. Phrases trailing after one another, playing tag, so many words. There wasn't a blank spot anywhere, *where did the whiteness go?*

I woke up, sweating, thinking *I can't go through with it. I'll just make do with what I've got.* I sat myself out of bed, glanced over at the telephone, but realized how easy that action had been. I didn't dwell, just reached out my hand to pick up the receiver, dialing with the other. *Hello? Is this the doctor's office?*

THE SCENE CHANGES
by Mysty Unger

Mysty is a lover of all things strange and macabre, a collector of body art, and a dedicated worshipper of the written word. Mysty writes primarily about what she sees when she closes her eyes—the wor(l)ds beyond the veil. She lives a happily reclusive life in the middle of nowhere, USA, with her best friend/husband Eric, and their furchild Horus. Visit her blog at mystymayhem.blogspot.com.

I don't want to spoil the ending for you, but I must say, this one took me completely by surprise . . .

She's lying on the filthy bathroom floor. Her pants are still around her ankles and her underwear are bunched at her thighs. Her hair is tangled and matted to her forehead with sweat. Her breath comes in shallow rasps. The clear blue of her eyes is invisible, only milky white orbs can be seen rolling restlessly in their sockets. Her tank top is bunched up around her chest and her stomach is a dull red, irritated by her nails continuously clawing the same spot over and over. Her blood is raging in her veins as the chemicals speed toward her brain. Her entire body is suddenly racked by one convulsive spasm as her mind is wrenched wide open in an explosion of colors—and the scene changes.

She's swaying slowly to the methodic drum and bass beat.

The floor rumbles and the throbbing moves from her feet, up her legs, into her pelvis, and rests in her stomach. Filling her womb with vibrations. Her shorts and sports bra are drenched with sweat. Her obnoxiously colored beaded jewelry clink merrily on her arms. She's in a room full of strangers and she starts to dance with wild abandon. The music moves to crescendo. She doesn't notice him, in the corner, staring at her. Eyes hungrily roving over her body. Watching her hips circle round and round in a frenzy. She continues her Shaman movement—writhing and lurching and lunging in oblivious ecstasy. She turns her back to him and he strikes. The quick snap of her neck drowned by the deafening music, no one hears it. She didn't even have time to scream. And the scene changes.

She's running down a spiral staircase, her voluminous skirts trailing behind her. She's laughing in a high-pitched trill of excitement.

"You'll never catch me!" she calls over her shoulder. The castle walls catch her voice and the shout echoes around the room, rolling off the high ceiling and rebounding from the great pillars at the front door. She reaches the bottom of the stairs and heads across the great marble room, headed for the antechamber beyond. She picks up speed and her bare feet catch in her petticoat. Her mother has been dreadfully insistent that she carry her skirts like a proper lady but she has never understood the fuss. She stumbles as her arms flail to regain balance. Face first, she smashes into the large cherry dining table. The very table she had meant to hide behind and await her lover to come and seek her out. Her teeth explode inward and she chokes as the shards of enamel and wood fly down her throat like so many small bullets. And the scene changes.

She's standing in a desolate landscape of twisted metal and

heaps of trash. The sky above is thick with dust and floating debris. She breathes in the relative clean air provided by her German WWII gas mask, making a mental note to scavenge for a newer filter as soon as the coast is clear. She readjusts her backpack and tightens the bullet belts around her waist. Her boots are grimy and worn, but they are better than the alternative. She can't bring herself to fashion a pair of human skin boots. Not yet. She ducks down behind a tall pile of scrap and tries to wipe some of the soot from her goggles. She thought she heard something coming from the other side of the derailed locomotive to her right, but the solitude of the past few months could be playing tricks on her. She doesn't hear the phantom noise again, and after several minutes of nothing she begins to creep to the end of the scrap pile. She peeks around the edge and the arrow lodges itself firmly into her forehead before she can blink. She falls to her side as the blood slicks down over her goggles, pushing through the soot like her dirty gloves could not. Four feral teenagers scamper over a pile of tires and a downed tower, toward her corpse. Immediately they remove all accoutrement from her body and disperse amongst themselves. The biggest one, a girl of 14 or so, pulls a rusty blade from the waist of her camo shorts and begins to carve flesh from bone.

"Tonight we eat, and tomorrow we have shoes for the others." she says in a deep gurgle. And the scene changes.

She's in an alley that reeks of piss and desperation. Her left arm is sore. Probably another fucking infection from the needle. He told her it was only used once or twice, and she gave him a free blow job for it.

"Can't trust a fucking junkie." she said out loud to no one in particular. Her miniskirt doesn't cover her bare ass and it's starting to get cold on the wet concrete. She stands up and moves toward the trash fire the bums are burning. She sees him standing there with another whore, groping her tits and licking her neck. Her arm throbs and she looks down, it's starting to ooze some greenish liquid. Definitely infected. Rage wells up inside her as she watches the puss bubble from the crusty black hole in her arm. She takes a step forward and wobbles on her 4 inch cum fuck me pumps. He sees her and thinks that she looks like shit, more so than she did yesterday when he gave her that needle he found in the gutter over on 4th street. He dislodges his cock from the current whore's hands, thinking to himself this other one might start some shit. Still staring at her arm she charges in his general direction, screaming incoherent words of hate. She can't really remember why she's so furious, or why she's staring at her arm. She runs right past the group of bums knotted around the blazing trash can. She thinks she should stop and say hi to a guy she recognizes, but it looks like he's got a date so she keeps running. She hears some chick screaming and wonders vaguely what the problem is. She runs out to the middle of Arlington Street where the 1030 bus from Downtown is picking up speed to run the yellow traffic light. The bus plows into her and she flies like a rag doll into the starless night. And the scene changes.

"TRINITY GET OUT OF THE FUCKING BATHROOM!" a disembodied voice yells from the other side of the door. "Come on seriously, your favorite part of the movie is coming on! You know, the part where that bitch gets killed? Get your ass in here before you miss it!"

She sits up groggily and looks around. Her right hand is clenched in a fist and she opens it. There's a tiny crystal vile there. It's empty except for a grain or two of white powder. Her left arm, forehead, mouth and neck all seem to be in pain.

"I must have passed out when I dosed. Fell off the toilet or something," she mumbles as she pulls her tank top down over her belly.

"What? I can't hear you! Are you coming to watch the show or not?!"

She identifies the irate voice on the other side of the door as her soon to be ex boyfriend. Abusive bastard. She's leaving him for real this time.

"Yea, yea, I'm coming, give me a second! Doesn't matter if I see it or not, she always dies in the end anyway. The scene never changes."

THE DIFFERENCE BETWEEN MY GIRLFRIEND AND A SEA CAPTAIN
by Katie Coyle

Katie Coyle is an MFA student at the University of Pittsburgh, a lover of awards shows, a baker of banana breads, and a middle child. She blogs at katiecoyle.tumblr.com. *I first encountered Katie while perusing* fictioncircus.com.

Her explanation for where the story came from is nearly as funny as the story itself. "In early 2010, my friend Steve Gillies related to me a conversation between himself and his then-girlfriend, now-wife, but his imitation of her voice was much gruffer and angrier than I knew her voice to be," said Katie.

"'You just made your girlfriend sound like a sea captain,' I noted.

"'No,' said Steve, 'the difference between my girlfriend and a sea captain . . .'

"His explanation of the difference might have been revelatory, but I had stopped listening, having just been provided with the best prospective title of a short story I had ever heard. In writing the story to match the title, I drew a lot of inspiration from the character of Quint *in* Jaws, *which I had just seen for the first time.*

"'Why are there no women in fiction like Quint?' was something I wondered, almost as much as I wondered, 'How many sea captain stereotypes can I fit into one story?'"

Note to self: swallow the coffee and set down the cup before reading anything by Katie.

I first saw her hunched over the bar at McLoughlin's one evening in November, the sleeve of her sweater rolled up past the elbow, displaying to Eddie the bartender a ghastly burn that covered most of her inner forearm.

"Does this scare your fucking plums off, or what?" she demanded. Her accent was Irish. "I'm serious, Eddie, you motherfucker," she said. "Put down the goddamn glass and feast your eyes on the tragic fucking state of my arm over here."

I was alarmed that anyone was speaking to Eddie this way—Eddie, the most angelic bartender in all of Queens County.

"It's a pretty bad burn," Eddie said, glancing quickly at her arm and then away. The skin there was purple and scabbed, infected-looking, layers of it clearly dead.

"You ought to get your fucking medical license, Eddie," the woman said. She sounded genuinely angry. The other men at the bar were silent, watching her out of the corners of their eyes. We were all, I think, a little afraid.

I stared at her profile. She looked like no woman I'd seen before. All the girls I knew then seemed like twigs and this girl—this woman—was a redwood. She had an explosion of red hair over which she'd pulled a dark wool cap. No curves were discernible under her thick blue sweater or her jeans, too big for her, which she had belted with a line of fraying rope.

"Would you like to know how I got it?" she asked Eddie, her arm still extended.

"How?" He sounded nervous.

"This past summer, it was, I fried burgers in Virginia," she said. "And one night shift I'm there alone, a couple of patties on the fryer for this lady and her kids, when this big beastly fucker sits down at the counter. And he's a hairy son of a bitch, mean-looking, skin like rare steak, you know? And he says to me, 'You a dyke or something?' Now, I'm used to that shite; I barely blink. But there are kids nearby, you know? And so I say, 'Is this about how small your dick is, sir? Is that what's really upsetting you?' And he's drunk, right? So. He leaps over the counter and knocks into me and my arm slams down onto the fryer and it *sizzles*, is the fucking thing. And now I'm pissed off, screaming. So he starts to stumble away, but I grab his legs and he falls—BAM!—onto the linoleum and then I get on him and hold my arm up to his face and I say, 'See this? See what you fucking did?' and it's bleeding and he's crying and trying to push me off but he's too drunk and crying too fucking hard." She took a breath and a sip from the short glass in front of her. "He got six months for that and I got the hell out of Virginia."

It only took me a moment of listening to appreciate that she had the most gorgeous voice I'd ever heard—heavy and low and expressive, the Irish a lilt that made every "fuck" a sudden jangling burst of music. As she spoke I moved towards her, slid silently onto the stool by her side. When her story closed, she grinned at Eddie and I saw that one of her bottom front teeth was missing. The shock of black space ran me through with love.

"That was an incredible story," I said.

She turned and took in my smile, my pale yellow polo shirt, my youthful haircut.

"Oi!" she exclaimed. "If it isn't Christopher fucking Robin!"

For the rest of the night, she let me sit beside her. She seemed to relish the attention. She called me a pussy when I asked if I could buy her a beer. She drank apricot brandy, no ice. Each time Eddie refilled her drink she took out a small silver flask of something clear and poured a swig into her glass. Her violet eyes seemed perpetually on the precipice of a wink. Looking into them I always felt I'd just missed one. How I cursed myself for missing those winks! She had a host of other gruesome wounds, which she was only too delighted to display, and I absorbed the sight of every jagged white scar, the strange misshapen bridge of her nose from the three times it had been broken, full chunks of flesh which at one time or another had been separated forever from her substantial gut. I wanted to put my fingertips in the empty spaces they left behind.

Her first name was Mary.

Long after midnight, she stood and produced from her pockets two handfuls of quarters, which she dropped onto the bar. She called Eddie over with a whistle and he slid the coins into the cup he'd made of his hand—happy, I suspect, to see her go.

"You're leaving?" I asked. "Already?"

Mary licked her lips. "Haven't you slummed enough? Isn't it a school night?"

"I'm out of school," I stammered, embarrassed that she took me for younger than my twenty-five years. She laughed and, without saying goodbye, hobbled to the door; she had a pronounced limp that made me imagine immediately a peg leg inside her black rubber boots. "Wait up!" I called, but if she heard, she took no shame in blithely ignoring me.

I had no cash and had to wait for Eddie's machine to read the magnetic strip of my debit card, all the while dodging the suspicious look he gave me. I'd been a regular since I'd moved to Queens in August, forsaking the trendy Manhattan happy hours to which my co-workers at the investment bank were forever inviting me in order to sit alone in this poorly-lit space and eavesdrop on the other patrons—men so weathered, they looked as if they'd come from a shift at a coal mine. Eddie liked me. He liked that I sometimes came in with a briefcase. When the newscasters on the TV said "recession," Eddie asked what it meant, then watched my mouth move as I explained. He'd never seen me interact with another customer, and now I felt he was moving purposefully slowly, as if to widen the physical distance between Mary and me. Finally I scribbled my name on my receipt and burst onto the sidewalk. She'd only progressed a block and half east. I ran to catch up but once I was beside her, she made no acknowledgment of my presence until, five blocks later, she stopped in front of a Greek restaurant.

"This is where I get off, Christopher Robin," she said, turning to me.

"Would you like to get dinner with me sometime?" I asked.

Mary squinted her left eye and looked at me shrewdly with

her right. "If you're here to see my papers, just tell me you want to see my goddamn papers."

"No!" I said. "I like you, Mary. I just want to know more about you."

"I'm not a bloody zoo animal," she grumbled.

"Of course not!"

We stood there for a full minute, maybe longer, while she sized me up with a scowl. I gazed into the large glass windows of the restaurant and saw a man and woman at a table looking back at me, laughing. Then suddenly Mary had her hands around my hands. Her skin was callused and hot. She pressed her thumbs into my palms so hard that her arms shook, and by extension, mine shook as well.

"These are hands that have never seen a day's work," she snorted. "These are city hands. These are *Harvard* hands."

"I went to SUNY New Paltz," I said.

Mary let go, and after a moment, she spit on the sidewalk. She took a large ring of keys off a belt loop and unlocked the door next to the restaurant's entrance. Then she turned to me with the door held open, as if waiting for me to pass through. "Alright," she said.

"Alright?" I echoed.

"Alfuckingright," she snapped. "But so help me Jesus if you try to *hold* me I will not hesitate to put a knife in you. Do you hear me?"

I nodded and entered the cramped stairwell. Passing Mary I breathed in her peculiar scent—sour and wet, like a piece of seaweed on a rock. She shoved me aside and began to climb the two flights to her apartment. More than once it seemed she was about to lose her footing, and I put out my hands to support her. But she never quite stumbled, and each time I pulled back quickly, wondering how seriously I was meant to take her threat. A thought flashed in my mind—how mysterious this woman was, how magical—and left just as quickly. I had a curious sensation in my stomach, like I was setting off on some necessary voyage, one I'd been led closer and closer towards with each step I'd ever taken.

The apartment was sparse. There was a kitchen on the left—

unwashed dishes on every surface—and a living room furnished with solely a couch. A few crude paintings of boats hung on the walls, unframed; from the tears in the canvas, I guessed they'd been picked up on street corners. I assumed the closed door on the right was Mary's bedroom. Beyond that a cluster of fishing poles leaned against the wall. I glanced up and saw the thin skeletons of assorted sizes of fish, hung by transparent thread from the ceiling like demented wind chimes.

I turned to Mary, burning with questions, with desire. She unceremoniously unbuckled my belt and pointed to the couch.

"There," she said.

She kept her boots on. When I tried to kiss her she put her hand on the top of my head and pressed me down onto her chest, into the stale wool of her sweater. She was strong. I pushed, tried to lift my head, look at her, but she pushed harder. Eventually I gave up. When it was over I sat beside her on the couch and gazed at the freckles that covered her thighs.

"Mary," I said, "Mary—"

But she pulled her jeans back up her legs, fished her flask from her pocket with one hand, and held up the other to silence me. "Please," she snapped. "Spare me."

From that moment on, we were inseparable. Or rather, Mary went where she pleased and I found it physically impossible to do anything but follow. The life I led before I met her, I abandoned. I never went back to my own apartment. I quit my job and took up dishwashing at McLoughlin's to be close to her. In a letter to my mother I said I'd gotten a job giving scuba lessons in Australia. It was the first thing I thought of. *Don't try to reach me*, I wrote, *you won't have any luck*. I threw away my cell phone. I fell off the grid. I tried to grow a beard. All I managed were patches that grew on my cheeks and my neck in imperfect squares.

But it was worth it, oh, how it was worth it to be close to her—or at least as close as she would allow. To hear her raspy, wet, tubercular laugh howl at my pitiful beard. To accompany her to every meal at McLoughlin's; to wash her dishes when she was done. She liked heavy foods—boiled potatoes dipped in cream cheese, sausages and fried onions. She'd rant about steak and kidney pie while Eddie winced. "I'll bring a lamb in here myself and cut it open," she'd cry, banging her fork like a gavel, "but if I don't eat a decent steak and kidney pie sometime soon, I'm going to blow my fucking brains out." She drank what Eddie poured and when she ran out of quarters she switched to her flask, but besides always seeming a little hazy-eyed, a little unsteady, and extremely belligerent, she never seemed drunk.

When I finished a shift I'd walk up and put a hand on her back, which she'd shrug off. "Christopher Robin needs attention again?" she'd say loudly. "Christopher Robin's not getting his cock sucked enough in the Hundred-Acre Wood?" But back in her apartment she treated me with an indifference that seemed to border sometimes on tenderness. She'd lie on the couch with her boots in my lap and play "Hard Times Come Again No More" on an accordion, singing raggedly along. She taught me how to smoke a pipe and we'd walk around in the early afternoons with a perpetual cloud of sweet-smelling smoke above us. On the rare night she did not eat at McLoughlin's, she'd cook for us both, fish—smoked sturgeon, red snapper, Scottish salmon—that she'd bought wrapped in white paper from the fish market on Broadway. When we finished she'd boil the bones clean and add them to her collection on the ceiling.

All the while I asked her the requisite questions about her past—where did you come from and why are you here and who have you loved and what makes you happy—which she never answered sufficiently.

"What's your favorite Christmas memory?" I asked her Christmas morning, as we sat on the living room floor, sharing a plate of bacon.

"Are you fucking kidding me?" she responded.

I'd gotten her a silver necklace with a charm in the shape of an anchor, which she'd smiled wryly at and placed in her pocket. She'd gotten me nothing.

I tried to not to take it personally. I suspected her resistance to my love was a cover for some deep and lasting hurt. I wanted to get inside her, to touch her internal scars the way I stroked the external when I could be sure she was asleep. I wanted to tell Mary about my own pain. But my stories lacked the urgency I figured would attract her—they were all about bones I'd watched other boys break, camping trips I'd taken with my parents—so I began to lie. She listened without apparent interest as I recalled fabricated fistfights, made-up women whose hearts I'd broken in despicable, implausible ways. Sometimes I felt I was breaking through. Most nights I stayed on the couch and she slept alone on the twin-size mattress which lay on her bedroom floor. But on cold nights, she began to call out to me, her voice a strangled mewing which I never heard otherwise. We'd lie on our backs, shoulder to shoulder, as she was adamant that my hands never rest uselessly upon her. It was when I awoke those mornings, the windows filled with sun, my breathing light so as not to remind her of my presence, that I was at my happiest, my most carefree in love.

Other days were harder. Once I walked into the living room to find her wiping a grimy-looking rag across one of the fishing poles. I was overcome with longing.

"Will you take me fishing with you one day, darling?" I asked, forgetting for a moment her strict edict against terms of endearment. Mary spat—onto her own carpet!—and looked at me with utter loathing.

"I don't sail," she snarled, "and if I did, you can be well fucking sure that I wouldn't want some noodle-armed American knobjockey tagging along, mucking everything up."

I didn't broach the topic again. And I began to start each shift at McLoughlin's with ten push-ups in the back kitchen. But I began, I admit, to grow a little frustrated. This was my *girlfriend*, this was *my* girlfriend, I said to myself, even though she would have objected to the word, possibly with violence. I'd spent every moment with her for months, but I was no closer to knowing her than I'd been the night I stood beside her at the bar and gazed at the revolting burn on her forearm. Mary had a past that she alluded to in general terms—a past full of knife fights and large blank spaces where memories ought to have been. But I knew there was something tragic about her, besides her inability to get through the day without a drink. Standing at the sink in McLoughlin's one afternoon, pulling soapy dishes out of the scalding water, I began to wonder about her unspoken affinity for the ocean—the fishing poles she never used, the paintings on her walls, the fact that she dressed as if she were expecting at any moment to step onto a barge. I imagined richly detailed disasters that might have befallen her over the anywhere between twenty-nine and forty-eight years she'd spent on this earth. Drowned siblings, shark attacks, icebergs, unexpected gales—anything that could shut a woman down, make her hard. I peeled off my rubber gloves and walked out into the empty bar, where Eddie was filling out the crossword in the free paper people shoved into your hands on the subway. Mary, to my knowledge, was still asleep at home.

"Eddie," I said. "Can you think of any story Mary's told about fishing?"

Eddie glanced up at me, his expression a little wary. He scratched the back of his neck with his pen. "Can't say that I do," he said, and he returned his attention to his puzzle.

"Me neither," I said. I sat across the bar from him. "But it's a little odd, wouldn't you say? Doesn't she seem preoccupied with the sea? The way she talks, and her peg leg . . ."

"Peg leg?" Eddie said, looking alarmed. "Is that why she limps?"

I remembered that I had never confirmed that her leg was prosthetic. "Yes, of course," I said, "but she doesn't like to talk about it."

"Well," said Eddie. He shrugged. "I guess she does have that sort of quality about her. But you'd know better than me."

"But I *don't*," I said. As if programmed by the sound of my whine, Eddie pulled a clean glass from under the bar and set it on the table in front of me. He selected a bottle of whiskey and poured just a taste of it into the glass. I gulped it down and my throat burned.

"Listen," said Eddie softly. "When you first started coming in here, I could see you were a kid with a real bright future. You're smart. Too smart to be washing dishes all your life. Before you met her, you used to wear suits. You used to get haircuts."

I glanced at my reflection in the wall-length mirror over Eddie's shoulder. I did look shabby, my hair well past my ears, my beard still sparse. I saw, too, the darkness beneath my own eyes, which gave my face a haunted appearance. I seemed, I was suddenly proud to notice, tough. Like someone who'd seen trauma and come out with stories to tell.

"I think I look okay," I told him.

"I'm just saying," Eddie sighed, "I don't know what you think you're gonna get out of this relationship. The guy you were before, he seemed like he was headed in the right direction."

I shook my head. "I was a chump," I said. "I was just a kid pretending to be a man."

"And what kind of man are you now?" Eddie asked.

I barely understood Eddie's point at first. I returned to my dishes and as soon as I heard the melodic hum of Mary's voice in the next room, I rushed to greet her. But in the days that followed, his words began to burn in me. I'd sit beside Mary at the bar, watching her shovel forkfuls of corned beef into her mouth, and I felt acutely all the ways in which she was making me look like a fool. I started to notice the looks Eddie gave me, the heights to which his eyebrows raised; I became paranoid when other patrons grumbled statements I couldn't hear, convinced that they were mocking me. I couldn't hack it. I took the rest of the week off. I knew that if I could only feel like the ground Mary and I stood on was the same ground, like she didn't exist on some plane I could never hope to reach, then I could continue to love her, happily.

That Friday morning—the day before Valentine's Day, which I was smart enough to know we'd never celebrate—the alarm on my watch beeped timidly an hour before dawn and I turned and lightly touched Mary's shoulder, whispering her name.

"Lay off, fuckhead," she murmured sleepily.

"Mary, wake up," I said. "I have a surprise for you but we have to take a trip."

She groaned and muttered something in Irish that sounded like it would be hurtful if I understood it.

"Please, Mary," I said. "This is really important to me."

Her eyes opened and focused on me. She ran her tongue through the space between her teeth and exhaled a breath that smelled like vomit. Then her expression came as close as I had ever seen it to softening. "This better be good," she said, sitting up.

While she filled her daily flask, I put on a wool cap I'd bought at the Salvation Army on Steinway and buttoned my double-breasted wool coat. I took stock of my reflection in the still-dark living room window, placing my hand inside my coat, Napoleon-style. Mary came and stood beside me in her denim overalls and a yellow raincoat.

"What in Jesus's name are you looking at?" she asked, squinting out into the dark. In the reflection, we looked like we could be siblings.

I led her up the metal stairs to the N train and we sat a yard apart in the nearly empty car—it was before rush hour and nobody else was riding but a homeless man a bench away, who slept on a layer of newspapers and screamed out in terror twice. I gazed at Mary, her face scrubbed pink, her mouth resting in a sneer, as she picked dirt from under her fingernails with a pocketknife. At Times Square we transferred to the 3, and when the doors opened with a chime at Wall Street, I led Mary up the stairs into the cold morning. We walked east in silence. I periodically wiped my sweating palms on my jeans. Eventually we began to smell the sweet stink of New York City water, and she eyed me suspiciously. "What's going on in that feeble brain of yours?" she asked, and I thrilled at how lightly she'd said it; I thought I could almost detect a note of affection under her brogue. I said nothing. I led her out onto Pier 11, to an old fishing boat tied to a post, white paint peeling off in strips. Mary regarded the boat coolly and then turned to me.

"I thought we could go fishing," I said.

"I don't sail," she said. "I thought I told you that."

"I thought it might be easier for you," I said gently, "if we went together."

Her eyebrows pinched together above the smashed bridge of her nose. She produced her silver flask from her pocket and took a swig. Then, after a pause, she handed the flask to me. She'd never done that before. I took a sip of what tasted like gasoline and handed it back to her.

"Stop acting the maggot, Christopher Robin," Mary said.

"I don't know what that means," I said.

"Why are you trying to get me in that boat?" she asked.

I cleared my throat. "Mary," I said. "I love you." She promptly erupted into laughter. "But I think you're keeping things from me," I continued loudly when she showed no sign of stopping. "I want to know why you don't sail. You don't have to keep your past from me. I want you to trust me, Mary. I want to help you."

"I don't sail," she said again. "I get seasick."

I was skeptical. "Why do you own all those fishing poles, then?" I asked.

"They belonged to my dad. I've been trying to hock them for a year now but I haven't gotten a good price."

"Oh," I said. I put my hand on her shoulder. "Did he die on the water?"

Mary looked murderous for a moment, and I anticipated the shrug that would dispatch my hand. But then she dropped her head. "He did," she said quietly. "I saw it. I didn't used to get sick, you know. I used to fish. He taught me how. I was brilliant, damn brilliant. One day, when I was seventeen, Da says, let's take a jaunt on the boat, Mary, and see what we can find. We leave from Schull and we get bollixed. And after an hour a storm wells up around us, and we're too pissed to move quickly. We capsize—we tip right over. Neither of us in a life jacket. You can see where this goes, can't you? I cling to the boat, but Da gets pulled away—up and down under the waves, screaming at me to help him, goddamnit, and I don't. The next morning another fishing boat plucks me up out of the water and we search for him. And we find him. He's shut-eyed, gripping a piece of driftwood like it's a pillow, and he's dead. When they pull the body up, everything from the waist down is missing. A shark got to him before we did."

"My God, Mary," I whispered. "Mary, that's terrible. I'm so sorry."

She began to whimper. I wanted to pull her to me; I wanted that massive ginger head on my shoulder. As I watched her face crumple in grief, I felt a sharp, unmistakable surge of triumph. I loved Mary for her dazzling strength, the brass spine I knew ran down her freckled back. But now, knowing that there was a difference between my girlfriend and a sea captain, and that the difference was in her soft center, her vulnerable edges—I felt a satisfaction I could not have anticipated. I'd never loved her more. Her whimpers grew into sobs, and for a moment she emitted nothing but guttural groans from the back of her throat. These gave way to what I thought was quiet moaning, but I realized quickly that she had begun to giggle. She let out a sudden shout of laughter.

"Oh, you gullible little turd," she cried, throwing her head forward and then back. "My father died of liver failure, last year, because he was a fucking drunk. Jesus Christ." She tipped the contents of her flask merrily down her throat.

My face flushed pink, and without quite thinking, I stepped onto the boat, grabbing the flask from her hand as I left the pier. I had no plan; I only knew that I wanted to be wherever Mary wasn't.

"Give it back," she demanded, still chuckling, her palm open.

I fumbled with the rope that held the boat to the pier. I was trembling, trying to get it done quickly. Mary leaned forward and tried to snatch the flask back, but I held it behind me and pulled at the rope with my free hand.

"Don't be cranky," she snapped. "I was only taking the mickey out of you. Come on now. Give us the flask, at least. Come on, Christopher Robin."

I'd untied the boat from the pier and I was floating softly away on a quick current. Mary's skin looked blue in the predawn light. She wasn't laughing anymore. I tossed her the flask, underhanded, because that was the only way I'd ever learned to throw, and because I knew it wouldn't reach her. I watched Mary watch the flask careen towards the pier. She leaned forward with her hands outstretched, but the flask's course was much lower than her reach; I saw her eyes widen as she lost her balance, and then I watched her topple forward. Her body met the East River with a splash. I kept my eyes on the spot where the water had gone white with ripples, waiting for Mary to emerge. A moment later, her drenched head popped up above the surface.

"You bitch!" she screamed. "You bitch! I am going to stab you through the heart! You dickless goddamned piece of shit motherfucker!"

I edged my way around the boat's perimeter so that I could no longer see her. If I closed my eyes and listened to her yells and the sounds the East River made when she slammed her fists down upon it, I could forget pretty easily that she was a real human being whom I knew, with whom I'd shared a bed. I imagined instead that she was just a man overboard, just a sailor meeting his inevitable end, and that her curses were meant for the sea, not me. I stepped up to the helm and put my hands upon it, despite having no concept of how to use it.

"Let's have a moment of silence for our fallen comrade," I said out loud, and I stood a little taller, trying to look both sad and noble. After a moment of quiet, I began to sing a song I thought sailors might sing.

"Show me the way to go home," I began, but I couldn't remember any of the lyrics that followed and I also realized that I didn't know the tune. The sun was a blurry hint on the horizon and my hands were freezing, but I stood there, pretending to steer my ship, until I could no longer hear my ex-girlfriend cursing at me from the water.

SAFE AS HOUSES
by Helen Burke

Helen Burke has been writing poetry for over 35 years and is widely published in magazines and anthologies. She also writes stories and plays and does some visual art. She has won the Manchester Poetry prize, the Norwich, the Devon and Dorset, the Southport Comedy prize, the Ilkley Lit Performance Prize, and the Sheffield Poetstars Prize—amongst others. She reads her work at many national literature festivals and music festivals—and having won a BBC competition was mentored to write for radio. She is currently putting together a retrospective of her poems.

"'Safe as Houses,'" she says, "was based on an actual flat I shared with a group of girls in Newcastle. The story does actually embroider on events that actually happened—but the memories I have of living there do not require de-frosting. The warmth and laughter of the people I met and friends I made, I would have to say, inspired the story. I'm glad to say—I didn't do much cooking!"

Friends *meets* Ab Fab *in a small slice of twentysomething angst . . .*

Trevor says it'll all be all right. That it's all about looking cool and innocent.

Melanie is so stoned even before we get to the party that it's difficult actually getting her there. People in the street are staring at her pink Wellingtons with hearts on and her one-rupee dress she bought bumming round in India. Mel is posh, she doesn't get a grant, (doesn't need one) and she doesn't care what people think of her.

Frankie is in love with Mel—but Mel is in love with Keith, who is half-French and looks like Rick Wakeman. Ain't life a bitch. Trevor is our leader and mentor. He's not a student. He's a plumber and he earns loads. He has his own flat where he grows pot on the windowsills, which he sells on the Uni, mainly via us.

"You're safe," he says, "as long as you don't look freaked out or weird, or (worst of all) hassled. *Do not* look hassled—else you'll be sussed within minutes. Always look them straight in the eye and *be cool*, man."

We listen, enraptured.

At the party, Mel and Keith vanish upstairs to one of the bedrooms to have sex underneath a pile of assorted Afghan coats and Biba army great coats.

Sarah—Keith's heavily pregnant wife—(they were married in a Druid pagan ceremony in Benwell Woods) turns up and understandably there is a bit of bother.

When I next see Melanie she has a big black bruise on her cheek and she is knocking back large plastic beakers of cheap cider.

Sarah has actually pulled out a piece of Keith's hair in her fury.

The kitchen is unbelievable. It looks like Ratty and Toad live there and have just fried up a few stoats and weasels for tea. Someone has cleaned a small area near the fridge—but cleaned it with what I wonder?

Trevor and me are rolling a joint on the cleanest available table when a woman called Liz comes in. She turns out to be a trainee policewoman. She agrees to keep quiet about things if Trevor slips her a wedge of the decent Moroccan. She says she is into bondage and Frankie follows her deftly back down the stairs. A girl called Nicky asks me if I'd like to be a lesbian for the night.

I decline.

I quite fancy Trevor and am hoping I'll go back to the flat with him.

I think he quite likes tattoos and have just had one done in a discreet area. It cost me an arm and a leg and I have hardly eaten for days because of it.

I should be at the library. I should be ordering a book by Marx on Engels—or is it the other way around, I can never remember. But, I reckon it's safer here, at the party.

You never know what you're going to catch in libraries.

The music is so loud from the next room, I can no longer hear my own brain working. Sweat is rolling down my green kaftan top and smudging my four layers of mascara. Someone has rung the pigs and there is the almighty sound of the front door being broken down. Then I can hear feet running up the stairs and crashing into one of the bedrooms. Unfortunately this particular room contains Frankie in various stages of arrest and the trainee policewoman. A bit of explaining to do there, I think.

Life's never fair, is it?

IN ANY MISTAKE
by Janis Butler Holm

Originally published in Caketrain 6 *in 2008, "In Any Mistake" is an absurdist response to U.S. military "interventions." Janis lives in Athens, Ohio, where she has served as Associate Editor for* Wide Angle, *the film journal. Her essays, stories, poems, and performance pieces have appeared in small press, national, and international magazines. Her plays have been produced in the U.S., Canada, and England.*

This sounds exactly like the political doublespeak I read in the newspaper every day. It was supposed to be absurd?

"In any mistake, Bill, find a rapid sequence of the mendicant squad." Clara leaped up from an estimate for nubbins.

"The torn red carpet," said Bill. "This projected audience is gruffly cease-fire."

There were no other allusions to prudence, and two hours trickled by. Madeleine, in epaulets, positioned herself before the next throttle. The window was just a Rotterdam window. Heat flanked the cuspidor.

"Each day, you've lamely resorted to flash." Madeleine distributed copies of her overcoat.

"So long carefully," Bill sang in his reflection. He had yet to see the fusillade resulting from her look. "The torn red carpet was maritime to you."

Clara made much of uniform garlands, almost laughably congruent. Against all demands, those lucky barrels sputtered, imperative. No, the synergy of pleated parts had proven irresistible, too slick for damage. Twenty dollars down, they'd made a present of the diode. Only snooty slacks had kept the press on every block.

"We could jive before the highball," Bill said quietly. "This shutter lacks a sternum." Plain spirit needed roughly six weeks. Though automotive, commercial demolition had made the limpets slide.

In some circles, kidneys loomed as overflow. Angular, befitting. In the stores, Clara had shrunk barley to a sign. Her hair had scuttled home. Several precious metals, Paleolithic, had quilted the work. Shortly thereafter, another striped blanket, wonderfully articulated, sighted armed debris. In the last month, the mystery of these was not unlike solvents or sniffling steadily. Even as the errors, more and more dazzling, bred sweet suspense, Bill could track Idaho. Their dialogue fostered Panamanian guilt.

Madeleine cursed the planes of wavy duplication. She was keen to send mail, to evict something nervously, while the boat was cold.

"You look like an oubliette," she said. Very thin and crystallized, she fired the hurdy-gurdy. There were no kissy chops. With the advent of bunting, clavicles soared. Compulsively, affinities burned through her thigh. An imperfect chassis, trained to overlook, resonated faintly in the narrative night.

"All I am, I was myself moved to moan." Clara could find no glandular taffeta. "In retrospect, Madeleine, one dollar filched the spot."

LION MAN
by J.S. Breukelaar

J.S. Breukelaar lives in Sydney, but is from somewhere else, blogs at thelivingsuitcase.com but not very often, and plays piano mostly in her dreams. One thing she is committed to is some of the weirdest, creepiest fiction I've had the pleasure to read in a while. I had the difficult task of choosing between several pieces the author submitted; each is a masterpiece of skin-crawling horror. You can find her work at Fantasy Magazine, New Dead Families *and other places; she has a collection of short stories and poetry out called* Ink. *Notable quote from an admirer of Mary Shelley, "She has no business to be a woman by her books." This is one of those writers who carves a generous chunk out of statements like that. With a particularly sharp knife.*

"'Lion Man' came out of one of those 'what if' moments," she said. "We'd moved next door to a really big Rhodesian Ridgeback, a giant of a dog. There was just this dark cast that would fall over his eyes from time to time, a look that had a voice and a shape to it, and Clint Eastwood seemed to be behind it somehow." Living in the city, she says, sometimes gets her thinking about how if it all went wrong, you'd want to head back to the place you were from before, where life seemed simpler, safer . . . but what if that were not the case?

When Turner blinked in the park in the glare of the morning, the hand was still there. It lay on the wood chips where Clint Eastwood had bitten it off at the wrist. The child whose hand it was stood staring at it, a bubble of spit between her lips. Turner shuffled forward once and back twice and glanced around him. The playground looked as empty as ever at this scant-shadowed time of day except for the mother, he guessed, talking on her cell phone over by the basketball court. Well, she had her back to them, to her child. And to the pale little hand lying amongst the scattered leaves, camouflaged you could say, if not for the bright bracelet of blood still clinging to the severed edge.

The child blowing spit bubbles and Clint Eastwood muttering to himself behind the roundabout.

Try eBay, the mother was saying into the phone, picking at a thread on her jacket. Or Craig's List. The one you have's an old model.

She was twitchy and rounded in the shoulders. She wore black leggings and a short jacket that rode above her skinny ass. She stood in boots with a crack in one heel with her back to the child who was probably in shock but not yet bleeding to death. Turner watched blood pour from the grimy edge of the child's parka sleeve. The fist of her other hand was tightly clenched. He heard a thwok-thwok building in his temples like a chopper and wanted to duck, wanted to pick up the hand and throw it into the bushes or screw it back on, Bob's your uncle, but all he could do below the runaway hammering of his heart was say, Fuuuuuuhhhhhhkkkkkk, or think it.

The mother thumbed a green shopping bag higher on her shoulder and hunched against the winter chill with her back to Turner. Her fine dark hair whipped around the phone grafted to her face. Turner pulled off his belt and took a step toward the child. He bent down and wound the belt around her right arm over her parka and he lifted the arm up so the blood would flow back to her heart. She stood there with her arm above her head. Look, ma, no hand. But the mother didn't look. The child's face as white as paper. From one small nostril an icicle of snot bungying up and down in time to the spit bubble from between her lips. Her eyes flicked behind him to Clint Eastwood. Turner turned away, looking back once, then followed Clint Eastwood loping off ahead of him out of the playground, past the tennis court and through the parking lot and over to Turner's truck. He drove carefully, with blocked ears and knifing bowel, to the apartment where he threw his possessions into a duffle bag and an hour later they were on the road.

The world was no longer a safe place for them. They put

dogs down for mauling kids, he was sure of it. And he could or would not live without Clint Eastwood, he was sure as hell of that. He felt too small in the world. Pain helped, made him feel bigger, but not big enough. He'd had his tragus pierced the day before at Industrial Art in Harrison and the thing hurt like a sonofabitch. He chewed another Advil and expanded into the pain, listening to Clint Eastwood snore in the back seat. They'd be coming for them both, he just knew it. Turner's heart fluttered unevenly, like a moth emerging from its cocoon. He tried to burp but all that came out was a foul taste in the back of his throat. Ridgebacks weren't all that common in New Jersey, at least he hadn't seen too many of them. He checked both mirrors again. The road stretched dimly behind him and ahead of him, the green signs popped out of the dusk to show him the way home.

It was a four-hour trip but he made it last for twelve. He stopped at the falls and for a late supper at the old diner in Red Hook just like he used to when they were kids before he'd ever even heard of Rhodesian Ridgebacks. Speedy, Gran's poodle-terrier-dachshund-whatever, wetly farting in the back seat beside him. His brother, Wheeler, in the front next to Grandad depending on who called shotgun, which was usually Wheeler and even when it wasn't, Grandad would call it for him. And Turner in the back of the green Vista Cruiser with Speedy panting beside him, and sometimes Gran, too, who liked to shop at Alexander's down in Hoboken. The cancer was probably already at work on her even then, and on Speedy too, Turner thought. The journey, or exhaustion, dropping down on him like a plank and making him feel like crying. He kept seeing the child's hand there pale as a lemon among all the winter leaves.

Night was lifting just after he left Utica. The early morning news reported that a girl had had her hand bit off by a savage pit bull in a Paterson park. She was now in a stable condition in the hospital, awaiting reattachment surgery. Her mother had seen the whole thing, the report said, and had been unable to stop the dog that lunged unprovoked—

Not likely, Turner objected.

—and pushed the girl to the ground, which would, said a

hospital official, explain the bruising and lacerations on her back.

You never pushed anyone, said Turner finding Clint Eastwood in the rear-mirror, incredulous behind his black mask.

The girl had tried to push the dog away, so it ripped off her hand, the report continued—

I was just going for the Chupa Chup she held out to me, said Clint Eastwood. Blueberry-Apple, my favorite.

—then the attack dog dropped the hand and ran off.

Bull-sheeet, said Turner. You never run from anything in your whole life.

What do you call this? said Clint Eastwood, his amber eyes flashing momentarily red in brake-light glare.

Listen, said Turner, twiddling with the radio dial even though the volume was fine, but the last thing he felt like was a lecture now from the dog about courage and facing your demons. Clint Eastwood could go on about such things but this was real. This was really happening. It was the mother talking now. Turner dialed up the volume.

I was prepared to pull it off with my bare hands. The mother's voice was high-pitched, a careful voice, aware of its audience. You just find the strength when you need to.

The mother described the dog as a white pit bull with yellow fangs and red eyes. Just trying to cover her skinny ass, Turner knew, like the rest of us, just trying to cover our tracks. He wasn't sure whether to be disgusted or sympathetic or just plain relieved. Authorities praised the mother's presence of mind in retrieving the hand and pulling off her belt and tying it around the child's arm. The report said the child was too traumatized to be interviewed at this time.

Clint Eastwood was listening to the report with his ears cocked and his brow creased in that strange vertical frown. Turner's heart swelled with the pain of his love.

A pit bull? said Clint Eastwood, the world's greatest director.

Doesn't matter, said Turner. They can round up all the pit bulls from Peterson to Poughkeepsie. Once that kid IDs you, we're sunk.

Coward, said Clint Eastwood, with his characteristic growl.

Fine, said Turner. What would you do if they tried to put me down?

Wrrooogh, wrrroooogh, said the dog, springing abruptly to life and leaning on his front legs over the passenger seat, then lifting his right paw with the white sock up to scrape at the air just in case Turner missed something. Like the fact that the white paw was the right one, same side as the one he took off the girl, and that they were in deep shit.

I get it, Turner said, shaking off the prickles of gooseflesh rising on the back of his neck. Clint Eastwood was scary sometimes, he had to admit.

The dog yowled.

Case closed, said Turner, softly. Now get down before someone sees you.

Dawn was breaking when he turned into Highway 15, the long pink stretch of it between the clapboard homes and clumped silos. He drove past the white fence that always loomed out at them and told them the next bend was the last. Then he pulled into the rutted gravel driveway beside the Georgian pile with its peeling paint, green shutters hanging by a thread, and drove around to the garage. He parked outside and they walked around to the back door. It was unlocked. The Vista Cruiser was up on blocks inside the garage. The garage was dark and bone-cold, with something in the air, like the taste in the back of his throat, foul and foreign.

He let himself into the mudroom, breathed in the rubbery smell of his boyhood. The kitchen was cold and empty and the red linoleum faded to the color of dried blood. Clint Eastwood's paws tapped behind him. He walked past the gleaming table and over the rag rug of the hushed dining room to the foot of the stairs and told the dog to stay. He went up to his grandmother's room, his hand on the railing that Wheeler had slid off that time and broke his arm—guess which one. Gran was propped on pillows in the bed. Her hands clawed at the bedspread and her eyes were open and staring out the window at the silver branches of the old white pine. He stood in the doorway and waited until she eventually turned her head and met his scared and lonely eyes with her own.

Kill me, she said.

He set himself and Clint Eastwood up in the little room off the front porch at first. Grandad had long ago converted it into a bedroom for him and Wheeler until Wheeler found God and left for Canada. Some New Age minister there legally adopted him, and then he moved with his new fish family to Australia, the last Turner had heard. Teaching at some fish college somewhere in the bush. Fish is what Grandad always used to call those born-agains. And the ones that were always trying to convert or blow up innocents he called Stinky Fish.

But there were too many memories for Turner out on the porch. Like the wallpaper with its repeating pattern of islands and anchors. So as soon as he could he fixed up the old shed by the pond so they could sleep in it, him and Clint Eastwood, at least for the summer. It had been his grandfather's workroom, gunroom, potting shed, machine and furniture repair room. He'd nailed a fox skull above the door after he finally caught the critter, two cats and a dozen or so hens later, and it was still there. It had turned pee colored, the bottom of the jaw gone and a big black spider hatching eggs in one eye socket and storing dead flies in the other. Turner cleaned it up nice and white and nailed it back on. The shed was cool and cluttered inside, dusty sunbeams crisscrossed overhead. Clint Eastwood looked doubtful. Stared at the ceiling with his hackles on the rise.

I see dead people, he said. Who's that hanging from the rafters?

I don't see anyone, Turner lied.

Truth was he always found it kind of soothing with Grandad swinging from the beam where he'd hung himself in his brown suit and Sunday shoes after Wheeler ran off to Canada. The gentle creak of the rope. Grandad didn't hardly know what to do with himself after Wheeler left. Gran had asked Turner to cut Grandad down, but he couldn't or wouldn't and he remembered hoping that no one else would either. He'd felt bigger with Grandad safely hanging up there, happy to have Gran and Speedy all to himself for a change. Then Gran made him call old Mr Lyons from down the road to do it.

Turner didn't now how Grandad got back up and he didn't care so long as the old coot was hanging high, and everything could go back to being the same. But suddenly Grandad opened one eye, only one. His face was deep purple and his one pale eye glared at Turner. He fussed at the rope around his neck. Fuck you, thought Turner.

Turner set up a camp bed for himself along the back wall. He kept Clint Eastwood in during the day; the big dog seemingly content to snooze on a blanket most of the time. Every so often he'd get up and bark at Grandad or mosey out for a pee. Every evening Gran's nurse came rattling up the driveway in her bright little Honda and Turner made sure he and Clint Eastwood were gone by then. He'd take him for long walks through the woods and across the moonlit fields of his boyhood. Fields like out at the Parson's farm where he and Wheeler used to drink beer and smoke weed and which they'd scream across in their dirt bikes. And where Judy Parson showed them her woo-woo in the tall grass by the creek. Wheeler asked later if Turner put his finger in it and Turner lied and said yes. Not long after that was when Wheeler left and Turner always thought Judy's woo-woo had something to do with that leaving.

Turner loaded Gran's ZipRoo into his truck and took her to Deansbridge during the day to shop at the Superette or to the doctor in Watervale. This was more just so she could catch up with her old friend than anything else. There was nothing Dr Thoburn or anyone else could do for her now.

Turner took care of the place. He fixed the fences and pruned the currant bushes and fumigated the apple trees and took the fruit over to Mrs. Lyons in Watervale who made pies for the church. He cleaned the pond out the back with its little waterfall that trickled down from the woods beyond. He watched DVDs on his laptop in the shed and daytime TV with Gran on the Magnavox he moved up into the bedroom, but the smell of impending death hung low in the air like a false ceiling or the lid of a coffin closing shut and he could hardly bear it. He offered to move her bed downstairs to the guestroom and when she refused he installed a Stairlift for her but she almost never used it. A few weeks after he arrived they were upstairs watching the news and a report came on about the girl whose hand Clint Eastwood had bitten off. She'd had the reattachment surgery and the doctors said she would regain sixty percent of the use of her hand. The mother yanked the little girl's arm above her head to show the reporter the jagged little bracelet of scar tissue around her wrist.

Wriggle your fingers, the mother told her.

The reattached hand looked a little off. Like it was put on too tight or had gotten too small for her. And it was a waxy color, like a prosthetic even though it wasn't. Turner figured that the child had been traumatized into silence from events way before Clint Eastwood's time. She made a feeble attempt to withdraw her arm from her mother's grip, and then miserably jerked her fingers around a little.

Turner felt compelled to rush out to his sleepout to tell Clint Eastwood all about it.

She can't talk! he said. Or won't. What a stroke of luck.

Lucky for who? said Clint Eastwood, getting all rhetorical on Turner again.

You know what I mean. We dodged a bullet back there. They'd rounded up all the pit bulls in the area but they all had alibis. Case closed.

Turner exhaled dramatically, trying to draw Clint Eastwood out of his funk.

So are we going back to Paterson now? said Clint Eastwood.

Turner wasn't expecting that.

You like it better here than in the city, don't you? he wheedled. All the fresh air. Hell we walk for hours every night.

But the dog just sank down then with his chin on his paws and looked up at Turner so he noticed for the first time how cloudy his eyes were getting.

Wroooogh wrooogh.

Gran died a year later and Clint Eastwood went a year or so after that. Turner had begun to expect it. The dog's whiskers had bleached almost white soon after they'd arrived at Forge Hollow, his black mask turned ghostly. Sometimes he'd freeze on their walks, rigid and stone still in the middle of a field staring at something just beyond. Something that only he could see coming. Whatever it was, it got him in the end. Turner sat with the dog beside the pond behind the shed from dusk to daybreak. Clint Eastwood had taken himself off there, where he lay on his side telling Turner his life story, stuff from his Atlantic City days that made Turner blush. The waterfall trickled in the background and the frogs burped and the mosquitoes bit. At times the old dog lifted his head and snarled at something and tried to crawl away from it and if Turner could have pulled whatever it was off him he would have, his fist clenched in sorrow and fury at his own cowardice.

Finally Clint Eastwood lifted his umber eyes to Turner and he was surprised at how clear they'd abruptly become. He could see himself in them although it was dark and the only light came reflected off the pond. In the dog's eyes he could see himself and the twin worlds they'd moved through together. Then those shapes slid off the edge and all that was left was Turner, weeping. He lay down beside the dog and closed the eyes whose emptiness he couldn't bear to look upon. He rested his cheek against the massive skull and held him all the way to the door of the next world.

This is goodbye, Clint Eastwood's gruff voice sounded faint.

But I want to come, said Turner.

I wanted to go back to Paterson, said Clint Eastwood. And look where that got me.

Why didn't you say? said Turner. Clint Eastwood snarled at him but Turner knew that was just because he was scared.

Home is where the heart is, said Turner.

Half a heart, maybe, said Clint Eastwood. Anyway, gotta go.

Will you come visit? said Turner. Please?

The dog barred black lips. Think I'll go back down to Jersey for a while. Maybe when I get back.

I'll kill myself, said Turner.

Make my day, said Clint Eastwood. And then he was gone.

Although he could have moved back into the house a year earlier after his grandmother died and after the nurses stopped coming, Turner had stayed in the shed because Clint Eastwood seemed to have gotten used to it—the swirling dust motes, the machine oil smell and Grandad bug-eyed and glaring down at them from the rafters. That was all changed now. The dog was dead and buried, with lilies of the valley budding on his grave. But still Turner stayed. He couldn't help it—told himself that Clint Eastwood would be back one day soon but that was a lie. Damn dog'd be back down in Atlantic City more like it, raising hell just like the day Turner found him in that alley, abandoned and filthy but with more guts in his toenail than Turner had in his whole body. Turner had always felt safer with Clint Eastwood around and that was the truth. Without him he felt small and insignificant in the world. So it was no surprise that he now fell prey to those old terrors, inexplicable chills and strange smells. He tried to resist the voices that woke him, calling to him from terrible dreams, racked by the sound of his own heart beating itself half to death. There was a part of him that just wanted to get up and leave and finally he understood why Clint Eastwood never took to the place. For the first time Turner felt afraid of it.

One late winter morning Turner woke up to a silence that sat on his chest like a stone, so heavy and final he could hardly breathe for terror. It was minute or two before he realized what it was. Grandad was gone, and in the sharp, cold space once filled by the creaking of the noose, there was nothing. A terrible burning nothing. Turner's ears rang and, nailed to the chair, he stared into the rafters day after day, but all he heard was silence and all he saw in the dusty sunbeams was the sluggish rotation of the seasons. Grandad was out there somewhere, and damned if Turner knew where. But he knew he couldn't leave, not now. It wouldn't let him.

Then one spring day he was cleaning the pond and heard barking from the house. His heart swelled. He couldn't tell if it was Clint Eastwood, his hearing not being what it was. But it sounded familiar. He headed toward the house at a dead run, banging through the garage and knocking over a drum full of worms and old coffee grounds. He thumped into the mudroom where in the dusty mirror he caught sight of his own reflection, scarred and pierced, wide-eyed and slack of jaw. A pale chicken bone through his septum and safety pins in both eyebrows. His mouth hanging open and dull studs visible on his tongue. One earlobe plugged in black, the other torn right through. A tooth missing and not too much hair left on his head. From inside he heard the uneven tap tap of paws on the linoleum.

And from outside he heard Grandad say, Where's that Wheeler?

Wheeler? That must mean they were going to the city. Turner loved the long trips to the city sitting in the back of the station wagon with Speedy on the seat beside him. He pushed through and ran to the kitchen window then swung around at the gimpy sound of the dog's paws on the linoleum. She stood in the dimness barking up at him and he bent to pick her up. His hands gnarled and shaky. Speedy could move like a sonofabitch, even with three legs, but he got her in his arms, surprised at how bad she smelled. Her breath smelling like shit and a slime where his hand cradled her ass. With the other he palmed the ridged empty patch where Speedy's right leg used to be before it got torn off in the spinning spokes of Wheeler's dirt bike behind the Parson's farm. Turner looked up. It was Gran.

Hi Gran, he croaked. I hope you're feeling better.

But Gran didn't look better. Charging through the kitchen wall on her ZipRoo, her face eaten away from inside by the cancer, bloated bags of urine dangling under the seat. Behind her came Grandad, the rope burn around his neck so deep that Turner could see the muscle slick with blood and bile. Turner started to cry.

It's all your fault Wheeler ran off, rasped Grandad, pointing a purple finger at him. The fingernail was gone and in its place a black goo, like mould. You were never a patch on that boy, you damn fairy.

At that moment Speedy did a three-sixty in his arms and sunk her teeth into his right hand, the soft web of flesh between the thumb and fingers. He screamed and dropped her on the floor where she skidded on her own feces and ran over to Gran's scooter and jumped up into the basket. The scooter advancing toward him and Grandad not far behind. Turner backed up against the counter, pain radiating from his hand and up his arm, but it was the axe Gran pulled out from her soiled and squalid nightie that had his attention now.

Give us your hand, child, said Gran. *The right one. It's time to take your punishment.*

PHAT IS A FOUR-LETTER WORD
by Deb Hoag

This story first appeared in Issue 7 of Polluto. Polluto *is a division of Dog Horn Publishing, which also debuted my first novel,* Crashin' the Real: One woman's search for Truth, Justice . . . and Steven Tyler. *Being both erudite and forward thinking, they will soon be publishing my fourth novel,* Queer and Loathing on the Yellow Brick Road. *For more info on Dog Horn and any of its many projects, visit doghornpublishing.com*

For health reasons, I'd decided to lose some weight. As I got smaller, I found myself wondering what it would be like to be able to revel in my poundage, instead of treating it like a problem to be managed and eradicated. There's such a feeling of power associated with size, but it's quite a different issue for women than it is for men. I'm a tad smaller now, but I like to think that there's a little bit of Sandy in most of us women, just bursting to get out . . .

Sandy Dennis was a hell of a woman. She had flaming red hair, great waving cascades of it, nearly down to her waist. She stood six-foot, five-inches tall, and weighed in at a voluptuous, steamy 410 pounds.

She was the Reference Queen at the local library, rising from her specially designed steel-reinforced rolling chair to assist the student, the researcher, the occasional *bon vivant* by virtue of her vast knowledge and succulent laugh.

The head librarian had tried to shush her, early in Sandy's career of service, education, and enlightenment for the masses, and had the rare opportunity to witness the other side of the jolly fat woman. Sandy had fixed her with a haughty and poisonous glare. "You're telling me to shut up? Is that what you're telling me? You know I could squash you like a bug?" Sandy rose to her feet and advanced on her pitiful prey like a rutting walrus, until there was nothing left in the world but Sandy and her flaming hair. Sandy raised her hands, framing the other woman's graying head between them, making little pumping motions as if she meant to squash the older woman's cranium right on the spot.

Wise woman that she was, Sandy's supervisor fled in terror, pursued by Sandy's laughter. Sandy's good humor had been restored. The head librarian developed an anxiety disorder, and ended up taking an early retirement for an undisclosed medical condition. Her replacement was both wiser and more easy-going. He left Sandy alone except for an occasional offering of chocolate.

So, all in all, Sandy was happy—more than happy—delighted in her lubricious, porcine size, her thick armor against the slings and arrows of everyday life. She could give a shit about airplane seating and big-and-tall shops. She wore her hair teased and curled into a Byzantine bouffant that added at least a foot to her height. She made up her face every day with the same care Botticelli had used for the pouting fleshy angels that rolled across his canvasses. She wore eyelashes made of mink and rhinestone.

Sandy also sewed, and made her own clothes, a rainbow of electric hues and shocking spandex creations that thrust her bulk directly in everyone's face. Fuck the polyester and the oversized tee-shirts with teddy bears and flowers. Sandy decked herself out in sequined cat suits and leather body stockings adorned with ribbons and feathers and chains and fringe.

For amusement, she viewed TV and ate. She watched the stock market and invested wisely. She took classes online and stretched her stunning intellect to its full potential. She wrote penetrating articles on a variety of obscure subjects for even more obscure journals of science and art.

Once in a while, she watched the weight shows and the exercise shows, and snorted with laughter or wept with pity, depending on her mood. She pitied their hosts and their targets—

pitied their skinniness, their earnest weaselly faces, their weightless, powerless pomp and pump and prostitution of their desire for love and admiration, male and female both. What lies they told! What magnificent drivel! They knew nothing of true power, true sweaty, beaming, glowing, weighty, rosy beauty, and never would.

She would hoist a cake in a sad homage to their impoverished hips and scraggly buttocks and lumpy triceps. Their twiggy penises and hollow, chilly, dried-up vaginas. How much better her own fleshy folds, hot, wet, secret scents, acres of milk-white, rounded rolling flesh! Standing up, she would strip off her clothes and pirouette naked in front of the dozens of mirrors that adorned her apartment, reveling in her own curves, running pudgy hands over those floating, jouncing, jiggling rolls of fat, bouncing a little to make them dance under her fingers. Was ever a woman more beautiful than she?

She had followers, worshipers at the alter of her zaftig corpulent beauty, mostly skinny young men who would drive for miles just to gawk and mumble, blushing if she looked at or spoke directly to them. Often, one or two of them would wait till the library closed, and then trail wispily behind her, as mesmerized as if she had been the Pied Piper rather than the local reference librarian.

She thought of them as her Shadow men, and the most dedicated of these she called "Shadow King," not caring enough to learn his real name, but admiring his perseverance—and his excellent taste in women. When the mood struck her, she would hold court in a local club, where one Shadow man would text another to spread the word of her appearance, and soon the facility would be stuffed to the gills with her lackeys.

Occasionally, one of the lesser Shadow men would forget himself in public and get arrested for pounding his pud under a library table as he worshiped her, or even while shadowing her on the street or outside her apartment window. But for the most part the Shadow King was quick to quash any inappropriate expression of their adoration. Her reward for their devotion was a thin shade and a bright table lamp. And mostly, they were well-behaved, her admirers. The Shadow King especially. So she tolerated them, accepting the gifts they left her—tributes, really—outside the door of her first-floor apartment, on the long counter where she worked at the library.

The gifts told her something about how they saw her—chocolate, flowers, perfume, poetry from the Shadow King, jewelry, exotic body oils, the occasional whip or set of restraints, redolent of submission and desire. More occasionally, a ball gag or a vibrator, a gift begging to be used on the giver.

She kept the gifts in her sewing room, the most fetching displayed like trophies. It was amusing, and rather flattering, but left her largely unimpressed—Sandy was and always had been a loner, content in her own company, and not much needing or wanting that intimate connection with others which most humans seemed to crave. Still, she allowed them, in an absent way, to continue their worship, entertained by their blushes and their adoration and their clammy masturbating palms, their gifts and their sighs and their skinny, toothpick thighs and meager asses wiggling as they trailed her to her apartment, to the market, to the fabric store, to the library.

And the super of her charming apartment, she came to realize, viewed her much the same way, not making a peep at these odd young men who came and went and cluttered up the bushes, as long as she let him enter her precious apartment once a month to collect the rent, chat for a few moments, and get the barest glimpse of the gifts that lined her sewing room walls. It made his breath catch, those glimpses, and his face go a strange mottled red that amused her. She pictured him leaving her apartment and racing back upstairs to his own, to lock himself in the bathroom and fist his cock in his Vaseline-coated hands wishing it was Sandy's jiggling flesh he was pummeling until he came hard enough to spot the ceiling and the walls.

When she heard he got married, and she saw the skinny, pathetic wench who had claimed him, she laughed outright, immune to the younger, slimmer woman's glare. From the miserable look that bloomed on the super's face as his wedded status took root, she deduced he felt the same. It pleased her, knowing that he was laid so low by his miserable choice of brides. Surely he would have been better off to remain single and worship her from afar, groveling and moping for the briefest glimpse of her smile, her curves, her fair, fair skin and glorious bright copper hair.

It was her due, after all, was it not? She was the best, the most beautiful and fearless of women. A treasure totally unique, a glorious Goddess deserving of worship and reverence. A Goddess sadly in need of a garment that fully revealed and embraced her divinity. Grabbing a pad of paper and a pencil, Sandy got busy designing an outfit that would once and for all proclaim her transcendent, nascent perfection for all to see.

While she sewed, she ate. And ate. As shimmering material wound through her fingers and her sewing machine, her breasts, pendulous gardens of earthly delight, grew and expanded. Her thighs quivered and splayed and thickened, her rolling belly and jellied ass, those huge dimpled calves, those amply padded toes and fingers got larger and larger and larger.

She kept her minions busy fetching ribbon and thread and sequins and fancy silver buttons, and monitored her steadily increasing bulk with satisfaction as she sewed. Some of it she did by hand, as the work was too delicate and precise to be left to the vagaries of a machine, even a Singer 6000 with super-surge.

Finally, it was ready. She donned her garb, her Goddess-wear, her superhero gown of light and power, and stepped out of her apartment, out of her building, pausing on the steps to test her outfit on the group of Shadows crouched on the pavement waiting. Around her ankles and wrists coiled links of platinum and glittering stones that would have served as necklaces on lesser women. Her fingers were adorned with rings, gems glittered at her ears.

The first of the Shadow men to spot her shot to his feet, made a brief, gurgling noise, and swooned on the spot, the Shadow King barely catching him before he cracked his head on the pavement. Sandy smiled, satisfied. Then she rolled down the sidewalk, juggernaut of passion and purpose, and headed to the nearby club she sometimes graced with her presence.

All along the way, pedestrians cleared her path in awe and astonishment. Shimmering, translucent fabric clung to every curve and dimple of her 450-pound frame. In the street-lighted evening, nipples the size of a man's fist, dark as cherries, thrust defiantly against the soft breeze. The outline of her flaming pubic hair, barely escaping the deep and brooding cavern that delved between thighs and belly, was clearly visible. The Shadow King ran up to catch the waterfall train of her garment, and followed proudly, holding up the flimsy fabric with all the honor of a flag of state, lest it get soiled or snagged on Sandy's journey.

For the entire two blocks they walked, Sandy nodded graciously to those who, having scrambled out of her way, gawked and stared in her wake. She could feel the sidewalk tremble as she passed, quivering at the beat of her lovely feet, encased in butter-soft, size-eleven silver slippers.

By the time she arrived, a vast crowd of her followers had materialized, waiting at the door, and oohed and ahhed as she passed. The evening was a smashing success, and Sandy arrived home gratified and beloved, beneficent Goddess who turned on the steps to wave queen-like to her hordes in dismissal.

There was a note pinned to her door.

She took it down, even as she flipped the key in the lock. It was from the super of her darling, rent-controlled apartment, and she read between the lines as easily as she read the words on the paper. It was the Goddess outfit, she realized. He must have seen her leaving from his window, and had finally been driven around the bend.

> Ms. Dennis
> *My Goddess, my Love* (she interpreted)
> The gawkers and rabble that hang around outside of your apartment can no longer be tolerated.
> *I am jealous to the point of rending my own flesh with your pinking shears, my darling, my heart, my love, and can no longer bear the agony. I would rather stab your sewing needles repeatedly into my eyes than go without you another moment.*
> I must speak with you regarding this matter at once. Please come up to my apartment when you return home.
> *My jealous wife has been sent away. I must be alone with*

you, no matter what the cost.

If we cannot reach an equitable solution to this problem, I am afraid I will have to ask you to seek housing elsewhere.

My lust knows no bounds, it cannot be contained! You must, you must be mine!

Sincerely,
Your Super,
R. Kadaship

Sneering to herself at his boldness, Sandy closed her apartment door and went to the elevator. The super lived on the second floor, and she had no intention of compromising any of her hard-won poundage to a jog up the stairs.

She knocked on the door and when the super opened it, she was rewarded by the look on his face as he took in the vision of her complete loveliness and reeled back, gripping the door handle for support. He didn't actually swoon, but it was a near thing. "You've actually come! I do not believe my fortune! Please, please come in, gorgeous one!"

She accepted this as an invitation and swaggered through the door into an apartment redolent of curry and Lysol. "Where is your wife?"

The super swallowed and hurried forward, eyes clamped to her nipples with all the force of a greedy mouth. "She's gone out. Lydia had some errands to run, and will be several hours."

"Did she know we were meeting? Did you tell her you left me a note requesting that I come up?" asked Sandy, almost coyly. She trailed a finger across the corner of a cluttered table and looked at the super from under a thick fringe of midnight-blue eyelashes.

"No, no," he said, breath catching. "This is business. I told her nothing."

"Oh, good," replied Sandy, stepping closer. "I'm so glad you're a discreet man, Mr. Kadaship. This could be so . . . awkward . . . otherwise."

She could see his Adam's apple bobbing as she got close enough to touch, and as if helpless to stop himself, his hands flapped at the end of his scrawny arms and he reached, up, up to stroke her silk-clad nipples, and she marveled at his daring.

"A man could drown in your garden, and never question the cost," he said breathlessly.

She moved slightly, allowing his skinny penis to ride up and down against her thigh, and watched his eyes glaze with pleasure. She left as if she were a St. Bernard, all bulk and muscle, being humped by a chihuahua.

"There's something I've always wanted to do with you, Mr. Kadaship," she said, as the lust built and flooded his eyes.

He never took his eyes from her huge, taut nipples as he responded with a sound that was less than a word, a simple humming note of inquiry.

She took half a step back, removing her nipples from his reach, her thigh from his dick, and he blinked, eyes finally refocusing on her face. "What is that, my princess?"

"Sit with you," she said.

He blinked some more. "Ah. Sit. Yes, of course. Please, what was I thinking, not to offer a seat to the most lovely, the most riveting woman in this universe?" He gestured toward the ugly plaid couch that took up much of the living room.

"Oh, perhaps I misstated myself," Sandy said, staying where she was.

"I beg your pardon?"

"I said sit *with* you. I should have said, sit *on* you." And that was exactly what Sandy did. She noted with both satisfaction and surprise that as he hit the floor, her on top, as his ribs cracked and shattered, puncturing heart and lungs, as blood welled and trickled from his ears and the corner of his mouth, his lips curled up in soft smile and his body jerked in orgasm—the last he would ever know.

As she considered what to do next, Sandy rocked back and forth on the increasingly boneless meat-sack beneath her pantiless buttocks. Just to see what it would feel like, she gave a little bounce, feeling more bones break and grind as she did so. She climaxed, a flash of blistering heat that bent her double and made her teeth snap together in shock, and her mouth formed a small, soft 'o' of surprise and delight.

Finally, Sandy stood, looking down at his flattened frame, the stain of jism on his cotton trousers, with fondness. She leaned over to give a final stroke to his engorged and bulging face. "I'm so glad we were able to have this talk and come to an understanding, Mr. Kadaship. I'm so glad you've decided to let me stay in my apartment and not make any more fuss about my lovely Shadow men. Thank you."

And Sandy sauntered back down to her own quarters, to await the sounds of the wife returning, the screams of horror and denial, the flashing lights and thrilling sirens of the police. Maybe she wouldn't watch TV tonight at all. Life itself was sometimes entertaining enough.

It didn't take long for the police to come knocking on her door. Sandy had changed clothes and stripped off her makeup, hair slicked back in an unflattering, lifeless tail when she opened the door.

The cop's eyes widened slightly as he took in her mountainous body, and she could see the dismissal in his eyes. He asked her a few questions nonetheless, but they were by rote—how long had she been home, what had she seen, or heard that might pertain to a death upstairs. He had already forgotten her, except possibly as a joke to repeat to his friends and co-workers, she saw, by the time he'd turned away.

Good karma for her divine nature, she supposed, she had drawn an idiot right out of the box.

Nearly two weeks went by before there was another knock at the door, and this cop was no idiot. His eyes also widened at the sight of her, but it was appreciation, not dismissal, and he stepped inside without an invitation.

"I was on my way out," said Sandy, with a carefully chosen hint of annoyance. "What can I help you with, officer?"

"Detective. I'd like to talk to you about the death of your

super."

He walked further into the apartment, caught sight of the trophies displayed in her sewing room, and whistled. In his sharp eyes she saw swiftly dawning comprehension. Now she *was* annoyed.

She stepped around him to close the door before he could enter her inner sanctum. Regret on his face, he turned to her.

"We've turned up some additional evidence in the case."

"What's that?"

He extracted a small plastic bag from a pocket and held it up for her to see. Inside, curled a single white thread.

She squinted and shook her head. "I don't get it."

"It's a very modest thing, actually. Plain white cotton. From a pair of woman's panties."

Uneasy, she shifted, remembering the resounding orgasm she'd had riding the squashed body of her super, and a blush of guilt crossed her ample cheeks. Then she shook her head. She didn't *wear* panties, Goddamn it. What was he up to?

He'd watched her expression go from alarmed to irritated to wary. He stepped closer, dangerously so. "Let me see your panties, Ms. Dennis. The ones you're wearing right now."

She stared back at him, alarmed again. "I'm not wearing any. White cotton, I mean."

"In that case, I've brought some that you can use." He reached into yet another pocket to pull out a pristine pair of women's white cotton panties, still in the package. As she watched, he opened the plastic and pulled them out. They were as big as a pillowcase.

The truth flashed through her. He too was a Shadow man, although bolder than most, and she smiled, knowing, even as she considered her options. "You live dangerously, Detective."

"Not that dangerously. I've got a gun. And, I'll stay on top."

"How did you know?"

"My mother was a big woman."

Slowly, she reached out to take the panties from him, and began to take off her clothes.

It wasn't so bad, as sex went, she supposed, except that it wasn't her idea. She felt a stunning slap of arousal at being his object—his toy. It was as humiliating as it was stirring to be a helpless victim of his lust. He insisted on making use of the various toys and appliances she had on display in her sewing room, in order to make sure the event would be consummated to his liking, rather than hers. Like the super, the detective had underestimated her. While he'd lusted after her phenomenal beauty, he had discounted her lethality, her deadly focus. He had no idea of the magnificent brain that whirled behind her smooth white forehead.

In shame, she put away her magnificent new Goddess gown. Could she deserve to wear it when she allowed herself to be so subjugated? Her mortification, ever new and endlessly nuanced, kept her tranced and docile for a good two weeks. She lost five pounds.

But it didn't take her long to shake off the initial shock of her violation, and realize that, like the cotton thread he'd tried to trick her with, his threat was illusion. He couldn't tell anyone about their illicit, garish, humiliating encounters, about how she looked with a ball gag in her wide, furious mouth, on hands and knees as he rode her from behind and still claim her as a suspect. He knew it, long before she did. Even entering her building was an event he handled with surreptitious skill; he came in through the alley, a basement entrance that was all but forgotten since the time of daily coal deliveries had passed. She doubted even her awed minions realized he was in her apartment, subjecting her to every depraved whim his debauched brain could come up with.

And he had not wanted anyone to suspect her, to threaten the fleshy Nirvana he had found. His report to his superiors suggested that the death had been the result of a Bananastani turf war, the super crushed by the ancient torture technique of placing a plank of wood on a man's body and piling rocks on it until the victim was crushed. It was an impressive theory. No one asked where the rocks had come from. Or gone.

No one but the detective ever considered that the object used to crush the super to hamburger was a human body.

He never relaxed his guard when pleasuring himself on her; but eventually he relaxed his mind, and Sandy was a patient woman. He began to tell her about his cases, criminals caught, puzzles solved. She listened as he talked, her fascination not a feigned thing, because she knew her salvation lay in there somewhere.

Finally, the opportunity presented itself.

A series of stakeouts, involving drug dealers, multiple murder suspects and the same Bananastani gang he'd blamed for the super's murder. He blathered on so endlessly about how boring it was to be on stakeout that she decided to give him a little excitement.

She probably could have sprung the trap with a simple phone call to one of the gangsters involved, but she really felt like she owed him a more personal touch. So late one evening she got up, carefully making up her face, her hair, donning her Goddess-wear, her jewelry, her best ermine lashes, and sauntered out her front door. The worshipers gathered there scrambled to their feet, watching as she walked down the steps, across the street, down the sidewalk.

When her adoring minions made to follow her, she turned and raised a hand, nails painted a sultry plum. They came to a halt, all piling up together line a gang of Larrys, Curlys and Moes, and she smiled, loving them. "I *vant* to be left alone," Sandy said, thinking fondly of Garbo and the many delightful hours they had spent together late at night in the flickering television light.

"But what about your train?" asked the Shadow King, in a plaintive voice.

She frowned, her lovely brow creased ever so slightly. "Very well. You may come. You alone," she said, holding up a hand to stop the onrush of eager would-be train carriers. "But you must wear a blindfold. I want my privacy tonight." She thought of the weapon she had packed in her bag, and smiled, taking it out, wrapping it around his flushed face, tying it so that he was blinded indeed. When she was done, she leaned forward and whispered in his ear, so that no one else could hear, "If you do not survive this night, will you die a happy man, to know you have my love and gratitude?"

The Shadow King's bottom lip quivered, then firmed. "Yes, light of my life."

"Very well, then. Come." And they set off in search of the detective, he carefully holding her train off the ground and she using it like a leash to turn and steer him in the direction she wished to go.

Finally, they arrived in the vicinity of the dingy warehouse the gang used for headquarters. It was nowhere near as well illuminated as the streets around her own darling sanctuary. She took her train, and her weapon, back from the Shadow King, instructing him to wait on his knees, eyes closed until her return. Happily, he complied. Strolling down the dark street, she made out the detective's dingy sedan, and swaggered over to stick her head in the window. He jumped a foot when she did, so focused on the buildings and its inhabitants that he hadn't noticed her approach. Foolish man, poor detective. Her lip curled in contempt.

"What are you doing here?" he said, scowling.

"Why, darling, I brought you something to help pass the time," she replied, and knotted her weapon in both hands. Before he could ask what she had brought him, she whipped her arms around his head and pulled tight, jerking the plain white cotton with such force that it nearly garroted his rattling throat. She pulled tighter and tighter, as his feet and hands shook in a death dance, and his eyes bulged wildly. When she was sure he was dead, and then some, she calmly removed the cloth from around his throat and placed it back in her bag. She returned to the Shadow King, waiting giddily for her, and rewarded his patience with a soft kiss on the mouth that nearly undid him.

"I rather think I like you, darling. I may be able to find a place for you on the mat outside my door, rather than amongst my bushes. Would you like that?"

She stroked his delicate cheek and watched his eyes fill with tears of gratitude. It was enough. She would let him live. She picked up her train and twitched it back into his waiting hands, then covered his eyes as before and headed home.

It was another two weeks before a new super was assigned to her apartment building, but a building can't be expected to run itself, and personally, she felt it was rather overdue. Soon enough, he made his way to her door, and when the Shadow King came to let her know they had company, she emerged from her sewing room in a cheery outfit of scarlet leopard-print and faux-fur trim.

He was already frowning as she stepped into view, but she didn't miss the flash of lust that crossed his face when his eyes rose to her massive breasts. The world, she was discovering, was filled with small men. Small men who yearned for big, big women. "Ms. Dennis. I'm here to talk to you about that crowd of perverts that follows you around everywhere and crowds the bushes at night. Not to mention the one who sleeps on your doorstep."

She bounced, oh-so-slightly on her toes, making her breasts jiggle, and underneath the scarlet leopard print, she could feel the plain white cotton panties she wore caress her like loving hands. She batted the thick ruby eyelashes that fringed her eyes.

"Why, Super. Have my boys been annoying you? I'm sure we can work something out that . . . satisfies us both. Why don't you come in, so we can discuss the matter?"

She shut the door on the Shadow King's wary face, giving him an absent look as she did so, then turned her attention back on the man standing before her. "I was just about to have a cup of tea. Would you like to have a seat in my sewing room?"

MINNOWS
by Carol Novack

Carol Novack is the publisher of Mad Hatters' Review, Blog, *and* Press *(*madhatarts.com*), and a former criminal defense and constitutional lawyer. Her writings may be found in numerous journals, including* Action Yes, American Letters and Commentary, Caketrain, Drunken Boat, Exquisite Corpse, Fiction International, First Intensity, Gargoyle, Journal of Experimental Literature, LIT, *and* Notre Dame Review. *Anthologies include* Diagram III, New Cross-Fucked Musings on a Manic Reality: Non-fiction of the Enigmatic Polygeneration, Heide Hatry: Heads and Tales, The Penguin Book of Australian Women Poets, *and* The & Now Awards: The Best Innovative Fiction. *Her fully illustrated collection,* Giraffes in Hiding: The Mythical Memoirs of Carol Novack, *was published in 2010 by Spuyten Duyvil Press.*

"'Minnows,'" she said, *"just flew out of the trap door at the hour of deaths and births."*

1. Wonder Book

My wonder book came with six vanilla minnows in satin pockets and a crazy rainbow of Crayolas. So I colored my minnows tangerine, plum, mint green, and cherry red. My twin sister Hattie snuck off with my minnows when I wasn't watching and colored the other two black. I'd wanted lime and lemon minnows. I screamed such a tantrum my mother thought I'd stop breathing and die; she was beside herself rushing around the room like dull blades in a blender, screeching *do something, do something.* Hattie whispered *minnows are black; you're so stupid* when Mommy was beside herself, not watching.

Hattie's wonder book came with six white giraffes. Before she'd finished coloring them yellow and brown, I poured water on two of them. They were ruined forever yes for always and she cried for always, cried like a minnow so quiet you can't hear those minnows with whetted hooks in their mouths, like plants when you cut their roots, voices of broken lutes, lobsters in hot pots. But I could hear her; put my fingers in my ears for always when she was around.

My wonder book was an ocean, hers a savanna. My minnows would play in water, darting in and out of rocks, safe beneath labile winds, oil tankers and battleships. The fish kissed and hugged and flew out of the ocean and into a sky I think I saw once when I was somewhere else. When I was somewhere someone else there the sky clapped and suddenly there were three baby minnows, wagging their tails. I told Hattie but she didn't believe me; I should've known. She went to the kitchen to make cookies with my mother: cookies with raisins I hate. She said minnows don't wave their tails. She said her giraffes eat raisins.

Daddy asked me what I was going to do with the babies. I sat in Daddy's lap while we discussed making extra beds for the mini minnows, whose names were Minnie, Mop and Mopetta. *Why are they all m's?* Daddy asked, sliding his fingers through the squeaky strings of my hair. *Because they're so small they remind me of M and M's*, I answered. *You are a chubby little Moppet*, said Daddy, patting my belly. I fled to my room and sulked, talked to my minnows. Daddy was a big bad whale. So I swam with my minnows where no one could find us, under the undulating green fingers of sea-creatures, till Mommy made me go to dinner to eat cookies with raisins. Daddy liked giraffes better than minnows I know he did. I know he liked things where he could find them.

Before dinner we always prayed, maybe because we had nothing we could say with ease. So we prayed for ailing sisters of sisters and parents of parents in nursing homes. We prayed for far away children with no bellies, please dear god give them honey. We prayed for Mommy who had a tumor in her belly, prayed for the tumor. Her belly was growing like my baby minnows were growing already too big for their beds, beds of shoe bags hanging in my closet. My baby minnows were jumping all over the floor, gasping as I held the book open for them to leap into its rivers, so they did and we hid as the tumor grew, invading the house till one day the tumor screamed and there was big idiot Nod bawling like a blowfish, full of nothing but DNA, wanting to devour the house.

Baby Nod grew and devoured my wonder book. The minnows were gone, maybe into the belly of the sky. I combed the ocean for my minnows while Hattie's giraffes multiplied like spider plants, all yellow and brown on the dry yellow savanna, propelled by their gauche necks, awkward in their bodies, bodies rooted to the feet of the humming planet. *Where can a giraffe hide?* I asked Daddy; wouldn't he know? *There's nowhere to hide*, I said to Hattie. *Don't be ridiculous*, she responded: *Why would giraffes want to hide?*

I asked for lions for my birthday, prayed hard for lions bigger than Hattie's giraffes. When the big lions arrived, I colored them the color of oceans. I sent them to the savanna.

The lions are on their way.

2. Two Temples

I was content in the Temple of the Minnows till Rock happened with his hooks. Rock with his Bluefish gods insisted Minnows were not; he would not leave me be on Fridays would follow me to the Temple of the not Minnows. Rock would hide behind trees so I wouldn't see him. He was giraffe thin and much too tall but full of sinews; snapped proof of the nonbeing of Minnows with his Polaroid. When I was basking in the solar beams of the yes Minnows, he would suddenly appear in front of me, as though from the sky, shrieking and sobbing like a spider monkey on a starvation diet. And then he laughed, but I wasn't fooled. He wanted moon, ached for moon. So much commotion!

When we wed, Rock insisted on a Temple of Bluefish ceremony, he said *yes, bluefish you must say yes yes yes you must or I'll drown* and I said *yes till death do us in*. If I hadn't he'd have gone on and on, boring me to madness I would've had to close my ears for good. When you know about Minnows as I do you know they are everywhere in the open; thus temples are unimportant I said to self, hiding my sorrows in shoe pockets in my closet. Whereas bluefish, well, we know where they are; check your microwaves, chandeliers and mirrors, so loud and cunning those fish, taking over oceans. I could live without attending the community of the Temple of the Minnows knowing I was living with them always in spite of Rock and the cameras.

The Temple of the Bluefish reeks of rotted teeth, not like the Temple of the Minnows. The bluefish are a sickly hue inside an ash gray blue, they with their black robes. Minnows wear robes of many colors, iridescent happy child shades. Those bluefish move like stagnant water. You have to be watchful; there's an epidemic of suicides in the oceans. Bluefish dine on the diamonds of the dead.

Why did I let Rock why did I listen I have wondered since that time, it seemed a small sacrifice. He was a man who knew how to design his fingers around my body; like a new lute, my body sang in his arms. His whetted bones like those of bluefish bruised my belly, but he had a way, a way of looking into what I thought I was that made me disappear slowly like a jellyfish, disappeared like a jellyfish under a malignant moon.

3. Movie Review

Minnie and Nod met on Nantucket by the sea by chance or destiny; already with minnows in the first scene, in the bucket minnows hard silver no safe gray tones, bones like the cracks in my lips, too much light, unlike those tender dull zips in the boy's khaki shorts she unlocked from their moorings fast forward to unleash the expected catch . . . *Ah, but now, my dear this is the first scene—don't rush me!* So we thought we thought anyway, you and I, she and he had to be circumspect with the light, I announced her eyes were *too much color*, too pronounced like neon violet contacts: *this will end badly* but of course she's young so young, both leaping minnows. *A woman's film,* you whispered to me in a back row. *Must I sit through the entire god damn thing?* You were raising your voice. *Ssh* I said, *soto voce,* the popcorn, your dentures, *dear, I can't hear* every word, any to tell the truth. *Ay? There are no minnows in the sea,* you spat.

So Minnie beseeched him: *Put them back, please do!* She repeated her entreaty for the frantic minnows, slippery slivers of iridescence leaping out of the bucket onto the sand into the sky, fearing extinction she said *this reminds me of early death, please no please no!* The heavens turned dense ash blue like hospice hair.

The minnows were gone with a sudden moon ascending to soften the glare of those gauche violet eyes and Nod tipped the bucket, obviously a gesture you wouldn't get. I know you didn't see she wanted big fish; remembering a shadow under the patio pool in Manhasset when she was nine, an apocalyptic clap of thunder, a spear in her father's mouth, lungs and lutes on the bottom of the oily red pool. She wanted more than a Nod.

Oh you slept through the scenes, you with your cataracts, acts one, two, three. After so many minnows who went to Yale and the Bowery and even Detroit, it was over. I think that looked like Rock till there was a white sheet covering him and he looked like anyone without a face. But then I recall you remember the over of it, the *WHAT?* The end, you appended, you old sea serpent in my pants; you asked, *what about mine?* I did not say your Viagra falls, DNA disappointment, the sickness of Modern Medicine; I unlocked your zip so long ago, no surprise gift, but smooth as a minnow. *Then what? Into the sunrise they went?* you queried, forgetting you had asked, no, told me; you always told me everything without your hearing aid imagined you'd related the whole ostentatious synopsis as well as the start of it all with the minnows in the bucket no, not a bucket, a net that stretched from Nantucket to Nova Scotia. Imagine! But I was tired and couldn't be sure I actually recalled stampeding giraffes, falling heliotropes, bloodstone storms, an old child with no eyes, wrapped in waves; I couldn't; and you had dropped like a minnow of a brittle star into my flat trap of a lap, my darling sour ancient fish.

SECTION 3
Strikingly odd or unusual

CAPPS AND CAVITIES
by Moira McPartlin

Moira McPartlin is a Scot with Irish roots, living in Stirlingshire with her husband. She has had work published in Northwords Now, Crannog, Countryside Tales, Brittle Star, Giggle, The Scottish Mountaineer *and a number of anthologies. Her debut novel* The Incomers *will be published in April 2012. Visit her website at* moiramcpartlin.com.

In regards to her inspiration for "Capps and Cavities," Moira says, "The story was inspired by a throw-away comment one of my characters said about mobile phones being so small you would soon be able to have them fitted into fillings. And then one day, while sitting in the cafe of the Centre of Contemporary Arts (CCA), the story came to me. The CCA is next door to the Glasgow Dental School."

A toothy look at where our technology is taking us . . .

Yati was spot on, there is a door halfway up the wall, how the fuck did that get there? It's one of those old-fashioned doors on an old-fashioned house, like a West End mansion or what not. And if being halfway up the wall isn't bad enough it's inside this building. Here I am sitting in this café amongst weird arty-farty students trying to sneak in their packed lunches and I am looking up at a stone house front suspended half way up an inside wall. ART. Man, what a load of shite.

Yati told me the house used to be outside, that, in the olden days there was a lane which ran along its front and they tore it all down, apart from this house, that is, and then built this building round about it. I don't know how come she is so clever about local history; she's not even from this continent.

At last—the waiter who thinks he's James Dean is bringing my cappuccino. His smile is reluctant but I know that deep down under that quaff he's gagging for a piece of me. I can tell from the leaf pattern that he's chocolate sprinkled on top of my coffee that this is going to cost me. I didn't want to wait here, I knew it would be like this, but Yati nipped on about waiting nearby and you don't argue with that girl, no way. She's got me well and truly screwed after that time I scored for her and then got mugged in The City Park. She didn't believe my story even though I had five fucking stitches on my forehead from where I tried to nut the guy and caught his Mickey Rourke chin instead.

James Dean has just sauntered past again. He's still looking to see if I fancy him. I wish I hadn't worn this short skirt now. To be honest I prefer the wee lassie at the next table to him, but I can't really be bothered with all that relationship stuff. I told Yati that but you know what these Orientals are like.

That's where she got the idea of this trick from. She was back visiting her folks for the summer. Her sister got hold of the kit for her. Yati hunted me out as soon as she made it through airport security intact. She knew where to find me. The bitch always does. Said she wanted me to help her out, just this once, would make it worth my while, knew I would understand why she could not do this through the usual channels. Said she'd rope her flatmate in too because she needed the additional expertise. Fuck knows how she coaxed the wee guy I had to see last night. He was shitting hisself, I half expected to end up with a needle through my eyeball the way he was shaking about. She must have something pretty big on him.

Man, that girl sure knows how to get what she wants. I reckon it must be her background. Word on the street is she is related to the King of Brunei, whatever that means. Sure sounds swanky though. And the gear she carries, she must be minted.

That guy last night said not to drink anything hot or cold for twenty-four hours. I forgot, had a swig of boiling tea this morning and my ear went ape-shit. Started to tickle and then there was a funny tugging, clunking sound, like someone had put a toilet chain in my head and couldn't get it to flush. Oh man, now my coffee's cold, I can't take coffee unless it's scalding. What a waste of a good capp and a leaf-patterned chocolate sprinkle.

I wish she would hurry up. I'm gonnae shoot the craw in two minutes if she doesn't come by then.

I can hear steps clip clop along that suspended gantry—it's not her. It's a guy with geometric hair and a pukey lime green jumper. An "Art Student Alert" buzzes my individual trend sensors. What is it about art students that make them think lime green is remotely artistic? The lime green jumper industry would be in dire straights if it wasn't for arties and their bowffin' taste. He doesn't seem to think there is anything wrong with the door halfway up the wall, just sashays right on by, clip-clops down the stairs, plonks hisself at the next table. Yuck, the smell of his aftershave—a mix of burger-dried clothes and Bachelor Uncle smell is giving me the boak. I'm definitely going to have to move soon.

I've been here nearly half an hour. Yati said have a coffee, don't look conspicuous. Should have worn a lime green jumper, shouldn't I? Conspicuousness is creeping round me and James Dean wants to clear my table.

My mobie rings.

"I thought I was to meet you here." I hiss at her while trying to sound calm.

"Don't be silly, they can't see me with you."

They, who's "they"?

"Come out the side door. Look up the hill, you will see me at the top of the road."

I feel my palms sweat and have a thirst on me that could choke a donkey. I give James Dean a couple of quid and leave. He doesn't say anything, just raises his eyebrow in an energetic way.

It's now my turn to clank my feet up the metal steps, along the gantry, past the stupid door halfway up the wall and out the side entrance. Then I get it. I totally get the door thing; all that about the lane and the mansion house. Man, I can practically see the carriage drawing up at the steps to pick up the master.

As instructed I look up the hill and there she is. I'm ashamed to admit I'm pleased to see the cow, but I am.

The phone rings again. She sounds breathless like she's climbed from the bottom. "Lying in the gutter is a MacDonald's cup." She puts on her secret agent voice. "Pick it up. Inside you will find a pass."

The theme tune to *Mission Impossible* hums in my head.

The cup leaks. The bitch hasn't emptied it first. Individual tracks of Fanta race each other down the hill until they run out. I pick it up and ping the lid off. Inside is a plastic card on a blue lanyard. It's my ugly mug that smiles back from the card but the name is Cindy Burk. Cindy for Christ sake, who thought of that? Despite it being sticky and wet I hang it round my neck.

Here she is again. I flip the phone.

"Come up the hill and in through the back door. I will take care of the security guard."

I daren't ask what tactics she will use for that.

The hill is steep and I feel a wheeze coming before I reach the end of the first building. Man, what a relief to hit the top. I head for the back door of the hospital, which sits just a couple of hundred yards off the junction.

Yati has disappeared. The phone bleeps, the text reads. *Room 402—find it*. Yes ma'am.

The automatic door gives me a fright, they always do, I never see them coming. I look for a handle and the woosh comes before it registers there isn't one.

An empty chair watches a portable TV. The guard has been dealt with. Spookily, I am on the fourth floor. I hunt for room 402, I don't have far to look.

"Psst."

She is at the far end of the corridor and now wearing a white coat that makes her look even more evil than usual. Her dainty features and Chinese hair compliment the garb. A Classic Bond baddie.

Room 402 is blinding bright. An executioner's chair sits centre stage.

"Where's your flat-mate?"

She giggles her geisha giggle. "No one else, just us."

"Great, but you're only a second-year student."

She holds up her tiny hand and masks it in front of her eyes.

"Ah, but a brilliant second-year student, and I will be even more brilliant if I can pull this off." Her mask becomes serious. "How did you get on with Clive last night?"

"My ear tickles and I can still smell his fear."

She laughs a hard tinkle. "That will soon be gone."

She presses me into the chair and wraps a blue plastic gown round my neck. A lamp is clamped to her forehead and suddenly I realise I've stumbled onto the set of that ancient movie *Marathon Man*. Lawrence Olivier pats the back of my hand.

"OK, this should only take ten minutes." She looks me right in the eye and says with a straight face, "You're not worried, are you?"

My sweaty palms and dry throat are permanent features these days, as are the shakes, but this is about more than my habit. I'm shit scared.

"Just get on with it, Yati."

"Open up." She peers into my mouth. I smell coffee on her breath.

"Goodness me, what a mess in here. When were you last at a dentist?"

Man, I knew she would be like this. " . . . et ong ef it," I try to say but the cotton wool tampons she's jammed in my mouth gag me.

The cold steel of the needle has an instant reaction with the ear tickle; a buzz kicks off and tries to bore a hole back out my eyeball. At least I don't feel the needle. My tongue swells to the size of a butcher's block.

Yati is humming *The Godfather* theme to herself, rattling instruments in accompaniment.

"Now you know this will soon be all the rage in Japan, I do not understand why your nanny government will not consider it. It is ridiculous."

She comes back over to my line of sight. I stare up at the light and try not to notice the bogie lurking on the end of her nostril. I better not tell her about it. These Orientals with their pride—it's all to do with face with them.

"How does it feel to be a pioneer?"

"Go'k," I lie.

Stupid cow doesn't seem to realise she'll be struck off or worse.

The drill reminds me why I haven't been to the dentist in years. Bits of shrapnel ricochet off the back of my throat and land on my tongue; water squirts in my face. I think I smell burning.

Thankfully the drilling doesn't take long. Her fingers feel nimble and small as she pushes something into the cavity. My neck hurts, my eyes hurt. My body and mind shout "get me out of here". I start to struggle but her hand pushes me back in the chair.

"Not much longer, just the final connection to make."

I hear a click and the pain disappears from my neck and eyes. The ear tickle vanishes. She wipes my face with the same gentle care I used to take with Mum.

"There, sit up. Time for the truth of the trick." She hands me a ring with a pad the size of a postage stamp to fit over my thumb. "For text," she says. "Stand over there and follow my instructions."

She takes her phone out of her whites and thumbs a number. A short beep happens just behind my ear.

"Bite down," she barks. I obey—of course.

She glides out the room and closes the door.

"Can you hear me," a voice says inside my head.

"Yes," I say and I hear her squeal from the other side of the door.

"After you bite down again and hear the connection break, scroll to Y on the pad and bite again."

I do as she says, a ringing happens in my head at the same time as I hear her ring tone trill from the corridor.

"Hello," she says behind my eyes

"Hello."

The door bangs open and a beaming Yati enters

"It fucking works."

She presses her phone between her palms and bends forward in prayer. "Fuck—I want one now."

I hold out my hand and she passes me my deal and more besides.

"No one should find out about this should they?" I say and

smile as I watch the smile drop from her face. She knows I know there is a lot more of this coming my way.

FALL ANY WAY YOU CAN
by Tantra Bensko

Tantra Bensko teaches Experimental Fiction Writing and writes esoteric articles. Her full length fiction book, Lucid Membrane, *is newly out from* Night Publishing, *and she has chapbooks, including* The Cabinet of What You Don't See, *from ISMs Press, and 170 creative writing magazine publications. She runs her own* Exclusive Magazine, *guest edited* Medulla Review's Lucid Fiction *(the genre she created,) and leaps about in a lot of strange directions, making sounds few people could have imagined.*

She currently is an orange poppy against a bright blue wall. She wrote this story specifically for the anthology, out of love. She falls out of the sky daily. No one ever told her not to. Sometimes she does it every moment. She wants to do it next while covered totally in orange poppies, and polarizing sunglasses to make the sky extra blue. She hopes this story will function as polarizing sunglasses for the readers who should look up at the sky and see what happens.

Smashing his way out of the giant hole in the sky that only he could see, the round man defecated onto the audience that had formed his ay below him, who were squirming like worms, and squealing in a way that made him want to rip the sky in two. He rearranged the relationship between the sky and the ground as he fell, making the wormy people turn much more civilized, standing up as they should instead of groveling at his apparent messiahship. Much better, he said, as he landed, his fancy collar opening out like a parachute just at the end, **POOF!**

The dogs however were less impressed, and the rearrangement

made them start to worry about their security, such as how much food would be in their bowls, and how few slugs. The started running around him in a circle, until it became clear the man was going to continue going downward. The ground around him started to crack very artistically, the lines pointing in toward him, the blackness in the center where he stood starting to amplify its saturation.

Tall drinks on the ground fell over, and poured their way, cherry and all, down towards him, and he kept his rather red mouth open as he went down into the hole in the ground, as the mixed drinks went into it. Sometimes he gulped and slurped, sometimes just belched a little, which made the tiny children cry. They hid their faces, as he reached too many scatological improprieties they have been taught to avoid.

He waved, his fancy suit all buttoned up but too tight stretched to accommodate his arm. Some waved back, some holding balloons, which they were therefore separated from. The balloons rose in the sky, red, echoing the cherries nicely. The balloons and the cherries both started getting larger therefore, once again, rearranging the relationships. It made the whole scene look a little unusual, but highly colorful, like a book cover, or a painting by a child-clown.

The people who were lying asleep started sliding towards the hole, oblivious, three of them. The nappers were going head first, the worst way to go into an opening hole, when the dogs ran to them to pull them back. This made the children scream with joy, and run circles around them. The day was becoming more circular than usual, thought a man standing beside it all, a thoughtful look on his face.

He was the newspaper reporter in the crowd, so of course, his thoughts were the most important. He heard the voice in his head as much more urbane than anyone else's there. He took out his large notebook from his pocket and wrote

C
R   I
A   R
L   C
U

He then burned a hole in the center of that with a cigarette. Satisfied he had done something superiorly creative, he threw the butt on the ground and let it smoke, looking around daring someone to look disgusted at that act. He found no one actually looking at him, a fact which he found repellant. All these people, he thought, looking at someone falling into a hole. It's like he's Charles Forte or something pooing in public. Who cares? he said aloud.

I care, said his wife, who had snuck up behind him and pulled his shoelaces. He fell onto the ground, which sucked him into it so fast, his wife could hardly remember he ever existed. Only the piece of paper with the circular message remained, floating in the air. She looked around and her eyes landed on the hole still caving in where the man had fallen from the sky. She shook her head and walked away, mumbling Factitious bastard, never had a chance with me. Small children were also sucked into the new hole, but their parents weren't looking, and so they forgot about them before long.

After a while the crowd noticed sounds coming from the original hole, which sounded vaguely like a song by Barry Manilow. **B M! B M! B M!** the crowd started chanting excitedly. No one thought to take a photo of it all, so I can't prove it, but there seemed to be some sort of apparition coming up from the hole. It was all an invocation, it seemed, all along, but how, and why, finally had to be superseded by a casual why not? if one were to remain sane.

But no, it was not to be explained so easily. The apparition didn't turn into the musician, but into a large porcupine. The crowd ran backwards, but were impaled by the quills as it grew larger and larger. Some of the quills reached the sky and popped the red balloons, creating turmoil in the crowd. Some of the quills reached into the hole and skewered the red cherries.

The porcupine luckily walked along not noticing the other hole which sucked it in so fast that no one there realized the day had been unusual at all, though they were of course also sucked in, as they were impaled on the quills. And just out of reach of the cherries, too, which made them mad.

THE GORILLA IN THE PHONE BOOTH
by Nancy DiMauro

I've known Nancy since we met on Orson Scott Card's writers' website, hatrack.com *several years ago. We've been critting and encouraging each other ever since. In addition to writing, Nancy is a mommy and a lawyer, who lives on a horse farm with her husband and two boys and far too many animals. She's received Honorable Mention for two of her stories from* Writers of the Future. *Find her at* fictorians.com.

"The idea for 'The Gorilla in the Phone Booth' arose from a Writing Excuses Podcast on Authors' Promises to their readers," Nancy says. "Howard Tayler mentioned that if you mention the gorilla in the phone booth, you'd better be doing it for a reason. I spent the rest of the drive home trying to figure out why a gorilla would be in a phone booth. Forty-eight hours later, the first draft of this story was completed." Evil Editor and his minions, who commented on the story, helped hone that first draft.

Men with good fur. Does a story need more?

The leaves of the magnolia trees surrounding the escalator opening disappeared as Mare and I rode down to the Metro. Mare stood next to me, trying to ignore the text messages from her boyfriend. The greasy smell of the hot dog cart didn't disappear. My stomach rumbled. I'd skipped lunch to meet a deadline, again. Maybe I'd pick something up from the Thai place when I got home.

We stepped onto the platform and walked to the turnstiles. The pleasant hot dog smell vanished under the stink of people, metro trains and the occasional spot where someone thought the mass transit system was a good place to relieve himself. I wrinkled my nose, all thought of dinner gone. This was one of the few stations that still had pay phones and the urine stench grew stronger as we walked toward the phone booths. Ugly things for creepy people. Speaking of creepy, a blur of dark hair seized my attention as we got off the escalator. A burly shape crouched in the second booth. The glass walls bowed around him. Thick fingers clutched the receiver. The other hand hovered just above the floor.

"You see that?" I asked.

"What?" Mare peered into the crowd as if hopeful for a fight.

"No, that." I pointed.

"I thought they'd gotten rid of all the phone booths."

"Doesn't that look like a gorilla?"

She stopped. Pedestrians flowed around us in the evening rush. "Halloween's in two weeks. Some guy going to an early costume party." She shrugged. "Whatever."

Inside the phone booth the man—It had to be a man didn't it? A woman would have more sense—hadn't taken the costume head off. Rather than the cheap party store faux-fur I expected, the material shone. When he turned to open the door, his thick fingers slid off the handle. Obviously frustrated, his fist slammed into the Plexiglas.

"Hold on a sec." I walked to the booth. The man continued rattling the door but it refused to budge. "Need help?"

Soft chocolate-colored eyes met mine. A sense of serenity and immense age washed over me. His fur, which first appeared a uniform black, had streaks of white. He nodded.

I pushed against the bi-fold door. It creaked and strained before creeping fractionally inward. His fingers stabbed into the gap, wrapped around the frame and pried the door further open. He levered a shoulder in and with a grunt heaved until it folded enough to escape.

He made a low sound that I assumed was a muffled "thank you."

"Lees, train's coming," Mare said.

"There'll be another in three minutes." I turned back to the man in the gorilla suit. "You okay?"

"Mask's stuck," he said, his voice somewhat clearer.

"Where's the zipper?"

"Lees, we've got to go." She tugged on my arm.

He turned around and pointed to the nape of his neck. He seemed to be taller. Rather than the five-five I'd assume he was he stood closer to six feet. Tall enough to make me feel feminine, not short.

I wanted—needed—to get my fingers into his fur. The warm strands slid over my fingers. Definitely not a cheap costume. Had it been made with real fur? I snorted softly. Like I knew anything about fur. Whatever the stuff was, it glided through my fingers. I bit my lip to keep from groaning.

After few moments, I found the zipper pull. He sighed as its metal teeth separated. Placing a hand on either side of the mask, he yanked it off.

"Thank you," he said again.

The scent of rich damp earth, growing things and musk enveloped me. His skin was nearly as dark as his eyes.

"Welcome." I smiled. "You're getting stuck in a lot of things today."

"You have no idea." Crow's feet carved furrows away from his eyes. "Can I buy you a drink?" His gaze darted to Mare. "Both of you. To thank you."

If he'd asked me to go alone, I'd have turned him down. But he invited Mare. That had to mean he was safe, didn't it?

"What'd you say, Mare? Catch a later movie?"

She had to go with me if I was interested. Her glare told me that I would pay later, but she said, "Sounds good."

"I'm Garrett."

"Elise," I said shaking his extended hand.

A tingle of electricity zinged through me and settled low in my stomach. Good God. The man was making me think of words like loins. Speaking of which. My gaze darted downward. It was hard to tell under the monkey suit, but I'd have bet a month's worth of Metro fares that he was all lean sinew and muscle.

"Mary from accounting at Jones, Wiles and Kenny."

I rolled my eyes. Mare always introduced herself as if her job was all that defined her.

"Nice to meet you," Garrett said shaking her hand. He had a streak of silver hair down the back of his head that blended into the slash of silver running down the monkey suit.

"Where would you like to go?"

"There's an Anita's on the corner. Great margaritas," I said.

"That sounds wonderful," Garrett said.

"Lemme call Pete," said Mare. "He worries when I'm late."

My fingers tingled with the urge to stroke Garrett's fur. I cleared my throat. "You going to take off the monkey suit?"

"As soon as I can."

We rode up the escalator while Mare checked in with Pete. Knowing Mare was flying wingman, Pete'd call regularly to check on us. More than one guy had warned me that Pete sounded like an abuser or at least a control freak. But, Pete's calls kept us safe so I put up with the fact that he was a complete dishrag.

Although it was still happy hour, the Thursday night crowd hadn't filled up the bar. We scored a table. Garrett held out our chairs.

"If I can impose on you one more time and ask you to start the zipper?"

I stretched my arms out. "Turn around."

He squatted. The man had rock hard thighs. My mouth went dry. Loins. Yep, the man definitely had loins. Once I could focus on the zipper, it parted without resistance. A silver oxford peaked out from under the costume.

"Give me a minute to get out of this. I'll be right back."

"Should I order you a banana daiquiri?" I asked.

His smile was self-deprecating. "I've had quite enough bananas."

As soon as he vanished down the hallway, Mare said, "What the hell're you doing?"

"Drinking with a smoking hot guy. Thought that was obvious."

"He could be some kind of serial killer."

"In a gorilla suit? Unlikely. Besides, you're here to protect me."

"I've got to go in an hour."

"Can't imagine we'll be here longer than that. He's got a party to get to. If I'm lucky, I get his cell. If not, I get a free drink. What's not to like?"

The waitress came over and we ordered two margaritas. Mine was banana. When he came back, Garrett winced when he saw my drink and then ordered a Famous Grouse scotch. He draped the costume on a chair.

"To freedom," he said as he held up his glass.

"To evolution," I said.

Garrett's brow creased.

"Making the transition from ape to man," I said.

"To appetizers?" Mare piped in.

Garrett's laugh was a rasping chuckle. "Get what you want. I'm not hungry."

Mare leafed through the menu.

My gaze kept straying past his shoulder to the fur. "Can I see that?"

He handed it to me.

Definitely not one of those horrible things from some party store. The costume weighed at least fifteen pounds. His musky earth scent lingered on the warm fur. I wanted to bury my face in it. "Where'd you get it?"

"You wouldn't believe me if I told you." His eyes twinkled.

"You're really going for that old line?"

"My . . . assistant arranged for it."

"Assistant?"

"I keep forgetting which term is politically correct this week. Secretary? Assistant? Evil Sorceress? It's all very confusing."

"What's her name?" Mare asked.

"Genia." He waved over our server. "Have you picked what you wanted?"

Mare ordered a cheese and chicken quesadilla. Garrett asked about our jobs. Mare's hour came and went. She gave me her "it's time" look. But I ignored it. She promised to call once she got to the theatre to see if I was still going to make the show.

After she left, Garrett and I switched to tequila shots. Probably not the best idea, but I sometimes get stupid when a handsome man seems interested in me. Mare begged me to leave when she called a half hour later. I told her to enjoy the movie—which we hadn't planned to see anyway—and I'd call her when I left the restaurant. The call I made sometime later was probably less than reassuring given that I giggled through it. Garrett paid for the taxi back to my condo near the Huntington Metro Station.

The wind rustled the broad magnolia leaves as we hiked three flights to my place.

"It's lovely," he said after he'd draped the costume over my blue Ikea armchair.

"Thanks. I try. Oh—don't go out there." I pushed the sliding glass door closed. "The balconies are condemned. Bad rebar or something."

He pointed out the glass door. Why had I thought his fingers were short and stubby? Long and tapered, they could belong to a pianist.

"There's a veritable jungle out there. You have to go outside to water them."

"My taking that risk is one thing. Your suing me when the damned balcony crumbles under you is another. I'm not insured for that."

"I'm not going to sue you."

The chocolate tones of his voice warmed me. I ran my fingers through the costume's fur and across the hard leather plates of its chest. "This real?"

He walked to me and put his hands on my hips. "I never thought I'd feel jealous that someone was rubbing my fur." He leaned down bringing his full mouth down on mine. The acidic taste of scotch mingled with something indefinably Garrett. Heat scorched through me and settled low.

"Don't you have a party or something to get to?" I said between kisses.

"I'm yours for the next three days." His hands slid under my shirt and settled on my rib cage.

"Why three days?"

"I'll have to leave."

"Business?"

"Yes," he whispered into the bare skin at the juncture of my neck and shoulder.

His breath sent shivers across my skin. I leaned back and pursed my lips. He held my gaze. I ran my fingers over his chest. Its planes were as firm as the leather from the costume. He slid his hands further up. Heat radiated out in ripples. My nipples hardened and ached for his touch.

"Do you want to show me the bedroom?"

Grabbing his shirt, I pulled him into the other room.

"Mare," I whispered into the phone the next morning.

"Thank God, I was thinking I needed to call the cops. Why didn't you answer my texts last night?"

"Shhh." I waved my free hand at the phone.

"He's still there. Isn't he?"

"I'm not going to make it to the office today."

"Oh my God. He's that good? You *have* to dish."

"Look just tell Margo that I have the stomach flu or something."

"Lees—"

"Drinks tonight?"

"Fine."

"I owe you."

I did *not* shriek when I saw Garret standing there without a stitch on.

"Plans?" he said as an easy smile spread across his face. My heart gave an extra hard thump that I was sure he could hear from where he stood.

"For, um, us—if you want."

He swaggered—and damn, the man could swagger—into the kitchen and grabbed an apple from the fruit bowl. "I want to take you back to the bedroom." The fruit crunched as he bit it.

"Um, ok." I scooted off the kitchen stool.

"Maybe not the bedroom."

He untied the belt around my bathrobe. His lips covered mine. "O-o-o-o."

"Are we making hot monkey love now?" I asked.

"If you want." He nipped my shoulder. "And it's hot *ape* love."

I took his cock in my hand and rubbed it. "Please."

He took a few steps back. Squatting with knees wide, he pounded his chest and grunted. "Hoo-hoo-hoo." Letting his knuckles drag on the beige rug, he lumbered close.

"O-o-o."

He sniffed my stomach. Teeth gently nipped my skin. His tongue laved me as he slowly rose from his crouch. My body warmed and tightened at the feel of him. Grasping his head by the hair, I pulled him standing. I skimmed his chest with my tongue, nipping occasionally, as I eased him between my legs. I shivered and tensed around him. His hands gripped my waist and held me in place.

"O-o-o," he whispered. The sound went straight to my core.

"O-o-o," I echoed as we moved together.

Mare and Peter met us at Ray's the Steaks several hours later. With as little sleep and food as I'd had, I'd probably look like I'd been ill all day if it weren't for the dorky grin on my face. Garrett's fingers intertwined with mine. We'd spent almost as much time talking about life, love and well, truthfully, nothing special as we had making hot monkey—no, correct that—ape love. The urge to pinch myself grew with every passing minute.

"Anyone miss me?" I asked after the introductions had been made.

Mare shook her head. "So what's the deal?"

"I had the privilege of being rescued by an amazing woman,"

Garrett said. He picked my hand up and kissed my knuckles.

"We're just seeing where things take us." I felt heat rush up my neck. Thank God the waiter chose that moment to show up. "The steaks are amazing, Garrett."

He smiled. "I'm a vegetarian. Mostly."

"Oh. I didn't know. Do you want to go somewhere else?" Mare blushed nearly red enough to match her hair.

"Isn't that just like a woman to forget to ask?" Pete said.

"The portabella looks wonderful." Garrett closed the menu and handed it to the waiter. His fingers tightened around mine.

"Do you want anything to drink?" I asked.

"Water."

"Where did you come from? The dark ages?" Pete said after we'd finished ordering.

"Pete!" Mare said.

"A bit darker than even that," Garrett said with a low chuckle. "And wine and ale is about all they drank back then. The water," he tapped his glass, "was too dirty to safely drink."

"Mare's a medieval ages nut," I said.

"Mythology," she corrected. "There's a difference."

"Mary told me that you got stuck in a costume," Pete said.

"Something like that."

"Embarrassing, man."

Mare dropped her head into her hands. "I don't know why I bring him out in public."

"You have no idea," said Garrett. "But I met Elise as a result. So I'm hard pressed to lament the difficulty."

"It reminds me of those stories about selkies," Mare said.

"Silkies? This a story for *Playboy*?" Pete nudged Garrett.

"Selkies are seals that become human. The person who loves a selkie hides his furs to keep him from returning to the sea. It always ends in heartbreak because when a selkie finds his skin, he leaves his human family."

Pete waved the waitress over for another beer. "I liked my idea better."

"Do you have any brothers?" Mare asked.

"Hey, Mary."

"Not that I'm looking for a trade in." She kissed Pete on the cheek.

"I had several brothers, but we lost touch."

"What do you do for a living?"

"What's this? The third degree?" I asked a bit ashamed that Mare was getting more information about Garrett than I'd thought to. After all, why wrinkle the sheets as it were when a sex god's in your bed? Well, why wrinkle them in a bad way. Heat flushed my features again.

"I travel all over the world," Garrett said.

"Sounds exciting." Mare leaned forward.

Pete's brow furrowed and he glared at Garrett.

"It gets old. Tell me what you do, Peter."

Now Pete was all smiles. Garrett spent the rest of the night shifting the conversation so Peter became the center of attention before his irritation levels rose too high. Garrett remained vague on what he did for a living. Working in DC you got use to it. If someone deflected the opportunity to talk about their job, it was probably because they couldn't. You assumed you didn't have the proper security clearances and let the matter drop. The thing is, Garrett's water condensed and sat untouched for the entire meal.

On Sunday afternoon we curled together on the sofa and watched the Redskins lose to the Cowboys. Again. Garrett put up with my yelling at the TV screen. Although, he jumped when I threw the popcorn at it. At least he wasn't a Cowboys fan. I'd have dropped him flat if he was. After the game, we adjourned to our bedroom.

Much later, he lay on top of me and kissed my forehead. Mingled with his earthy musk was the scent of sweat and sex. "Do you love me?"

Yes. The word almost jumped from my mouth. Sure we'd had three amazing days of sex, but that wasn't love, was it? "I barely know you," I said instead.

With a groan, he rolled off me. He lay on his back with his forearm over his eyes. I traced patterns in the coarse dark hair on his arm. When he didn't lift it, I moved lower and drew a ship in his chest hair. I'd never been partial to furry men, but on him it seemed right. I bent my head to the juncture of his neck and shoulder. His musk seemed deeper, wilder somehow.

"We'll have plenty of time to figure out what this is when you get back."

"I leave at midnight."

"Should I call you Cinderella?"

Now he did look at me. Shadows darkened his chocolate-colored eyes. "You might just."

I didn't like seeing him down. He'd been full of life and light since I'd rescued him from the phone booth. "When'll you be back?"

"I'm not sure. It might be awhile before I can even call."

He must have been a Federal agent of some kind. I knew an accountant whose husband who worked on one of the early satellite projects. He'd vanish for months at a time leaving her with just an emergency number. My gut twisted at the thought of Garrett going into danger. Truth was, I ached for him.

"In that case," I said as I rolled on top of him. "Let's make the most of the time we have left."

Now he grinned. "I couldn't have said it better."

Midnight came too soon. Standing in my living room, I ran my fingers through his costume's fur. His fingers entangled mine. A slow kiss heated my blood even though we'd only finished making love half an hour earlier. He hefted the costume as if it weighed as much as my heart at his leaving.

"Call me when you can." I bit my lip ashamed at my need.

"I will."

He paused as if hoping I'd say more. I'd made the mistake of telling someone that I loved him too soon and scaring him off. I wouldn't do it this time. Three days was way too soon. But what if the government shipped him off to someplace and he never came back? Should I tell him?

"I have to go."

"It's been fun." The room was too warm. I wanted to throw up.

"More than that." He kissed me again before he turned and left.

I walked onto the balcony pushing the fronds of a dracaena plant out of the way. My urban jungle closed around me. Shoulders hunched, Garrett appeared in the parking lot. Light beat down from a pole. It looked like he'd put the costume back on without the mask. Maybe to ward off the chill. He turned. I waved and he returned the farewell before getting into the cab.

"You still moping?" Mare leaned over my desk. Christmas was almost here but I didn't feel like celebrating.

"I'm not moping," I said.

"He hasn't called."

I shook my head.

"Where do you want to go for lunch?"

"Ugh. My stomach's bothering me. I must have the flu that's going around."

Mare sucked on the end of a pen. "You sure that's all it is?"

"What're you talking about?"

"Hon, when's the last time you had your period?"

I had to think about that. "Oh my God." I ran from the office. I needed a pregnancy test.

Fifteen minutes later the traitorous thing read a clear "pregnant."

"Son of a bitch," I murmured from the restroom stall.

"I take it that means a positive result?" Mare said.

I stepped out of the stall, wrapped the test in paper towels and then shoved it down in the trash can. Mare consoled me back to the office.

My cell phone chirped as I sat down at my desk. "Elise Willard."

"Miss me?" Garrett's voice warmed the line.

"Are you back in town?"

Mare mouthed "Garrett" from where she stood in the doorway. I nodded.

"Not yet. But I had a chance to call."

"When are you coming back?" I mouthed "damn it." I didn't want to sound as desperate as I was.

"I don't know. Look, I'm needed again. I have to go."

"I love you," I said.

I heard his sigh through the phone lines. "I wish you'd said that before I left." His voice sounded heavier, almost sad. "I'll come back to you when I can."

"I'll be here." I held the phone a long time after the line went dead.

"Why didn't you tell him?" Mare asked.

"He didn't say he loved me too. Stupid I know, but . . ."

She put her hand on my shoulder. "We'll do this together."

"Thanks."

The doctors reassured me that the pregnancy progressed normally even though I was nauseous all the time. According the busybodies at work the continuing heartburn meant that the baby would have a full head of hair when he was born. When I went into labor at thirty-eight weeks, I still hadn't heard from Garrett. Mare was my birth partner.

The nurse handed me my son. Unfocused dark chocolate eyes looked out at the world. My heart swelled and the ache I'd felt since Garrett left eased. The world shrank down to the tiny bundle wrapped in a blue blanket. The little biddies were right; Mitchell had a full head of straight black hair.

"No wonder I had all that heart burn," I said.

"He's amazing, Lees." Mare unwrapped Mitch to tickle his toes. "Um, what did the doctor say about all the hair?"

I nuzzled the baby smelling his innocence. "That it'll probably fall out in a few weeks and his real hair'll grow in."

"Can I hold him?" At my nod, she took him from me. "He's so beautiful. Can you say that about a boy baby?"

"Only when it's true." I peered up at Garrett's son.

"Not to put a damper on this or anything, but is he suppose to have hair on his knuckles?"

"What?"

I unswaddled Mitch. His hands ended in five perfect digits. Between the back of the hand and miniscule fingernails, black hair dusted his knuckles. A fine coat of hair covered his body. His toes looked longer than they should be. I ran a finger down his forehead. The brow did seem a bit more pronounced.

"That's crazy. It's just baby hair," I said. "You saw Garrett. He wasn't . . . he wasn't—"

"A gorilla in a phone booth?" Mare winced. "The offspring of a human/selkie mating has webbed fingers and toes."

"It's not possible."

"Land selkies."

"You're insane. It's just baby hair." I clutched Mitch closer.

"I'm tired. Seeing things that aren't there. All that matters is he's my Godson." She brushed a finger lightly over his cheek. "He's amazing. Even if he's a little fuzzy."

Mare met my gaze and smiled. Whatever it was, whatever he was we'd be okay. Hopefully, someday his father would return. Petals of magnolia flowers danced in the breeze outside my hospital window.

GRETEL BY FIRELIGHT
by Roberta Lawson

Roberta Lawson lives in Brighton in the UK. She likes hats, the woods, and Shamanism. Her writing can be found in venues such as Prick of the Spindle, Mung Being *and* Sein und Werden. *Her twist on this classic fairy tale sheds a warm light on two charmingly witchy women.*

She was barely more than a babe in arms when she first started visiting. Aged six, seven, she would tear down to my cottage. Past gnarly trees, around winding forest paths. You trust the forest, you earn its respect. Each one of my trees, owls, wolves, watched over Gretel. She would dash in, toss herself onto my knee, or curl in front of the fire, and urge me to tell her stories. A wily little thing she was, always a trail of rye or pumpernickel crumbs to guide her home.

Fleeing the groping hands of corpulent Hansel, her limp father, her cruel-tongued stepmother, Gretel was always searching, starving. She would sink her teeth into my gingerbread cottage, nuzzle against my shoulder, and curl herself against me. Later she would dash home—with the deer and the rabbits, the doves and the bluebird, pouches of herbs tucked inside her stockings. Grabby-handed Hansel would keep far from Gretel upon her return, no idea in his head what so repelled him. A magical girl she was, bright and fattened on my stories. As she grew, so my stories deepened. By the time of her eighteenth birthday, I vowed to leave out no details in my stories to her—the truth of my people, from our beginnings to this day.

Before the storybooks were written, before God or churches, long before armies and priests and burnings, my people lived here in the forest. Once this forest stretched on endlessly, becoming other countries, landscapes. My people lived in harmony with the land—honouring the creatures, dancing and singing to bring in the seasons, cider in Autumn, mead in the Winter. The land loved us, and we slept warm and safe in its arms. No weddings, but sweet, sweet couplings—men with women, women with women, men with men, sometimes all these combinations at once. We knew such delight, such earthy love and lust. The Summers were never-ending, sunshine that lit up our faces. We would fly with the eagle, fish with the heron. Dance with the pixies and the elves, swim with the mer-people. In Winter we would huddle around the fire, play ballads to the moon. The cries of the wolves were our religion, the hooting of owls our only prayer.

We were rarely ill. Yet we knew the lore of the herbs as well as we knew our own minds and bodies. The knowledge of the earth passed down through the generations—how mandrake brewed right could plant a baby in a maiden's belly, how hops could clear a blocked head, a pouch-full of cloves cool a fever. The very ground we walked fed us each lesson we needed, opened each door to our magic. Beyond that, we would travel freely between the worlds, via sea and air and our own imaginations. We knew the ways of lust, how to milk orgasm into a state of such ecstasy we could emerge immortal. Spells, potions, elixirs. Darkness and light dripped from our tongues like ambrosia. Snakes coiled and nuzzled against our legs. We loved—oh how we loved .Our teardrops, blood-drops, were transcendent, our sexual fluids doors to new realities.

I would murmur these and other stories to Gretel. The tales of the leprechauns, the goblins, the selkies, of the many inhabitants of this rich green-brown land. We, its dwellers, had only to think of abundance and still more buttercups and tulips would spring up, oak trees, deep wishing wells. Gretel—pink cheeked, black-haired, dark-eyed, drank up each drop.

Things changed, of course, as they must. The landscape, the stories. So many of my people had carried their homes on their backs, their healing herbs in their pockets. As more and more of Gretel's family and all the huddled townspeople had ridden into our sacred forests, from the cities and from far, far away, our stories had to change. When the burnings started, so many of us knew it was time already. Fire had always been on our side, so much a part of our rituals, so intrinsic to the women amongst us. It burned in our bellies and our wombs. Then the newcomers turned our fire on us, and we knew it was time. In darkest night, by the light of the moon, scores of my people rode out—to newer safer pastures, countries, forests. They called upon the corn, the moon and the animals to shroud them, and quietly they fled.

Let me tell you the newcomers, the people of the new towns, said the acts of bloodshed they enacted were the works of their God, their ways of civilization. So the forest became stilted, haunted. The wolves grew fearful, the hooting of the owls became a mourning cry. The faeries, unicorns, mer-folk, fled; some underground, some to the skies. Some left this world entirely, entered deep into the place of mythos. That was how, almost imperceptibly, the forest folded in on itself. God crept in, and schools and farms and pain. Lust was almost entirely bled out, along with ritual and joy and healing, and slowly our abundance tailed off.

Yet I remained. Let me tell you that I am the mother of this place, if those are the terms you favour. My people had a particular name for me, but the name is of little consequence. They say my womb is the earth itself. The wolves and deer may be frightened now, but they never leave my garden. I am the beginning, and I will be here until the end.

So we come to this. My people so greatly dwindled, the forest a shadow of its former self. The newcomers despise me, fear me, but there is no protection on this earth I lack. So I remain, here in my cottage, in my seat of magic. It is a November evening that Gretel calls upon the stealth of the forest, calls upon every disguise I have taught her. On this particular evening, her stepmother—ensconced in her selective blindness—is sitting in the kitchen. Hansel and Gretel rush in, and Hansel—fat and raucous with beer and Bratwurst and grabby-handed as ever—forces Gretel's skirt up and tries to push himself upon her. On this occasion Gretel bares her teeth, and with the strength and fury of every woman who has ever fought this particular violation, Gretel bundles corpulent Hansel into the oven and strikes a match. She leaves him to flame and sizzle, and chop-chops their house right down. Now she turns on her heel and flees.

Here we arrive. Late in the night, and here stands Gretel, aged nineteen and unholy beautiful, knocking at my door, pushing herself inside. Those blood-red lips, that thick dark hair, and all the frenzied lust of a murderess in those coal-black eyes. Gretel throws herself into my arms, finds my lips with hers. *I'm all grown up!* she cries. *Oh witch, oh healer, oh earth mother, the things I've done, but finally I'm home!* She presses me to the floor, sobbing, ripping at my clothes. My fingertips stroke her neck, and I hold her to me. Gretel moans, tears off her clothes, twines around me like ivy. She tastes of cardamom and spices, blood and salt-tears. She smells like apples. How she rolls and tousles with me, grinding herself against me. *My other*, she moans, *my Goddess, my dream*. Gretel tells me how long she has waited for this, pleads softly that she wants this—*Please*, she whispers, *please?*

She reaches inside me, soft fingers slowly unfurling into

whole fist, and I am soaked, dripping, open. She brings her mouth down to me, tells me I taste of sugar and gingerbread, of the earth itself, and her hot red tongue curls inside me. We groan, we fuck, we meet in this burning, throbbing place. I feel her whole body—whole being—unroll under my own tongue, and I cry out. She rolls her body over mine, and we tangle, rut, writhe; kissing, biting, moaning. She is not content until she knows the taste of each drop of my blood and juices. So I learn sweet Gretel who I have known for so long in these new ways, taking her in through face and mouth, tongue, fingers, orifices. Together we fall deep, deep inside the earth's belly, tumble into our stories, into soil and magma, magic, lust, secrets. We writhe, we fall, we scream. *I am home* cries Gretel, and I wrap my body around her. We are home.

THE STRAWMAN
by Candy Caradoc

Candy Caradoc has been dreaming up stories for as long as she can remember (some of which have made their way out of her head and onto paper). She is interested in the nature of the mind, creative and independent thought and personal epiphanies. She is not interested in polite chit chat, the common opinion or "personal achievements". She lives in Melbourne, Australia, teaches a creative writing course for the general public and is completing a Postgraduate Diploma in English.

"'The Strawman' came to me, initially, as images." Candy said. "First, of a young woman with a stuffed 'man'—having a nice day out at the park like a little girl might do playing with a favourite toy. I looked at this situation and thought; That's rather concerning. Particularly if this is a 'real' relationship. And they're gazing into each other's eyes and such (her eyes, his buttons), but at the end of the day he's material and unreal. So then what? Showing a relationship as an artistic creation makes for a deeper, more emotional revelation than trying to describe a relationship realistically, I feel."

I'm not sure what creeped me out more in this story— the nonresponsive strawman, or the self-absorbed main character.

Part I

It's a bright, sunny day and my Strawman and I are spending it at the park.

We hold hands as we walk along the footpath between the leafy, green trees. The Strawman's hand is fibrous but snug.

We sit on the swings and twist the chains around so that we face each other, gazing into each other's eyes. The Strawman's eyes are black shiny buttons. Sometimes they catch the sunlight and sparkle at me.

We sit at a wooden table in the middle of the park and chat. The Strawman and I have thoughtful conversations. We have compatible views on many things.

"I like summer days. They last longer and feel optimistic—make you feel like you're doing things with your days."

Yes, summer days are, on average, longer than winter days. Except at the equator.

"I especially love the days like this: warm but with a cool, dry breeze. I can't stand humid days."

Strawmen don't do well in humidity, either. The moisture makes us uncomfortable and sluggish. And your hair looks pretty blowing in the breeze.

I brighten up as though a thousand Christmas tree lights have switched on inside me and rush to the Strawman's side to embrace his scrunchy waist. I kiss his cushiony cheek and smile at him. He looks back at me with his shiny black buttons. I'm sure he sees the light in my eyes.

It's getting late: the sun is low and there are pink and orange streaks on the horizon.

"What a great day. Isn't this better than sitting at home?"

I'm glad you had a great day.

"But, did you have a good time?"

I think it's good when you have a great time, yes.

The sunset is very pretty, but it makes me a little sad. Like endings.

"It's a beautiful sunset."

Yes. Shall we go home now?

I look at the Strawman and see that he is not watching the sunset at all: his button eyes are facing mine dead-on. It's not so easy to see the shades of light and color in a sunset with button eyes. But he always looks at me with love.

Part II

The Strawman likes to stay at home, and it is difficult to persuade him to do otherwise.

I catch him outside, checking our letterbox.

"Any mail?"

Only an advertisement. I'll bin it.

I walk with him to the nature strip, where our bin is awaiting rubbish collection. I strike up a conversation about the flowers in the grass and how I never noticed them before. The Strawman throws the pamphlet away and turns back to our apartment.

"Wait, I'd like to continue our conversation and I have to walk down the road, to post a letter."

I hold up the envelope.

I'll see you when you get home.

"Please walk with me, it's not far." The post box is close enough that I can point to it in the distance.

The Strawman turns his button eyes in the direction in which I was pointing and I take his hand and start walking.

I launch back into conversation.

"I think I'd like to plant some flowers outside our window."

We don't have a garden.

"No, of course. But we have a balcony. We can put a planter there, full of flowers."

Okay, flowers.

"What sort of flowers can we plant?"

You can plant any flowers you like.

"Don't you like flowers?"

Flowers are nice.

"Maybe flowers that match your eyes. Oh, and some that match mine. Black and blue. Black orchids and bluebells!"

All right. Let me know when the flowers are planted.

I look at the Strawman; an imploring look. He doesn't notice. He stops abruptly and looks behind us.

We passed the post box.

"Oh, you know what? I don't have a postage stamp on this

letter. The post office is just a couple of streets away."

The Strawman looks at me. He says nothing. I don't know what he's thinking, but I don't think he's very happy. He loves me, though, and I think that's why he keeps going when I start walking again and squeeze his hand tighter.

We don't say much for a while.

The Strawman is slowing down when I catch the first gust of fresh, salty air.

"Almost there, come on!" I pick up speed and pull the Strawman along with me.

Wait!

I'm running. I can see crystal-blue waters on the horizon and now I'm running across the road towards them. It occurs to me that I did not look both ways (*either* way) before crossing the road. But I'm on the footpath that's now sloping down towards the shore and the fine white sand and it's beautiful: the sun glints off the tops of the waves like the reflected light in two shiny button eyes . . . And this is when I realize that I've lost the Strawman's hand.

I turn around. The Strawman is standing at the top of the sand hill, on the footpath, standing straight and silent and unnervingly still in the blustery sea breezes.

I walk back up the sand hill, back to where the Strawman stands facing me, waiting for me. I don't like the way he's looking at me.

I wait for the Strawman to say something.

I think he's waiting for me to say something.

"Want to come into the water with me?"

Strawmen don't go into water. We get waterlogged, damaged.

"Not even to walk along the edge, just to get your feet wet? You can dry your feet –"

I don't think so. Let's go home. Now.

I'm a little fazed by the insistence of that final word, but I continue. "Sit on the sand, then, and wait for me to take a quick dip."

Why do you need me here to do that?

"I like being with you."

I like being at home.

"I don't understand why you don't want to be here with me."

I don't want to be here. Ever.

Now, without really thinking yet feeling the truth of the words but at the same time wanting to stuff them back into my mouth even as they are falling out, I say:

"Well maybe we should go our separate ways, then."

The Strawman's mouth falls open. Wide open. Round and empty beneath his fixed, shiny black button eyes. Like a cavernous 'O' of horror. Then he begins to unravel. He unravels into reams and reams of spiraling thread and straw falls out in tufts. His mouth is a dreadful void, and everything around it is coming undone.

I try to hold my Strawman. There's a dry rustling sound as his body gives way to my touch: like embracing a pile of dead leaves. Straw spills out over my arms. For a second I look at the Strawman's face swimming in my tears, then it falls, falls away with the unraveled thread and straw, passing over my hands like loose pillow-down.

I look down. I'm standing in the strewn, scattered remains of the Strawman, but what I notice are my hands: there's a shiny, black button in each palm.

I swallow my tears.

I pocket the buttons.

I turn around and walk home.

Part III

When I reach the apartment I see that there is a pillow with half its stuffing ripped out sitting in front of my door. I'm extremely upset that someone has left junk here. But now, as I'm looking closer, I see that it's not a pillow after all. It's a baby. A cotton baby.

I take the baby inside, stitch it up, clean and dry it and make it comfortable. I sit it facing me, but it doesn't look back at me.

I remember to check my pocket.

I pull out the black buttons.

I go back for the needle and thread.

My cotton baby is starting to crawl now. His button eyes are a bit big, but he'll grow into them. He bumps into things a lot. It's hard to look where you're going with such big button eyes. But when I pick him up and hold him in front of me, he always looks at me with love.

THE SEASONAL WITCH
by Rachel Kendall

Rachel Kendall is editor of ISMs Press and Sein und Werden. Writer of twisted fiction. Mother of Violet. Photographer of obscurity. Collector of all things meat and bone. Her website is kissthewitch.co.uk. *"The Seasonal Witch" was originally published in* Screaming Dreams *in 2007.*

"This story is based loosely upon the Pendle Witches who were tried and hanged in Lancashire gaol in 1612," said Rachel. "But to offset the crones' business of midwifery and pleasure in hallucinogens I decided to add a little spice to the pot and make the daughter, Alizon, a mistress of the devil: a role her mother could only dream of."

A story about what a real worshipper of the devil might have made of the goings on in Lancashire— but the real magic in this story is in the author's way with words . . .

Two figures of the same substance but taken from a different mould; bearing a likeness of texture, half-baked and still a little warm. A mother and daughter whose looks could not be further cast from two shores, but whose grave intentions were twinned. Elizabeth, the mother, bearer of child and beast; ugly as sin with a roving eye. She had nurtured her three children, brought each one to her breast, fed them her own liquid core. But it was only the daughter Alizon who had drawn blood from those two bolts of flesh. She had sucked so hard in her greed that had she any teeth she would have bitten the nipple right off, said Elizabeth. And from that day forth the mother had taken a dislike to her daughter, who had blossomed into a beautiful swan, a pauper's princess, while she herself was shrinking into the shadow of a fairytale hag. Far from these simple aesthetics mother and daughter were one and the same. They fed on other peoples' anger and shared a bitter broth.

In these superstitious times, when babies were thrust violently out onto a bed of discontentment and dead souls silently searched for a vessel in the dark of every night, no one could escape the gnarled finger of guilt. One day a woman may be made to walk the cobbled streets clad in chains for her sin of adultery and then called a whore. The next a man may have his neck broken in the noose for the act of lycanthropy, the blood on his beard barely dried from the young girl's throat he had recently ripped out.

Elizabeth and Alizon did not go unnoticed. The whole family, siblings and grandmother Demdike, were under observation from the local gossips. But it was Elizabeth's name that fell fresh from their mouths. Being so very poor and of a tempestuous nature, her name just seemed to catch in the cracks of their lips, roll around ulcerated tongues and stick to blackened teeth. If the butter were spoiled or baby Anne fell asleep and did not wake, it must be the fault of Elizabeth Davies. If John Turnpike failed to arouse his member upon the gaze of his succubae wife Ursula, naked and trembling, it was because Ursula had forgotten to return Elizabeth's spindle, borrowed the week before.

The bond between Alizon and her mother had been shared for nigh on sixteen years. A bond based on an intense dislike and a mental dependency made clear by their behaviour towards one another, which was simply a mirror image. A curse and abnegation were their formal salutations. But together they were part of a puzzle which as a whole made up a small community.

There were distractions. Alizon had a friend, Mary, someone she could fall out with when she felt the need. And Elizabeth had Ball. Since the day she had produced milk and had stopped bleeding nine months since, she had found a mouth to feed, a physical dependent. When her own children had grown too old or simply too vicious she had taken every opportunity to attach another's new-born to her sagging teat. When the mother is away, the crone will play. But once she was caught, the baby exhaled its last a few hours later, and this mother was no longer invited to visit either labouring women or those whose thighs were still sticky with amniotic fluid.

And shortly after this, Ball crossed her path. On four padded paws he followed her home and instantly latched his velvety muzzle onto her breast where he was rocked back and forth in the arms of an anti-mother.

There were others, women who knew of this familiar, who knew of the clay figures, the Wolfsbane and Belladonna remedies. There would be get-togethers. The women, rowdy, raucous, bestial women from around Lancaster would come over, broomstick in hand. Talk of a play by Middleton where the women had cooed their way through each jolting scene. Now to be replayed over and over in slow Jacobean motion to music they could dance to. Music which Alizon could not hear. From a darkened corner she would watch between long lashes and spider webs as the women began an incantation. Between two palms she rolled a doll, the symbol of a past quite different from that of her friends. She would sigh and watch as the women undressed to fill the room with the crinkled flesh and stench of a dozen harpies, who never bathed and who still wore the perfume of their husbands' semen in their hair and the imprint of his hand on their thigh. A potion was collected from the hearth and the women would howl and inhale through flared nostrils as they lathered its magical properties onto the handles of the brooms. As their laughter turned into screams of ecstasy with each penetration of the handle into the darkened portals of withered flesh, Alizon chuckled and backed out of the house.

The texture and colour of her music was velvet mulled wine, warm and enveloping, a lining to a fantasy. Another mother may give the child the dream. But the anti-mother, the antithesis would not allow it. A child could have no interplay, only a doting, yearning, craving, to follow in the footsteps of a Mother Superior. Without this there would simply be ignorance and detachment. And so those desires became like coils of apostasy, barbed wire springs that poked metal fingers through velvet undertones. So, she took her song elsewhere, buried it in the bosom of someone stronger, cushioned it in the throes of a sentient flesh.

"Devil take me, I'm flying!" A woman's voice permeated the cold air outside. Hallucinogens, old glamour trick. The women were all lunatics who would one day hang. And Alizon would personally like to slip the noose around each withered neck.

A clown painted face of wood and strands of her own flaxen hair. The doll was always smiling. The white dress torn but still a perfect gift. A gift from the heart, a gift from her soul. Alizon rambled slowly towards the dark of the forest where her highest bidder and most fallen angel awaited her. Who needed a mother when a father could be found? She would kiss the gem between Beezelbub's buttocks and sell herself flesh and soul for the sake of one simple loving gesture.

PRAYERS FOR AN EGG
by Sara Genge

Before beginning her medical residency three years ago, Sara Genge wrote speculative fiction with a gender and social focus and a sickly twist. She hasn't written since then but it's ok. She'll come back to it when people stop getting sick.

"'Prayers for an Egg' was my first story in Asimov's*," says Sara. "Its origins are shrouded in the mysteries of bad memory but it may (or may not) have been born in an effort to explore the effects of extreme oppression to the point where the oppressed come to believe the dominant narrative. Also gender. And pink shiny tentacles. Because, hey."*

Master Gundaro chooses an auspicious time to come claim his bride. The wheat is ripe and mobile, and surges out of the fields and into the garden, poking at the windows, growing through the cracks in the marble portico and even under the stilts that support the house.

Lasa stands behind the intended, Mistress Jandala, on the portico and clutches the egg bead Dia has given her. She closes her hands into fists and hides them in her robes, ignoring the pain from her cracked calluses. The state of her hands shames her, as does the sunburn on the tips of her tentacles, earned by the long hours spent with the other servants attaching pink ribbons to the swaying stalks of wheat. Old Dia says this is what it means to be a good servant: to be forever shamed by your condition, forever proud of your good work.

The wind pulls at each ribbon, lifting the stalks by their

bountiful heads for the new Master to see and Lasa allows herself a smile: she's helped turn the estate into a sea of pink and yellow, and pink and yellow are good colours for a wedding.

And, oh, how beautiful is her lady, Jandala! It makes Lasa proud to look at her Mistress, so refined and perfect, the best example of the High Caste. Jandala's pink mane floats in the air and her tentacles, thin and wispy, surround her head in a delicate corona. Even as she sings, her forked tongues remain close to her face so as not to smell the unpleasant odours of the low caste servants around her. Droplets of sweat and saliva collect on her tongues. To Lasa, they look like a dozen small pearls shinning in the sunlight.

Lasa wants to cry from happiness. She can never be more than a servant, but this woman has chosen her to be her jaja-maid and, for a servant, there can be no greater honour.

When Gundaro jumps out of the carriage, Jandala's shoulders quiver and the sunlight bounces off her nacre skin in subtle iridescence.

Everyone waits while the trunks are opened and the wind-organ is pulled out in clanging pieces and assembled noisily on the front lawn. When the wind starts moaning through it, the household breaks into cheers. Master Gundaro has claimed his wife and his estate. Their life together has begun.

"We are married now," he says, pecking his wife's cheek with a sturdy tentacle.

"The bonding will be at sunset," she replies.

"As you wish," he chuckles, "although why you women put such store on that ceremony is beyond me."

Master and Mistress retreat into the house and Lasa starts preparing for the jaja ceremony. She has already washed and purified herself to meet Master Gundaro, but she still needs to scrape her skin with pumice. Hopefully, pumice stone will also help her calluses.

"Jaja-woman, Mistress Jandala wants you," Master says, standing under the doorway with his tentacles in disarray.

Lasa is embarrassed, although she knows she needn't be. It is appropriate for a jaja-servant to see a Master dishevelled. Gundaro has broken protocol and come to fetch her himself, and she realizes that Master must be eager to impregnate his bride. It is not the first time that he tries to hurry things up: a couple hours earlier, as Lasa listened behind the door at the ceremony, she heard Gundaro urging the Ceremony Master, muttering that he didn't have time for "prayers and roses".

As he turns to open the door, she notices his clenched buttocks. His musk is strong so she moves quickly, wrapping her tongues closer to her face to avoid his smell. Being on such intimate terms with the Masters makes her uncomfortable, but she steps into the room, fingering Dia's egg bead for luck, anxious to get it over with.

Judging by the way Jandala's smell clings to the dry moss, Lasa guesses Mistress is more than ready. Lasa's stomach tightens as her tongues dance to the taste, and she tiptoes up to the bed and stares at the Mistress, deep in fecundity trance.

She doesn't want to break the spell, so she hesitates for a few seconds before placing her hands on Jandala's body and caressing her skin, which shines like egg-shell in the candlelight.

When Jandala's skin turns pink, Lasa parts her Mistress's nether lips and breaths jaja into her oviduct.

The woman shivers with pleasure and calls out Lasa's name. Jandala's grip on her servant's hair is not the stately pat Lasa is used to. Mistress keens and the windows rattle. For a second Lasa fears that her newly wed Mistress will be one of those deviants who prefer the breath of a casteless servant to the rhythmic thrusts of her rightful husband, but then Mistress ovulates and it's over. Lasa presses her hand on Mistress's abdomen and helps the gelatinous egg lodge into the oviduct.

Mistress sits up and arranges the quilts around her, covering her glowing skin in silk and dignity. She pats Lasa on the head and orders her to fetch her husband. She is back in control, and her jaja-servant sighs with relief.

Master orders her to leave, but she can tell he does not want her to go. Lasa is painfully aware of the jaja breath still clinging to her. He inhales deeply, as is custom, and hesitates. She can read the contradicting impulses playing out in the knot of his shoulders and the ripple of his neck-flaps. Masters are always torn between temperamental wives and docile servants, but most of them don't feel such lowly impulses on their wedding nights. How sad for Mistress Jandala! It seems forever, but he finally waves her away and she's free to run out of the room.

Getting down the stairs proves to be hard. The after-taste lingers on her tongues and she trembles as each spasm brings up another wave of jaja breath, which trails behind her in a scented cloud.

She tells herself that she's done what was required. It's not a servant's place to feel shame, but she hides under the staircase anyway, wiping her mouth until she stops convulsing and starts crying, the tears strange on her breath-scented face.

After a while, Old Dia slips into the darkness and places a wrinkled arm around Lasa's shoulders.

"Shh, don't cry, you've done well. The Masters will be pleased with you."

Lasa cries harder.

"It's all right, it's all right. You'll get used to it. First jaja is always the hardest, but it's a great honour."

Lasa whimpers and sinks her face into the wrinkled crevice between the old woman's arm and first tentacle. Dia smells of jimba beans, soap and roast, and the hay filling of the servant's beds. Lasa digs her head further into the smelly pit and feels safe surrounded by Dia's sagging flesh and the soft noises her body makes to keep her alive. She listens to the older woman's heartbeat, the rattle of her lungs and the occasional puff of her neck-flaps as they open to expel gas.

Old Dia is the kitchen boss. She can be hard if you let her down, but she always treats Lasa like she's special. Lasa stops crying.

"Come on into the kitchen," Dia says, "we are going to shell pods. Purple peas make a good breakfast for newlyweds."

The servants gather around a tub brimming with warm water and vines. The pods move against the servants' fingers, trying to escape, twisting and tickling until one by one, the women retrieve them, bite off the stem and release the wriggling peas back into the water. Peas die fast off the vine, but because the servants are devoted and do the shelling at night, Master Gundaro and Mistress Jandala will have live peas for breakfast in the morning.

The women joke about the thumping noises coming from the ceiling. Lasa works at good pace, but she doesn't talk much. Suddenly, she feels warm wet peas wriggling down the back of her dress. She squeals and turns around to catch Dia purple-handed. The old woman has a look that says the girl won't dare retaliate. As if! Lasa grabs a handful of husks and smears them on Dia's face.

"See what you've done! How do I explain purple face to Master tomorrow," Dia says, exaggerating her accent because she knows it will make the women laugh and because she won't let them forget that she wasn't born to this house, that she was bought in Quei and that she was originally a free woman. Dia always wears the egg necklace her mother gave her before she was sold. Now it's missing a bead, the one Lasa carries in her pocket. The necklace is a symbol of Dia's power, and the closest thing to a sceptre any servant ever wielded in the kitchens of a house.

"He won't notice," Nin shouts. "I doubt he'll even leave the room."

A husk fight erupts. Beans fly from one corner of the room to the other. Purple stains their faces and clothes, but they're drunk on gossip and jitter. Today is for happiness and washing can wait.

As fast as the fight started, it's over. The servants quiet down and give each other guilty looks. In the garden, the wind-organ moans. The servants heave a collective sigh and get back to work, shelling the peas to the beat of lovemaking from the first floor.

Two weeks later, Mistress Jandala gives Lasa the egg. It wouldn't do for a mistress to become attached to an egg that might grow up to be servant. Lasa takes it with both hands and places it in her marsupial pouch, daring to glimpse into her Mistress's face from beneath lowered eyelashes. She wants to read something in the way her mistress carefully wipes the egg with her handkerchief before thrusting it into Lasa's hand, but, no, she is only projecting her own lowly thoughts. Mistress feels nothing but proper disregard for her and for the hatchling.

Lasa hopes that the egg will be High Caste when it hatches. If it turns out to be a Master or Mistress, Jandala will bring it up herself. If it's a servant, it will be Lasa's job to teach it its place in life. At least the egg has hope.

Mistress sits down and lets Lasa comb her. Lasa makes each brush stroke linger. When Mistress leans back and closes her eyes, she steals a puff of hair that has come lose on the comb and tucks it away into a fold of her dress. Afterwards, when she's alone, she'll pull it out and bring it close to her tongues to smell, before putting it away again and glancing guiltily around her.

The servants gather in the kitchen to fawn over the egg and bury Lasa in advice.

"It's a great honour."

"Yes, indeed."

"You must drink crushed shells so that the egg won't break."

"And no more jimbisters for you, lady, it's servant food and we don't want it to hatch into a servant."

"Pray every day: breathe on the statue of the Name God and ask him to make it a Master or Mistress."

"You'll do all right, it has that tint. It'll be a Master, I'm sure," Nin says.

The women fall silent, and a couple of them whisper a warding. Nin should know better than to bring the egg bad luck. The egg could be anything at this point, servant, Master, Mistress, or even . . . a monster. Many eggs don't even hatch. Dia breathes on the egg's surface to protect it.

"Put it away," Dia says. "That's enough excitement for one day."

That night, Dia says Lasa must sleep tied up. The egg is still so small that it's unlikely to break if Lasa turns over in her sleep, but Dia isn't taking any chances. She gives Lasa an old moss mattress, which used to belong to Jandala when she was young, and ties her hands to the sides of the bed.

"Will the egg be all right?" Lasa asks. "I mean, after what Nin said . . . " She's been thinking about this all day.

"Stupid Nin should know better! But I think the egg has a good chance. I'll light an incense stick for it tonight. Don't worry about it, there's nothing you can do."

The old woman busies herself with the coverlet and cushions, kisses Lasa goodnight and heads for the door.

"Dia! Don't leave yet."

The woman plods back.

"I've been thinking . . . If the egg is a servant, I'll get to keep it . . . I know I shouldn't, but I want my own hatchling. Is it wrong to feel this way?"

"Yes. You don't really want to keep it. Imagine how it will suffer if it's a servant. You must pray for it to be a Master or Mistress, hear me?"

"Yes, I know," Lasa sighs. "I just . . . Do you think my wanting a hatchling will harm its chances? Oh Gods! What if I've already turned it into a servant by thinking this all day!"

Dia chuckles and shakes her head.

"Everyone feels like that at first. What matters is what you pray for."

Over the next three days, the egg's shell grows porous and the hatchling begins to take nourishment from Lasa. She knows because the egg is now stuck inside the pouch and she's ravenous all the time.

"Lasa," Master Gundaro grunts.

Lasa freezes, poised on the tips of her feet, almost of a mind to pretend she hasn't heard and leave. She's had trouble sleeping, she's irritable, and she has discovered that a pregnant servant can get away with things. She sighs but obeys, taking only a couple steps into the room where Master sits playing a game of solitary *wass*.

"Your pouch is small for five months," he says.

Lasa nods; she secretly wonders if something is wrong with the egg.

"They feeding you enough?"

Lasa doesn't know what to say; Dia won't let her eat as much as she wants, claiming that it isn't good to spoil the hatchling. If they'd known it'd be High Caste, there wouldn't have been much harm in spoiling it, but just in case it's a servant, it must learn to make do with what it gets.

"Yes, but I'm always hungry," she says, head lowered.

"I see. Tell Dia to let you eat. Enough eggs die as it is, I won't have servant superstitions hurting my chances. You should be glad you have Masters to take care of your lot. You people would be all dead if we left you on your own."

Lasa blushes with caste-guilt. She'd give anything to be free of it.

"Do you know how to play?" Master asks.

She nods; even servants play *wass* from time to time.

"Come. Sit. You're the only one around who isn't supposed to be working, and Mistress Jandala doesn't like this game."

Master calls Lasa back to play more and more often. Mistress stops calling Lasa in the morning to comb her hair. Dia frowns at Lasa as if she's done something wrong and servants stop whispering when she approaches. Outside, the wind-organ has changed its tune to a low, disquieting moan.

A month into their *wass* sessions, Master wraps a tentacle

around Lasa's wrist. She wriggles lose and he smiles without lifting his eyes from the game, sending a chill down Lasa's spine. It's the smile of someone who knows that he'll get what he wants and isn't bothered by the wait.

"Do you know what the rebels of Quei say?"

Lasa keeps her eyes on the board.

"They say that eggs aren't only the fruit of a Master and Mistress's love. They claim that hatchlings often resemble the servant who attended at the jaja ceremony. They believe that a hatchling is part Mistress, part Master, part servant. It's a curious idea, neh?"

Lasa has heard the rumours, but she doesn't understand why a Master would bring this up. It's the kind of talk that Dia doesn't allow in her kitchen—filthy speculation designed to tarnish the High Caste's reputation and give servants "notions."

"But it must be wrong, don't you think? Imagine, Masters being one-third servant! Disgusting," says Gundaro.

Lasa's heart starts pounding and her breath crystallizes on her tongues. What has she done wrong? The Master is going to punish her. Why else would he speak like this? Is he trying to trap her? What does he want her to confess? She starts inventorying her small transgressions.

"Your turn," he says.

She moves the angry god figurine without thinking, leaving the pig and the cat exposed for Master to take with his air and water pieces.

He reclines in the chair, pleased with himself. The household spider, almost half a foot tall, tiptoes up to him and he pets it.

"Yes, it's disgusting," she ventures.

"You're a good girl," he whispers. His hand falls casually on her lap as he grabs Lasa's hand to keep her from leaving.

Dia is waiting up for her with a scowl to tie her up before bed. When the old woman starts scolding, Lasa breaks down. Lasa's confession spills out like a flood.

When she is finished, Dia stares at her from the corner of the bed. The old woman's cheeks are red and her tongues are dry and flustered.

"I was free," Dia mutters, and then louder, "I was free."

Lasa nods, Dia repeats this often enough.

"It's not much, but I have something," Dia continues. "Other jaja-servants have borne High Caste hatchlings. Some have only their cooking to be proud of, but we all need something to keep us alive. Pride in something. It can be a secret that only you know, but there has to be something."

The girl thinks she understands what Dia means. The old woman fingers her bead necklace, bought with the hungry days of her childhood. The necklace is there for all to see, saying *here, watch, this is me. I am not a slave,* or at least, not *only* a slave.

"He's taken that away from me," Lasa whispers.

"I know." Dia sits next to her in silence, caressing her hand. In the yard, the wind-organ grows shrill.

"You need to get it back. You need a secret," Dia mumbles. She gets up and leaves, forgetting to tie Lasa down this time.

Lasa lies back. She can't smell the hay cot beneath the moss mattress and wonders what it would feel like to sleep face down again. She misses working with the servants. It's all the egg's fault. No Master ever looked at her before she got the egg.

Lasa marvels at the freedom in her arms and legs. It's been months since she could turn in bed as she pleased. She turns, just a little, to rest on her side. She's playing with an idea, which scares and tantalizes her at the same time.

Eggs die all the time.

She settles comfortably on her side, rocking back and forth slightly. Lasa closes her eyes and pretends to be asleep.

When she rolls over on her stomach, the crunch is faint. She doesn't have to put her hands inside her pouch to know that the egg has cracked. The spilling yolk is proof enough. She knows they'll make her pay for this, but she's not the first servant to have lost an egg. Content, she falls asleep.

Lasa isn't the first servant to have lost an egg and Master only cuffs her, sending her reeling to the floor. Then he storms into the kitchen, demanding to know why she wasn't tied up. Like a spool of ribbon snagged on a bramble, Lasa's plan starts to unravel and she is powerless to stop it.

They blame Dia. She is old and not worth much, so Master has her beaten.

Lasa watches, clutching her eggless sack. The marsupial pouch will take months to regain its shape and it's unlikely it will ever be full again. High Castes have their own superstitions.

The stick beats down in rhythm as the wind-organ keens. The beater starts to sweat, but even the most obedient servant won't bring him water and he knows better than to ask.

How was Lasa to know? Eggs die all the time. She bites back the frost jellying on her face.

Some part of Dia's body cracks and the hunger-beads in Dia's necklace fly up into the air and scatter. One of them rolls beneath Lasa's foot. She picks it up, although she can't think of anyone who deserves it less and puts it with its sibling in her pocket. Those eggs never hatched. Some eggs are never meant to hatch.

When it's over the servants retire to the kitchen while the beater goes to bury Dia. The women leave food at the back door so that the beater won't come knocking. Lasa sits by the basin and cleans out her pouch, removing the crusted yolk and broken shell. She rocks back and forth and hums to herself. She even laughs a little, though she doesn't know what is so funny. Her body moves automatically while she herself is far away. The women look at each other and start muttering that she's going mad. They expect her to grieve, but Lasa doesn't know how to begin. Guilt and pain have not caught up with her yet, but she senses them creeping up on her and she wonders how she'll be able to live with what she's done.

In the meantime, Lasa clutches her belly. She has her secret.

BRAIN BOX
by Gina Ranalli

Gina Ranalli is an award-winning author of numerous novels, including Dark Surge, Unearthed, House of Fallen Trees *and the YA fantasy,* Peppermint Twist, *among many others. Her short fiction has been published dozens of times in a wide variety of venues. She currently lives in Washington state and can be contacted via her website at* ginaranalli.com.

The man sat weeping over the cardboard box.

He'd lined the inside of it with clear plastic, taped it down good to keep the inside as cool and moist as possible. It had worked well enough until a few days ago when the power had finally quit and the refrigerator died.

Now he didn't know what to do with it.

Trailing the tips of his fingers along the top edge, hot tears streaming down his cheeks from his shocked blue eyes, he said, "I'm so sorry, sweetheart. I don't think we have a choice."

From across the room, Johnny stared at him with sorrowful eyes, which made the man feel even worse. He sniffed, wiped his nose on his sleeve. After a moment, he said, "I'm open to suggestions, John."

Johnny blinked and looked away, either embarrassed or bored; the man couldn't tell which.

Returning his attention to the box, he wondered if he should wash what was left of his wife. Scrub her clean. Make her . . . what? Presentable? It was almost funny, if you thought about it.

The man had watched his wife become more and more sick. He'd watched her die a slow agonizing death. And then he'd watched her live again, if what she and all the others were doing these days could be considered living. Which, of course, it couldn't.

Not really. They were dead, all of them. All but their brains, which lived on and did nothing but command them to feed on the flesh of the living.

For a long time, he'd managed to keep his wife under control, chained to his heavy oak workbench in the basement. But it was summer and it wasn't long before her skin had begun to sluice off her body in pink, dripping sheets.

He'd done what he had to do. Preserve the brain and get rid of all the other parts of his beautiful wife. The brain was the only part of her that was still alive and therefore, the only part worth saving.

The dismemberment had been the hardest. The sawing and hacking. And even after he'd removed all of her limbs, she'd still tried to bite him, still tried to continue *living*.

"A mistake." The words caught in his throat, nearly choking him. "I think I may have made a mistake, baby. I think maybe I should have just let all of you die. Even your brain.

"I'm sorry," he whispered, his stomach rumbling. It had been nearly a week since his last meal. Same with Johnny, whose ribs were now showing through his thinning coat. "If it makes you feel any better, Johnny and I will be with you soon."

The man began to tear the tape off the box and called his dog over to share a final meal.

THE BUNNY OF VENGEANCE AND THE BEAR OF DEATH
by Eugie Foster

Eugie Foster calls home a mildly haunted, fey-infested house in metro Atlanta that she shares with her husband, Matthew. After receiving her master's degree in psychology, she retired from academia to pen flights of fancy. She also edits legislation for the Georgia General Assembly, which from time to time she suspects is another venture into flights of fancy.

Eugie received the 2009 Nebula Award for Best Novelette and was named the Author of the Year by Bards and Sages. Her fiction has also received the 2002 Phobos Award; been translated into eight languages; and been a finalist for the Hugo, Washington Science Fiction Association Small Press, and British Science Fiction Association awards. Her publication credits number over 100 and include stories in Realms of Fantasy, Interzone, Cricket, Orson Scott Card's InterGalactic Medicine Show, *and* Fantasy Magazine; *podcasts* Escape Pod, Pseudopod, *and* Podcastle; *and anthologies* Best New Fantasy, Best New Romantic Fantasy 2, *and* Nebula Awards Showcase 2011. *Her short story collection,* Returning My Sister's Face and Other Far Eastern Tales of Whimsy and Malice, *is available from Norilana Books. Visit her at* eugiefoster.com.

"Over time, I've come to regard the rabbit as something of a personal totem animal," says Eugie. "I admire its grace and winsome features, its fanciful personality, and its mystical heritage. Also, I think people underestimate rabbits. In the immortal words of a character from *Buffy the Vampire Slayer:* 'They might not look it, but bunnies can really take care of themselves.'"

How right she is.

Rabbit crouched in a corner, unseen, as the men in the orange jumpsuits slammed their fists into the bad man. She preened her ears as a heavy foot dislocated the bad man's kneecap and twitched her whiskers when the bad man screamed in pain. His shrieks seemed to encourage the other men to greater excesses of violence. Blood splattered the dingy white walls.

Rabbit's eyes gleamed gold, and her nose wiggled at the tang of copper in the air.

"Bunny?" A great round paw, shaggy of fur and sharp of claw, appeared through the solid wall. A second joined it, and then the jagged muzzle, thick shoulders, and burly haunches of Bear entered the cell. The men continued their sport.

Rabbit raised a paw and sketched in the air. She left behind sparkling trails of words in an archaic script older than memory. Bear could read them for he, like Rabbit, remembered a time when the stars moved in a different dance and the mountains were young.

Yes, O Bear of Reason? Rabbit wrote. The words hung like gossamer threads before fading away.

"What're you doing?" Bear said.

Rabbit's paws flowed through the air in a ballet of lettering, leaving behind spangled words in her wake. *I am overseeing my domain, O Bear. That man yonder*, and she dipped her nose at the flailing, screaming bad man, *abducted three young boys and took his pleasure of them, reveling in his own brutality. Thereupon he strangled them, tore out their eyes, and cut off their youthful manhoods as trophies.* She stroked a paw over her soft ear. *He also drowned five kittens and crucified a puppy.*

Bear read her words with great solemnity. He nodded his head as she listed the man's crimes. "But what are *you* doing here, Bunny?"

I am fulfilling my purpose. I heard the prayers of the kittens as death water closed over their heads, and I felt the rage in the heart of the second boy's father when he saw the mutilated remains of the joy of his soul.

"I thought we agreed not to get involved anymore."

O Bear of Reason, you and our celestial brethren decided to withhold your influences. If you will search your memory, you will remember I kept my own counsel.

Bear sat on his haunches. "That's not nice, Bunny. I should take you back to the sky pagoda."

Rabbit lifted a hind leg and scratched at a spot behind her ear. "Don't be such a pook head." Her voice was high and nasal. It squeaked out of her throat as though squeezed from a crowded chamber.

She raised her paw and continued writing. *The object of my attentions will soon flow from my jurisdiction to yours, if you wish to take him.*

Bear glanced at the bloody figure in the corner. The bad man had lost consciousness. A thickset man with a tattoo of a red scorpion on his arm lifted him up.

"You won't hop away, will you?"

I will stay, she sketched in the air.

Bear lumbered forward as the scorpion-tattooed man bashed the bad man's skull against the steel lavatory. He reached into the broken man's chest with a sharp-clawed paw. He groped for a moment and then pulled forth a murky shape that jiggled in his grasp. Bear sat down, lifted his paw to his mouth, and popped in the oozing grayness. In a single gulp, it was gone.

Blood and brain matter spilled from the dead man's cracked skull.

"See?" Rabbit said. "Wasn't that yummy?"

"I suppose." Bear licked his muzzle. "Will you come with me to the sky now, Bunny?"

I do not wish to return, O Bear of Death. You are stronger than me, and larger, so you may force me if you will. She thumped her foot on the smooth cement. "But you won't, will you?"

"Why don't you want to come back?"

A ribbon of elegant script streamed from Rabbit's paw. *When I saw that words would not sway our kindred nor the fire of vengeance kindle them, I kept myself quiet and still. You may do as you like, O Bear of Reason, but I will perform my function.*

Suddenly, Rabbit's ears pricked up. She snuffled the air, her pink nose busy. "Hsst! I smell a bad man." Her paw flashed. *I hear the thoughts of a murderer, unrepentant. He raped five women and forced them to swallow a poison that burned through their bodies. They died screaming in agony, vomiting up their innards.*

She leaped into the air, but Bear reached out. He caught one of her strong hind legs and shook her by it. "Bunny, no. I invoke your other manifestation. No longer Bunny of Vengeance, I appeal to Bunny of Words."

Rabbit hung upside down from Bear's paw; her long ears trembled. "I wanna smack the bad man."

"This place is full of bad men. They are being punished for their crimes without your intercession. Justice has been done."

"Justice isn't vengeance and you know it." Rabbit swung in Bear's grip as she sculpted the air. *And you know as well as I that justice is neither swift nor true in the world of man.*

Bear tipped his head so he could better read Rabbit's inverted script. "I know. But it's no longer your job to watch over them."

"Is so."

"Is not." Bear turned, still dangling Rabbit by her hind leg, and jumped.

Both animals passed cleanly through the stone and metal walls, and fell through the open air outside. They plummeted several stories before landing softly, cushioned by Bear's wide paws. Bear padded past the guard towers and razor wire. Large searchlights swept over them. They elicited no outcry.

"You're not taking me back," Rabbit said. "If you do, I won't talk to you ever, ever again."

Bear found it awkward walking on only three legs. "You don't mean that."

"Well, maybe for a week. And anyway, I'll wait until you fall asleep, and I'll hop away. You can't stop me, and you know it."

Bear broke into a clumsy trot as they cleared the penitentiary gates. The scenery around them flickered by in a blur of shadow and light. "I'm not taking you back. We're going to a special place, one dedicated to both of us."

"Vengeance and death? Really?" Rabbit clapped her paws together. "Yay!"

"Not those, the other ones. Reason and words."

Bear halted. Rabbit twisted her body so she could take

in their destination. A plaque at the top of a large set of stairs, watched over by two stone lions, read: *New York Public Library*.

Bear lollopped up the steps. His paws were too large to take them individually, and he stumbled, off-balance.

"You're gonna topple us over," Rabbit said. "Put me down."

"Hush." Bear shifted Rabbit from his paw to his mouth, clamping his teeth over her ears.

"You're getting my fur all goopy."

Bear did not reply, as his mouth was full. He bounded up the stairs and passed through the glass doors, swiveling his head from side to side, searching. Rabbit flopped back and forth in his mouth. He carried her over to a thick, much-handled tome lying open upon a podium and dropped her on the bared pages.

She glanced down. "*Webster's*? Fooie. I want the Oxford English one."

Bear dropped to his haunches. "Sorry."

Rabbit, her eyes wide and reverent, gazed at the different colored spines, lined up neatly around them. "Lookit all the words." She breathed in, her nose a-twitch. "All the words and words and words and words."

Bear put a paw gently on Rabbit's head. "Feel better now?" He watched her swivel around, her eyes bright and glowing at the array of books.

Rabbit rose on her hind legs. *I was fine before, O Bear of Reason*, she wrote. *But I have always found temples of devotion to me and mine soothing.*

"Me too." Bear surveyed the tall shelves lined with scientific journals bound by year and series. "Here in our shared holy place, I think we should talk."

Very well. Let us converse.

"I don't think you should go around revenging people."

"How come?"

"We agreed to leave the world alone."

You may have done so, but I did not concur. I do a service for the wheels of balance. I am karma. I am righteousness. If I do not oversee my domain, then who will punish the wicked?

"You are not improving the balance, Bunny. You're making it worse."

Rabbit stomped her hind leg. "I am *so* doing good!" Her paw darted in the air. *In bygone eras, crimes such as the ones I read in the minds of those men carried true penalties—entrails torn from flesh and salted with brine, skin flayed from bones, the sear of red-hot iron. What is the penalty now? A few years in a clean room with regular meals, and then returned whole and hale so they might wreak havoc anew? Or at best a quick, clean death? Where is the fairness in that? Where is the right?*

"It isn't up to you anymore. The man who killed those children—did it help them, what you made the other men do to him? Did it bring back his victims, erase their suffering?"

Of course not, O Bear of Reason. But he will not commit new atrocities.

"He wouldn't have anyway. He was serving a life sentence."

Rabbit ignored the interruption. *And the kinfolk of the slaughtered will hear of it and rejoice.*

"What of the criminal's loved ones? Won't they be sad?" Bear closed his eyes. "I tasted a sister on that man's soul." He smacked his mouth. "She cherished her brother, sins and all. Won't she grieve?"

Rabbit crossed her paws and glared. "What's your point?"

"You do harm. Leave the world of man to itself. In the end, I will take them all."

"Easy for you to say. Everything comes to you. But so what? Death doesn't solve anything. It just finishes it."

Bear sighed, a great exhalation that fluffed through Rabbit's fur. "Death solves everything, O Rabbit of Words and Vengeance."

"Wanna bet?"

Bear eyed Rabbit. "What sort of bet?"

Rabbit's paw, limned in spangled light, became a blur of motion. *Relinquish the life of the man you took. We will watch him and work upon him together. I will work one instance of my aspect on him. You work one of yours. Then we'll see which way leaves the world the better.*

Bear considered this.

But only our eternal aspects, O Bear of Death. If reasonable words were enough to sway men's hearts, then vengeance would be unnecessary.

"Death versus vengeance? If I win, you come back to the sky pagoda with me. No more Bunny of Vengeance hippity-hopping about."

And if I am victorious, you must accompany me on this plane as I will it, and together, we will cut a swath of retribution and death as this time has never seen before. Agreed?

Bear nodded. "I get to choose what parts we visit, and I get to go first."

So be it.

Bear concentrated. His muzzle twitched and his jaws strained apart. He gave a great cough, spitting up a viscous gray ball. It bumped and rolled to a stop on the thin library carpet.

Rabbit bounded off the podium and landed beside it. She jabbed a paw at the globule and peered in. Close up, the gray resolved into a snarl of many colors, swirled together into a morass of gray. "This one's all messy."

"They usually are."

She pulled her paw out, dragging a colorless line. "I got the beginning."

Bear plucked Rabbit from her perch and wrapped her in a hug. "Best you pull hard."

Rabbit yanked. The lump of life unraveled in a shining filament. It unkinked itself—for a moment, a single strand before them. She gave the end in her paws another tug and it wrapped around and around as they watched. At last, the end knotted itself anew and the man's life sprang up around them.

"Is it a boy or a girl?"

"A boy, Mrs. Highland. A wonderful, healthy baby. Have you thought of a name?"

"His father's name was Jacob."

Rabbit sat in a corner and eyed the squalling newborn, a shriveled red bundle of flailing limbs. "You could take him now, at the very beginning. Then he wouldn't live to hurt anyone. You gonna?"

"Nope."

"I didn't think so."

As he did every school morning, Jacob knocked on the door of his sister, Ellie's, room. He juggled a ragged backpack over his arm and a windbreaker a size too small.

He heard a soft moan from within.

Jacob dropped his pack and pushed open the door. Instead of finding Ellie dressed and ready, she lay curled up in bed, huddled under the covers.

He ran to her side. "What's the matter, El?"

"My stomach hurts."

"Your stomach always hurts. You gotta get up." He tugged on the blankets to uncover his sister's slender frame, the nightshirt she wore revealing bruises in various stages of healing covering her legs and arms. He was accustomed to seeing the purple, yellow, and black hurts on his sister's body; they matched his own.

"Stop it, Jakie. I'm really sick."

Jacob shifted from foot to foot. "Can't you be sick at school?"

"Get your asses out here!" Their mother's voice rang through the tiny house. The thin walls bounced the sound in the confined area, warping and magnifying it.

"It hurts," Ellie whispered.

The sound of heavy footsteps brought both pairs of eyes to the door. Sister and brother shared a fearful look.

The door slammed open. Their mother stood in the entrance, glowering. Her mouth twisted, the red lipstick she wore stark on her pale features.

"What are you doing in here?" Before Jacob could answer, she grabbed a handful of his hair. "You filth!" Pinioning him in place, she punctuated every other word with an echoing slap. "I told you never to go in your sister's room. You're never to touch her, ever, ever, ever."

Rabbit watched as Mama rained blows on the boy. *Do you intend to take the woman?* she wrote. *Perhaps truncate the root cause of the maddening guilt that roils in his mind?*

"Nope."

Rabbit shrugged.

The rain was cold, and the eyes of the man in the purple sweater, colder. But the hollowness in Jacob's belly made him reckless. Twenty bucks would buy some food, and maybe the man's place would be warm. Surely, nothing he wanted Jacob to do could be worse than starving.

"Bear?"

"Not now either."

"But if you take that man, it'll stop him from making a bad man out of—"

"No."

Ellie smiled, radiant in her white, sequined gown, her sandy hair peppered with rice, as she drew her brother into an embrace. "I'm so glad you could make it to the reception."

Her hug was tender. Jacob broke from it. As he always did, he felt like he was sullying Ellie by touching her, being near her. Yet at the same time, he yearned to hold her in his arms, like they used to do when they were children. She was the sanctuary, the harbor he'd always looked to.

And now she belonged to someone else.

The woman's mate would be a beneficial choice, Rabbit wrote. *I can scent the violence and anger fermenting in her groom. For many years he will belittle a psyche already traumatized, and it will place a wedge between brother and sister. Removing him now would revive their relationship, mend it before it becomes forever sundered.* Rabbit let her paw droop to her side. "And the bad man would have Ellie back before she gets all broken and sad—"

"Not him either."

"When're you going to do it?" Rabbit knew she was whining, but she was growing antsy, seeing all these unpleasant scenes of the bad man's life. It was enough that he had been wicked. She didn't like standing witness to these previous episodes. It did not matter that he too was a victim, that others had helped to spawn the monster he had become.

"I will when I'm ready," Bear said.

Through the prick-prick-prick in his mind, Jacob could hear the voices, though he struggled to shut them out. He was disgusting, an animal, to even think those thoughts. Touching, skin upon skin, the taste of sweat in his mouth, the living warmth salty against his tongue. It was wrong to yearn for such comforts. Evil.

His mother had known from the beginning about the disease, the sin festering in him. There were pictures of him as a baby, dressed in pretty dresses with yellow bows in his hair. Mama delighted in showing them to him, proving that she had tried so hard to fix him, make him clean and nice, like Ellie.

But if you mixed shit with water, you didn't get half shit and half water, you got shit. That's what Mama always said.

The puppy had been dirty too. He'd licked it clean, but it had still been dirty. There was nothing else he could do. He despaired when he realized it would grow up, awash in sin. The devil was in all beasts.

Until God had told him how to save it. He'd shown him through his holy son.

Rabbit lifted her paw. *He has crossed the precipice. Linger, and he will beget only evil. If you took him now, you would prevent the deeds before him from transpiring.*

"I know."

And still you refrain?
Bear met her question with silence.

The voices battered inside his head. Jacob lifted his eyes to the clear partition, the bulletproof glass. No one ever visited him.

The whispers and chants in his skull silenced when he saw the woman watching him, tears bright in her eyes.

"Ellie, what are you doing here?" His voice was dull, although his heart tripped in his chest, so fast, so hard. Had it been beating before?

"Aren't they feeding you in there, Jakie? Why didn't you call me?"

"You know."

"I don't. No matter what they say you did, no matter if you actually did those things. It's not your fault. When Mama—"

"Go ahead and say it."

Her voice faltered. "You're not a bad person. I know you're not."

"I am. I have been since I was born. Mama knew it from the start. She tried to save me, but I was too evil."

"That's not true!"

"I don't want you coming back here. I don't want you seeing me again."

"Jacob—"

"Go away."

"I'll always love you."

Jacob waited for the voices to shrill their mockery and jibes. Love wasn't for him. He wasn't good enough for it.

They remained uncharacteristically silent.

The guard stepped forward. Their time was up.

"I'll get you out of there," Ellie said. "We need to be there for each other, help each other. Like when we were kids, remember?"

Jacob touched his hand to the thick, smeared glass. "Ellie—"

Here is proof that my services are still required, O Bear of Death, Rabbit sketched in the air. *Through a quirk of man's justice, he will be released. Will you take him before he is freed to wreak more havoc in the wide world?*

Bear shook his head.

The street light was still out, the sickle moon the only illumination. The city didn't bother fixing it anymore. It had been dark for years. Still, Ellie would call the utility people again. Maybe they'd listen to her this time.

She hated walking home at night, especially having to pass through this one, dark block.

Why have you brought us to this moment, O Bear? The evil man is not present.

"Watch, Bunny."

In the darkness, Ellie didn't see the cluster of men waiting for her in the shadows.

Rabbit's ears flickered. "You going to take the head bad guy? Ellie might get away if you do."

"No."

The two animals watched as figures coalesced from the gloom, surrounded Ellie, and cut off her retreat. They were featureless in makeshift masks and shrouded by the night.

"Pretty lady, let's have your purse."

Ellie froze. Her handbag was full of the tips her customers had given her that night. She needed that money, and safety was one block away—bright lights and populated streets.

Putting her head down, she charged, knocking into the man in front of her. He went down, oaths spilling from his lips. But the man beside him leaped, tackling her before she could make good her escape.

They didn't like it when their victims fought back. To teach her a lesson, they tore her clothes off, raped her, beat her with bricks and boards, and left her bleeding, broken, and half-dead on the ragged pavement.

Rabbit knew a passerby would find her and summon aid shortly. Ellie would survive. But the bad man would learn of the assault. It would break his mind, shatter him when he learned of her violation. While she lingered in the hospital, mending from her injuries, he would succumb, totally and utterly, to the voices in his mind.

Bear put Rabbit down and padded forward on his wide paws. He reached into Ellie's broken body and drew out, with infinite care, a flickering shape—her soul. He inserted it into his toothy maw and swallowed.

The woman's watery breathing stopped, and a burr hummed from her chest—the rattle of death's embrace. She lay still.

"I am done," Bear said.

"You killed *her*," Rabbit said. Her eyes glistened; she blinked. Tears darkened her fur and trembled on her whiskers. "She was the only good thing in his life. How could you take *her*? How could you?"

Bear picked Rabbit up and rocked her in his paws. "Shh, little bunny. Don't cry. They all die. It is the way of things."

"But she was good!"

"The good die as well as the bad." Bear pushed his paw at the shining image before them. "If you wish it, his purpose can now be for vengeance. In avenging her death, he will act justly."

Bunny rubbed her eyes with a paw. With the other, she shaped words in the air. *What would be the point? It would not fix the wrong.*

"Exactly." Bear took the life string out of Rabbit's paws and flung it away. It shrank, growing dimmer and dimmer until it was a single shining mote of light, then nothing. Gone.

"When bad things happen, it hurts," Rabbit whispered. "It makes me sad and frightened. I want to fix it. Make it better."

"Poor Bunny." Bear cuddled her against his chest. "There is no fairness, no true justice. There is only what we make, here and now—and then there is me. You can't change that, little one. No matter how many bad men you get, there will be other bad men, bad women, and bad things that happen."

Rabbit sobbed. "I don't like it down here anymore! It's scary and mean. I want to go home."

Bear nuzzled her head. "I won't let the bad things hurt you. I'll keep you safe, and I'll take care of you forever and ever."

Rabbit sniffled. "Promise?"

"Promise."

Bear leaped, sending them hurtling into the sky. He carried Rabbit, still weeping softly, in his arms.

Dog Horn Publishing presents...

a preview of Deb Hoag's upcoming novel

Chapter One
Dorothy: The Meeting

I don't know much, but I know this: magic is all around us, every day. It's in the air we breath, the water we drink. Sometimes it's wonderful, and sometimes it's absolutely horrid. Magical things are happening to all of us, all the time, without rhyme or reason, without a care in the world about who deserves it or who doesn't.

Magical things have happened to me. My name is Dorothy, and this is my story.

*

I met Frannie in the spring of 1890, the night I got thrown into the hoosegow for getting overly friendly with a couple of guys at the local saloon. I stomped into the cell and threw myself dramatically on the bunk, except it wasn't the bunk I landed on – it was another woman. I hadn't seen her there in the dim light leaking in from the booking room.

She made an 'oofing' noise and I jumped off the bed faster than I had jumped on, and the guard laughed. A small horde of adolescent jitterbugs that were prancing around on the ceiling giggled shrilly, but my mundane companions didn't notice.

"Well, excuse me," the woman said with a sniff, sitting up and putting a hand to a hairdo that had seen better days.

"Sorry, sister," I replied, scooting over to the wall, where I slid down into a sitting position.

The jitterbugs went back to their endless, intricate mating dance, having approximately the same attention span as the gnats they so closely resembled.

The tiny flashing disco light was annoying, but I did my best to ignore it. I'd learned early that people who see things no one else does get a one-way ticket to the nearest loony bin.

Even jail was better than that, which reminded me of exactly where I was. Jail. Fuck!

I thunked the back of my head against the concrete. It hurt like hell, so I did it a couple more times. Stupid, stupid, stupid getting caught like that! A few more dollars and I would have been on my way back to Kansas, chasing cyclones till I could find one that would take me back to Oz.

"Hey, honey, it can't be that bad," said the woman, eying me with alarm.

I stopped banging my head and sighed. "I was this close to going home, and I got picked up by some needle-dick copper for soliciting. Now I'm stuck here until I can see the judge, pay a fine, maybe a bribe, and then earn the money I'd saved all over again. And I'm on a deadline. I need to get back to Kansas before cyclone season hits."

She laughed. "If you can make enough money out of these hayseeds to bribe a judge, you're even better than you look. Most of these hicks would rather boink a sheep than pay money for a tumble with an actual woman."

I sighed again. Completely true. I should have known two guys with cash money in a frontier town like Aberdeen, South Dakota were too much of a good thing.

"Look," I said, "I didn't mean to sit on you. I really didn't know you were there. I'm Dorothy. I just blew into town a couple of weeks ago. Who are you?"

She shook her head sadly. "I'm Frannie, from right here. For the last few years, at least. I hale from back east, originally."

"God, you actually live in this podunk town? You poor thing."

We sat in companionable silence. Eventually, my thoughts brought me back around to what I'd been doing that landed me in jail, and from that to what my cellie had been doing that landed her in jail.

"So, what exactly got you thrown in here?"

Her face grew sulky. "I committed a lewd act in public."

"Wow. What constitutes a lewd act around here?"

She shrugged and looked annoyed. "Looking cross-eyed on a Tuesday, if the constable is in a bad mood. It wasn't really even in public. We were in a perfectly respectable alley. It just happened that the alley was behind the police chief's house, and his wife picked that very moment to look out the bedroom window."

"Gee, that sucks."

"Yes, and so did I. That's why I got arrested."

I laughed out loud. Frannie started laughing too. Just like that, I knew we were going to be good friends.

When we stopped laughing, Frannie stretched on the narrow cot and stood up. "I've got an extra blanket," she said. "It gets quite cold in here at night. You want it?"

"Sure," I said, and she walked over to drape it around my shoulders.

When she stood up, the jitterbugs' disco ball illuminated her face and figure. She had a square, short jaw, and lush, full lips. Her nose was a little large for her small face, but it lent humor to an otherwise serious visage and her eyes were beautiful and large, thickly lashed. In the dim light she was altogether pretty, and she had a grace of movement that gave her lithe frame an inviting wiggle when she moved, top-heavy the way men liked. The farmers probably ate her up. She looked closer to thirty than twenty, but I prefer older women, myself. She wore boots she must have sent all the way to New York for, and had the goodies wrapped up in a scarlet silk dress that suggested all kinds of mischief.

If I wasn't heartbroken over Glinda, that wicked bitch, I might have eaten her right up myself.

I must have been staring, because she blushed, and reached up a hand to check her hair again. Her hands were large but well-shaped, with long, sensitive fingers. When she tucked the blanket around me, I smiled up at her, and noticed an unfortunate Adam's apple, nearly as large as a ma--

Was that a wisp of mustache on her upper lip?

"Are you . . . ah, you wouldn't happen to be . . . I know this sounds crazy, but are you a man?" I blurted out, watching as her painted cheek turned even rosier than it already was.

Frannie raised one of those large hands to tidy hair I realized now was a wig, askew on her head. I reached up and gave it a tug to set it straight.

She slid down to the floor and leaned against the wall a scant distance from me.

"You've found me out. Our guard doesn't know that I sat next to him on a pew just last Sunday in a suit coat and tie. Are you going to tell him?"

"Your secret is safe with me. It's no skin off my nose."

Frannie blinked. "Really? That's a refreshing attitude. You didn't grow up around here, did you?"

"Well, I'm from Kansas, originally, but . . . "

"I've been to Kansas. I didn't realize they grew 'em so liberal there."

"Oh, Kansas isn't really my home."

"Then why do you want to get back there?"

"It's a long story."

She laughed. "Sister, time is one thing we both have plenty of, given the present circumstances."

I had to agree.

I didn't suppose for a second that she would believe a word I said, but I didn't think she'd call the local loony bin about me, either.

I nestled in more comfortably to begin my tale.

"It all started in New Orleans . . . "